Cailean McBride is an author, screenwriter and journalist who has lived and worked in Italy, Australia and the UK and currently lives in Ayrshire, Scotland. He blogs regularly at www.cailean.info.

JOHNNY ZERO

© Cailean McBride 2015

The right of Cailean McBride to be identified as the author of this work has been asserted by him in accordance with the Copyright, Designs and Patents Act 1988.

All rights reserved

No part of this publication may be reproduced, stored in a retrieval system, or transmitted in any form or by any means, without the prior permission in writing of the publisher, nor be otherwise circulated in any form of binding or cover other than that in which it is published and without a similar condition including this condition being imposed on the subsequent purchaser.

First published in Great Britain by the Calenture Press in 2015.

ISBN: 978-0-9575018-2-9

Printed and bound in the UK
A catalogue record of this book is available from the British Library

Cover design by Calenture Press (Design)

I. DREAMS OF EMPIRE

ONE

JOHNNY hung helplessly from the skylight, his fingers struggling to find purchase on the crumbling window frame. He felt bloody ridiculous as his feet flailed uselessly into empty space and was relieved when he felt Jack grab his ankles from below and guide him towards attic floor.

"Cheers," he whispered. His feet hit rough wooden floorboards that were grainy with dust, grime and several decades of neglect. Jack was still invisible in the attic's murk and Johnny waited as his eyes adjusted to the blackness and he regained a sense of balance. As he did so he began to make out several shadowy forms, including a tall, obviously human configuration leering out from the shadows directly ahead, scowling, hooded eyes fixed malevolently upon him.

"Jesus Christ."

"Relax," whispered Jack from behind him, unable to quite keep the amusement from his voice. "It's only old Bela Lugosi, ain't it?" Jack's torch beam cut through the darkness and revealed the flimsy cardboard cut-out of Lugosi in full vampire regalia, with the words

'The Bride of Dracula. Saturday Matinee' emblazoned in lurid type across his be-caped chest.

"Figures," murmured Johnny. "That bugger always did give me the creeps."

He looked around, his eyes now adjusted to the gloom. They were surrounded by similar promotional cut-outs. Bogart. Cagney. Shirley Temple. And piled between them were old film cans, stacked boxes with rolled-up posters, programmes and the like. They'd clearly landed in the cinema's storeroom.

Jack shone his torch upward. "Let's get Frankie in."

Both men looked up at the skylight. Silhouetted in the patch of icy starlight was the massive, square head of Frankie the Pliers, so named because of his persuasive skills with said instruments.

"Give me a bloody hand 'ere," said Frankie, his hundred-Woodbines-a-day growl sounding like a furtive cement-mixer.

As Jack and Johnny helped guide Frankie's bulky frame inelegantly through the skylight, the fourth man in the attic, Sam Silk, was already busy at the lock of the storeroom's internal door. It sprang open under his masterful fingers with the lightest of clicks.

"Piece of bloody piss," whispered Sam, professional satisfaction on his sallow features. He began carefully stowing his picks back in their battered leather pouch.

"Right then," said Johnny, stepping forward to lead the way. "Let's get bloody to it."

All four men padded out of the storeroom, their shoes sinking in the soft pile carpet of the cinema's opulent public interior. Johnny flashed his torch up and down the corridor until its beam caught the unlit 'exit' sign at one end. "This way," he said. "Office is on the ground floor."

They crept along the corridor, past the double doors that led to one of the cinema screens, a large framed poster of the Marx Brothers proudly displaying that week's feature. A Night at the Opera.

"I like 'em," gravelled Frankie under his breath. "They're funny."

"Yeah, well, I'm afraid you've missed this evening's performance," whispered Johnny. "Shame that."

They descended the wide, white marble stairs to the long lobby on the ground floor, also done out in the same ornate art-deco style, with yet more flecked white marble and angular signage in beaten brass. The place felt cold and even eerie in the darkness, more like a tomb or a mausoleum than somewhere you'd expect people to go to enjoy themselves. Johnny and the others flitted across the open floor, past the long refreshments counter towards the ticket booth, their torch beams bouncing off the smooth, stone surfaces.

Johnny lifted the hatch at the side of the cylindrical booth and led them through a secondary door into the cinema's back office. The cheesy Classicism of the front of the house made the office seem even more utilitarianly drab than it might otherwise have appeared, but the room held only one attraction for the men – the sturdy iron safe in the corner. Johnny crossed the room and fell to his knees by the safe, lovingly running his hands along its smooth corners.

"Perfect," he whispered. "Hello, darlin'. Ain't you a one?"

"Can you break it?" asked Sam.

"'Course I can bloody break it," said Johnny. "No trouble whatsoever. Give us the stuff."

Jack passed the bag hoisted over his shoulder to Johnny who set to work. A hole was drilled in the lock and a French letter filled with gelignite and water stuffed into the opening. A fuse was then also threaded into the hole. Johnny worked with practised efficiency but still taking the care needed in handling the unstable explosive.

"We're good to go this end," said Johnny, once his preparations were complete. "Make sure they're ready outside."

Jack and Sam slipped out of the office and flitted to the front doors of the cinema, keeping low and to the shadows where possible. Through the closed iron grating, they could just make out the fifth member of the team, sitting behind the wheel of their parked car, ready to rev the engine and cover the noise of the detonation when given the signal. Sam started to raise his arm to do so when he was stopped by Jack.

"Hold on," he whispered. "Something's up."

They watched as another black car glided out of the darkness and four burly men in dark suits got out. They surrounded the other car and pulled the driver roughly out of his seat, slamming him roughly against the bonnet. Jack could just make out the thud of bone against metal, the man's cry of pain.

"Christ," said Sam. "Where the hell did they spring from?"

Jack scrutinised the grim faces of the men around the car. He recognised some but not all of them. "Come on," he said, withdrawing back into the cinema. "Better tell the others."

They ran back across the stone floor and into the office.

"Johnny," said Jack. "We've got trouble. The Law."

Johnny, still busying himself with the fuse, didn't look up. "You sure?"

"Not just any Law either. The Heavies."

This did make Johnny look up. It was not good news. The Heavies. The Flying Squad. Thief Takers. Serious detectives from the Met.

"Who?" asked Johnny, doing his best to keep his voice nonchalant, his fingers still playing with the fuse. "Anyone we know?"

"Does it matter?" said Jack. "Same old faces and a couple of new ones too. One of them looks like a right mean bastard too. Come on, we've got to get the hell out of here."

"We're nearly done here," said Johnny. "Everyone take some cover."

Jack took a step forward and plucked the fuse from Johnny's fingers. "Johnny, forget about it. They're already here." He could already hear the boom of urgent, male voices, the rattle of the iron railings over the front entrance. "We've got to go and go now."

Johnny cursed and got to his feet. "Alright, alright. Up the bloody stairs, boys. Double quick."

They all ran from the office and across the lobby. Sure enough, the shadowy outlines of the policemen outside could be seen against the frosted glass of the main doors. There were cries of alarm when they heard the movement inside and the gates were rattled more insistently as someone tried to get a key into a lock. Johnny and his team sprinted up the stone stairs, no longer remotely concerned with keeping quiet, and returned to the storeroom. They set about helping each other back through the still-open skylight with practised, agile movements, urgently aware of the sound of male cries and of heavy footfall in the cinema below them. The Law were inside.

"Right," said Johnny, once they were all through and back in the chill night. "They'll have this place covered. We'll have to get some distance." He pointed across the flat roof of the cinema towards the adjacent building. The gap was not huge but it was still wide enough to present a challenge.

"Are you bloody serious?" growled Frankie. "I can't jump that."

"It's either that or the Scrubs then," said Johnny. "Because those blokes downstairs ain't playing. Now, move."

He set off across the roof, sprinting to pick up speed, keeping his eyes firmly fixed ahead, never looking down, and focused only on where he wanted to be. And then he was over, rolling on the hard, gravelly surface of the roof opposite. Moments later, Jack landed beside him, closely followed by Sam and finally the less-graceful form of Frankie.

"Come on, keep moving," said Johnny, on his feet again and sprinting across the roof, towards the vista of moonlit roofs that stretched beyond. It wouldn't be that easy to shake the Heavies and they had to keep moving. The next roof was easier and all four managed it without dropping the pace.

Johnny stopped at the far end of this roof at the point where an iron ladder fire-escape was bolted to its side.

"You two down there," Johnny said to Sam and Frankie. "Give 'em two targets to play with. Keep it quiet and get as much distance as you can and you should be alright. Don't go back to the hotel. They'll probably be waiting for you there. Just start heading back to London as soon as you can. But no direct routes. Keep it roundabout. Liverpool. Manchester. Wherever. Keep 'em guessing. They'll have all the direct trains and roads to London well covered."

Both men nodded and began descending the ladder. Johnny didn't have too much in the way of concern about them. They were good blokes and they'd been well drilled in how to get out of a job gone sour. And even if they did get nicked, they knew enough to keep their mouths shut. Which was why they'd been picked in the first place.

Johnny nudged Jack. "Right, come on. We ain't out of this yet either." They started running again, picking up speed to leap across to another roof. This one wasn't so easy. Gabled and slated, with a lot less purchase. Johnny felt his foot slipping against the wet tile but then Jack had him by the arm and both men were able to start scrambling up towards the peak of the roof.

"Black!"

They heard the voice roar across the stillness of the night. Johnny looked back across the roofs to the top of the cinema. A bald, bullet-headed form could be seen framed against the skyline, the round, white skull as pale as bone against the moonlight. He was too far away for the features to be made out clearly, but the broad, powerful physique seemed to effuse menace, even at this distance.

"Who the hell is that?" asked Johnny.

"Dunno," said Jack. "That's the one I was telling you about."

"Well, he ain't doing nothing tonight. Come on, let's go." Johnny gave the spectral figure a cheery wave before they both started running again.

They slithered down the other side of the slate roof and then across another couple of buildings to be on the safe side, both men discomfited by the pale apparition still howling at them across the rooftops. When they were sure they were no longer being pursued, they found another fire escape and descended to the relative safety of the darkened streets below.

"So just what the hell are we supposed to do now?"

Jack looked up and down the deserted street, half expecting to see a car full of Heavies come screaming around the corner at any moment.

"Dunno," said Johnny. "Find a bolthole till morning. Then get out of this God-forsaken shithole."

"Any ideas? Because I don't know Cardiff all that well. In fact, come to think of it, I don't know it at all."

Neither did Johnny. They had only arrived in the town the previous morning. It had been the final stop on a brief larceny tour of the UK. Hit a different place in a different town every couple of days. Manchester. Bradford. Glasgow. Liverpool. And now Cardiff to finish it off. They'd hit a different kind of place every time too. Pawn shop here. Jewellers there. Everything to keep the Law off balance and the money flowing in. And it had been a string of brilliant successes. Until tonight.

Something small and bright caught his notice. The twin points of light of a cat's eyes, blinking out from behind a couple of dustbins at the mouth of an alley. He nodded in the puss's direction. "In there," he said.

The alley was stinking, littered with discarded, decaying rubbish and they could hear the scuttle and squeak of rats in the shadows. But it was dark and more or less invisible from the street. It would do for a couple of hours, or at least until the inevitable search got too close and they had to move on again.

Jack wrapped his overcoat around him to fend off the cold. "Well, this is nice, ain't it?"

"Hey, no one's more pissed off about this than me. Can't bloody believe it. I hate leaving empty-handed. You should have let me blow it."

"If I had we'd all be in the nick now. You've got to know when to bail. I keep telling you."

Johnny grinned. "Yeah, you're right, you're right. They got Dennis then you think?"

Jack offered Johnny a cigarette. "Yeah, they did. Saw them get him."

"Think he'll talk? Land us in it?"

"Nah, boy knows better. He knows we'll take care of him. Besides, he knows what we'd do to him if he opened his trap."

Johnny's expression relaxed slightly. "Yeah, suppose." He was silent for a moment and then he started chuckling in the darkness.

"What's so bloody funny?" demanded Jack.

"The Heavies," said Johnny, something like elation in his voice. "You really think it was them?"

"Yeah. I'm sure of it."

"And you know what that means?"

"Yeah, I know what that means. It means trouble. Trouble that won't go away anytime soon."

Johnny shook his head. "It means that we've made it. We're getting noticed, Jacky Boy. We've arrived. We're playing with the big boys now."

"I always kind of thought the point of this game was not to get noticed," said Jack. "Not by the Law anyway."

"No, getting noticed is the whole point. Making a name for ourselves. That the Law is starting to sit up and take notice, that's a good thing in my book."

"Tell that to Dennis. And you don't think it means we should dial it back for a bit?"

"Nah, to hell with that. It means we've got to push even harder. Show that we're not to be messed with. We can't bottle out now, Jack. We've still got work to do."

"Such as?"

"Well, the Danellis for a start. It's time we took 'em on. See if we can't slice off some of that action they've got going for themselves."

"That's some big talk. And we wouldn't be the first to try."

"You think we couldn't take them?"

"I didn't say that. I'm just saying we better be sure, that's all."

"Never been surer. I just want to get back and start getting on with it. Still," he broke off regretfully. "I wish we had got to do that safe. It was bursting full, I'm sure of it. Folk love those Marx Brothers."

"There'll be other safes."

"But that ain't the point. That ain't the point at all. I wanted that one. One of these days we're coming back here and we're going to pop that bastard wide open. These Taffs ain't getting away with it."

Jack chuckled. "You're kind of on the crazy side. Did I ever tell you that?"

Johnny returned the grin. "Many times. Mind you, I don't recall ever saying I wasn't."

TWO

THE girl's singing was the first thing that registered with Jack as he walked into the Tap Club. The smooth, bluesey tones broke into his preoccupied train of thought and scattered his concentration, making him look around almost dazed.

"Evening, Mr Spinks." The doormen nodded with friendly but respectful familiarity as Jack handed his overcoat to one of the counter girls. Everyone knew him here. And not just as a regular but as someone bordering on being a VIP.

"Alright, lads," said Jack. "About, is he?"

One of the doormen nodded through the double doors of the lobby towards the main area of the club. "Through there."

The place was busy for a weeknight but what with things being the way they were, people seemed to be partying like it was the end of the world. So what if it was? thought Jack. It seemed like it was good for business.

He'd not gone three steps before Johnny came bounding up to him, his face alive with joyful exuberance.

"Where the hell have you been? I've been waiting for here for you like a right 'erbert."

"Been working, haven't I? Sorting out the bloody mess that was Cardiff."

"Oh yeah? And what's the upshot?"

"Pretty good, on the whole. Frankie and Sam got away without a hitch. They took your advice a bit too far though and ended up in Edinburgh. They'll be back tomorrow though. All safe and sound."

"And what about Dennis? Did the Heavies lean on him?"

"Without a doubt. But he gave them nothing. But they ain't charging him. Not after Sharkey went in and put the screws on a bit." Sharkey was the Black Mob's tame brief, a conniving Irishman who seemed to know every crooked inroad and loophole in the law and was worth every penny of his hefty retainer. Jack continued: "And I did some asking around about that big, bald bastard."

"And?"

"Name's Harry Blum. He's been working Clubs but he's just moved into the Heavies. And going through them like a dose of salts, apparently."

"Never heard of him."

"I have. By reputation anyway. Meant to be a right hard nut. He'll be one to watch."

"Talking of which," said Johnny, his concentration already wandering, "there's somebody I want you to meet."

He took Jack by the arm and led him deeper into the club. The dancefloor and stage were a wide oval set lower than the main level by a few steps. On the stage, under a moody, blue spotlight was the singer who had entranced Jack even as he had entered the club. Her looks matched the voice too, thought Jack. A real looker, with curves in all the right places, blonde hair coiffed and curled, blue eyes and full lips, that were coiled into just the slightest of sneers, giving her an expression of defiance, of disdain that only somehow managed to add to her attractiveness.

It only took the quickest of glances at Johnny to see why he wanted Jack to see this girl. He had a look on his face that Jack had seen too many times before. The usual besotted admiration but also something like pride, perhaps even incredulity that something so strikingly beautiful could exist and also be within his reach.

"So, this is the new one, is it?"

Johnny gave him a disarming grin. "She's something, ain't she? And it ain't like that, Jack. Not this time. She's the one, I'm telling you."

"Like I haven't heard that before."

"Nah, it's different this time. I've never met anyone like her."

"She's a hell of a looking woman, I'll give you that."

"She's a lot more than that, let me tell you. Come on, I'll introduce you."

The singer had finished her set and was descending the steps from the stage towards the dancefloor. She beamed when she saw them approach and embraced Johnny, giving him a chaste kiss on the cheek. Jack couldn't help notice just how tightly and for how long they held each other and he watched her slender hands travel down Johnny's shoulders and grip him in the small of his back, pulling him firmly towards her. It was a sensuous and passionately direct gesture, and it made Jack wonder whether this new romance might in fact be as serious as Johnny had claimed.

Johnny clapped his arm around Jack. "Billie, sweetheart, this is Jack." His voice was suffused with a pride that Jack found difficult to tell was for her or for him, or possibly for both.

Billie gave Jack a cool, evaluating glance before smiling and holding out a slender hand. "I've heard a lot about you, Jack. Johnny here says he couldn't get by without you. Which, I suppose, means that I couldn't either."

Jack took the hand, feeling a slight thrill at the cool, but surprisingly firm, touch. "I'm sure that's not true."

Billie held onto his hand for just a moment longer before releasing it. "Let's not find out though, eh?"

A figure hovering at Billie's elbow cleared its throat ostentatiously and took a step forward. "Um, Billie, my dear."

It was only then that Jack registered the grey, gnomic individual hovering as Billie's sequinned elbow. He was a small, wizened man somewhere in his late 40s, with thinning hair of a grey almost exactly matching his pallor. He was dressed in an equally bland suit, cut in a style at least a decade out of date.

"Who's this?" whispered Jack to Johnny. "Her old man?"

"Her manager," said Johnny, with a grimace. "How are you doing, Mr Siddell? Nice to see you again."

"I'm afraid I'm quite unable to say the same," sniffed Siddell. He took hold of Billie's elbow. "Shall we, my dear?"

Billie shrugged free, taking a step closer to Johnny. "Actually, I think I'll stay here for a while. The night's young and I could do with a drink."

"Now, that sounds like a plan," beamed Johnny, putting an arm around her waist. "What would you say to some Champagne?"

Billie returned his smile. "I'd say it sounds like a bloody good idea."

But Siddell wasn't giving up that easily. "I'm afraid that won't be possible. Billie, we do have rather a lot to discuss, and an early night would do your voice the world of good. As your manager, I'm afraid I shall have to insist."

"Didn't you hear the lady?" said Johnny, his tone still quiet but with a sharpness that put Jack on immediate notice that he was suddenly on duty again. "She said she wanted to stay. And that's what she's going to do." He led Billie away from Siddell, heading in the direction of the bar.

"Do you think I don't know what's going on here?" spluttered Siddell. "What you're up to, you damned hoodlum?" He leaned in towards Johnny and hissed, "And if you think I'm going to just sit still and let a guttersnipe like you steal my livelihood from right under my nose then you've got another think coming."

The smile didn't drop from Johnny's face, almost as if he had not heard Siddell's words at all. He turned to Billie, still beaming charmingly, and said, "Let's go and see about that Champers, shall we?"

"Yes, let's."

They sashayed away, with Johnny giving Jack one final significantly raised eyebrow, and Billie too giving him a smile. Siddell took a step forward to pursue them. "Billie, my dear," he managed to say before Jack put a restraining hand on the older man's chest.

"How dare you," blustered Siddell. "Get your damned hands off me."

Jack pushed Siddell, gently but firmly, to the side of the stage until the older man's back slammed against a drinks' shelf, making the glasses and ashtrays rattle. Siddell's face went even paler as Jack leaned in, exerting more pressure on his chest.

"This is outrageous," wheezed Siddell. He looked imploringly over Jack's shoulder, appealing to the two waiters at the side of the dancefloor who had seen the whole thing but who were studiously pretending they hadn't.

"They won't help you," said Jack. "No one will. Not in here. Johnny's got an interest in this place. You're on our turf."

"You're making a big mistake. I have powerful friends."

"And Johnny has more. So if I were you I'd shut up and listen for a moment. Because I don't want to hurt you. Not anymore than I have to anyway."

To Jack's surprise, Siddell did stop struggling for a moment. "Now," said Jack, "it's clear that Johnny and the young lady are something of an item, isn't it? I suggest you just let them get on with it. You don't want to be standing in the way of love's young dream now, do you?"

"I have a contract," Siddell began.

"But it don't mean you own her, does it? And if you think it does then it might be time to start thinking about tearing up that contract. Before someone does it for you."

"I won't be threatened by a couple of gutter thugs like you. I'm not afraid of you."

"Then I'm afraid that doesn't show much, what do you call it, business savvy, on your part. Sounds like Billie should definitely think about getting herself some new representation." He released Siddell. "But like I said, I ain't going to hurt you. Not tonight. But if I see you around again, I might have to. So I suggest you piss off home and think about what I've just said."

He took a step backward to give Siddell some room but the older man just stood there, glaring at his opponent. He's got some balls, I'll say that for the old bugger, thought Jack. In his own little world, he was probably not someone to be messed with. But he wasn't in his world anymore.

"Go on," repeated Jack. "Hop it."

And this time Siddell complied. Jack didn't take his eyes off him until he had left the club and only then did he go looking for Johnny.

He found him sitting with Billie at a table by the side of the stage, their hands entwined. Jack couldn't remember ever seeing Johnny quite as happy as he was now.

"Here," said Johnny, pouring him a glass of Champagne. "Take a load off. Our geriatric friend gone, has he?"

"Yeah, past his bedtime, I think."

"Thanks for doing that, Jack," said Billie, flashing him another brilliant smile. "The old goat never leaves me alone. God knows what I was thinking getting involved with the likes of him in the first place."

"Think nothing of it," said Johnny. "Our Jack here can be very persuasive. It's one of his real talents."

It was only then that Jack realised this was the reason he'd been invited along this evening. He knew Siddell was going to make an appearance and wanted it dealt with. Jack didn't mind as such, but it was a timely reminder that with Johnny there was always an agenda. Always another angle.

THREE

FREDDIE Winner had a nose for trouble. Always had. He also had a nose for gossip, for money, for where a lucrative deal, or a useful contact, might be made. Freddie worked the street, haunting all the places where Johnny could not now go without calling too much notice to himself – the bareknuckle bouts, the cockfights, the dives and the street corners where arrangements were struck, information exchanged, alliances formed. Johnny called him the Ferret, a name which Freddie hated and told himself that only Johnny Black himself could get away with calling him. In this, as in many other things, Freddie was mistaken.

And it was trouble that Freddie was detecting as he saw the two burly men making their way along a crowded Peckham High Street towards him. He recognised them both. One was called Phil Illingworth, a fairly straight-up copper, now with the Heavies, who Freddie had had dealings with before. The other was a detective Freddie had heard of but had always made a point of steering clear of, primarily because what he'd heard was far from good. Name was Harry Blum, or something like that.

And now this Harry Blum was walking up the street towards him, his slabbish features set and grim, taking off his jacket and handing it to Illingworth as he went. Rolling up his sleeves. This tallied with what Freddie had heard about Blum. You only got nicked if he thought it was worth the effort, if your crimes had reached a certain level of severity. Otherwise, chances are you'd be dealt with summarily on the streets.

"What—" was about as far as Freddie got before Harry's fist hit him square in the face. Freddie went down, the taste of his own blood sharp in his mouth. And then he was being dragged towards a doorway by the scruff of his neck before being hauled roughly to his feet. Illingworth stood a few feet away, his back to them, acting as a barrier against anyone who might feel public-spirited enough to interrupt their 'discussion'.

"You're Freddie," said Harry, leaning in close enough that Freddie could smell the stale beer and tobacco on his breath.

"Yeah, that's me," Freddie spat through saliva and blood.

"I've got a message for you. For your boss."

"Ain't got a boss."

Harry shook Freddie, twisting his grip on the lapels and flesh he had bunched in his fists and was grinding his knuckles into Freddie's scrawny chest. "You really think that's a wise way to go, Freddie?"

"Alright," Freddie gasped. "You got a message. For Johnny. What is it?"

"You're it," said Harry.

The beating did not take long, nor was it particularly severe by Harry's standards. A piledriver to the solar plexus that folded Freddie in half and had him retching in pain. And then a cuff to the ear on the way down. Not too hard, but enough to send his brain ringing, enough to draw blood.

Harry bent down beside the gasping, vomiting Freddie, now on all fours on the ground. "You tell Johnny that the game's up," he whispered in Freddie's bleeding ear. "You tell him that I'm coming for him. Tell him that his only chance is to stop now. To quit while he's ahead. Otherwise, I'm going to fucking take him apart. Him and anyone else who happens to be standing with him. Got it?"

"Got it," groaned Freddie. And when he had stopped puking and gasping long enough to look up there was no sign of either Harry or Illingworth. Just the rushing pedestrians, the housewives and the businessmen, scurrying by, pausing only to throw a quick look of disdain and disgust in Freddie's direction before hurrying on.

Alun Symons was the operational commander of the Flying Squad and it was not something that delighted him as much as it had in days gone past. Now in his final years before retirement from the Force, part of him had already left the building and was halfway back to Oxford to complete the English Literature degree he'd been forced to abandon as a young man. He'd had bills to pay, a family to feed and Shakespeare and Donne weren't going to help with that. But literature and Oxford had remained Symons's dream all his adult life. This was the reason that his men had given him the nickname 'The Professor', part affectionately and part mockingly at their Guv'nor's long-held academic pretensions.

But close as it was, Oxford was still a few years away and in the meantime he still had duties to perform, a squad to run. And its newest member was now standing in front of his desk and Symons wasn't sure how he felt about him at all.

"Detective Sergeant Harold Blum," he read from the file laid out in front of him. "Your reputation precedes you, son."

It felt odd to Harry to be referred to as 'son'. His youth was far behind him now. But he supposed that next to Symons, he might still seem like a relative youngster. Pretty much anyone in the entire Met would.

"Yes, sir," he said, standing in front of Symons's desk and feeling very much like a schoolboy being sent up before the headmaster. "Thank you, sir. And I prefer 'Harry', sir."

"Harry it is then. Just thought I'd have you in for a little chat. Say hello and all that. You've got a hell of a CV here. Eight commendations. A conviction rate that's, well, let's put it this way, I've never seen one like it. And it looks like you're hitting the ground running here too. I've been meaning to get you in for a chat for the last few weeks, but it's quite the challenge finding you at your desk."

"Job's out there, sir. Not in here."

Symons scowled, sensing a rebuke. But he didn't mind too much. It wasn't taking him long to get the measure of Harry Blum. Never tread softly when you can go in with both fists flying. And it hadn't escaped his notice that the fellow had never shown up in the squad room once without sporting grazed and barked knuckles. A bruiser, rather than a thinker. But that was alright. The department had need of both.

"I see you've spent time in just about every serious squad in the Met. And now you've come to us. What, was it just my turn? Why did you want to come to the Flying Squad?"

Harry shrugged. "Don't know really, sir. Reckon I can do a bit of good here."

"I don't doubt it, son. Tell me, what do you see as our main priorities at the moment?"

"People out there are hurting," said Harry. "War left them in a hell of a bloody state and now they can see another one on the horizon and they just don't want to know about it. And things are tough anyway. It's hard getting a job. Tougher keeping it. They want to feel good, want the finer things, but they just don't have the money to get them. Situation like that is just ripe for the gangs to move in. And that's what's happening. They're trying to carve up this whole town between them. Succeeding too."

Symons nodded. It was a fair summation, if a little on the blunt side for his taste. "And what do you suggest?"

"How about not letting them? How about taking the fight to them? Letting them know that they're not going to get away with it."

"I see. That's your plan, is it? And is this why you've had my men tearing about the length and breadth of the country these last few weeks?"

Harry had a feeling that this was where the conversation had been heading. "Johnny Black's mob on a spree. Serious hits on major targets right across the country."

"And how did that work out? Any arrests? Recovered any of the stolen goods?"

Harry shook his head. "No, sir. On both counts."

"So, a bit of a bloody waste of time then. Unless you count the expenses and overtime clocked up in the process, that is."

"Is that what this is about? A couple of hotel bills? A few train tickets?" The fact that Harry had dropped the "sir" did not escape Symons's notice. No respecter of authority either.

"Harry, I don't give a damn about the money. I'll go upstairs and fight to get you gold-plated bloody truncheons if that's what you need. But I want to see some results. Because that's what they'll want to see too." Symons tapped the side of his head with a long forefinger. "Think, Harry. You've got to be using this as well as your knuckles. Otherwise you're going to get nowhere. And all that's going to happen is people are going to get hurt. People who don't need to. People who, lest we forget, pay us to protect them."

Harry nodded. "Yes, sir."

"So, we're understanding each other, are we? We play it a bit savvy round about here, you got me?"

"Yes, sir."

"Right, off you go then. Go and catch me some wrong 'uns."

Symons watched Harry leave the office and return to his desk, wondering just how much of a problem his new addition was going to be. He liked an orderly team and hated loose cannons, usually finding them more trouble than they were worth. But Harry, he felt, might be different. And he was not wrong that things were changing out there. Symons hardly recognised the job from what it was when he'd signed up. The mobs were tougher, more sophisticated, harder to crack. And it was getting more dangerous too. Respect for the Law was being gradually eroded. Maybe a blunt instrument like Harry Blum was just what was needed.

FOUR

JACK scanned the house numbers as he walked down the street, looking out for the one he'd been told to find. In the end, it didn't turn out to be too difficult, as parked outside was the midnight blue Bentley that he'd specifically advised Johnny not to buy less than a week before.

Johnny himself was leaning against the motor, shirtsleeves rolled up, the pomade in his hair glistening in the sun. He beamed at Jack. His smile was coy, smugly guilty, like a child who knows they've been caught being naughty but who also knows they're going to get away with it.

"So, you went ahead and got it, did you?" said Jack, unable to keep the smile quite off his own face. "And what happened to keeping a low profile?"

"To hell with that," said Johnny. "That time's past, Jacky Boy. It's time for us to start making waves. Let people know we're here. And we ain't going away. Besides," he took Jack by the arm and started leading him towards the house, "You ain't seen nothing yet."

He led Jack through the open front door and into front hallway. The floorboards were bare and the whole place smelt of must and emptiness. A couple of doors led off the front end of the hallway with a narrow staircase to the upper level opposite. The hallway then narrowed into a long-ish passageway with a single door at the other end, from which emanated the sunlight that was giving the whole place a warm, golden glow.

"Christ," said Jack. "This place too?"

"Had to, didn't I? We're stepping up, Jack. Can't very well run my whole mob from a bedroom at my mum's, can I?"

"I dunno, Johnny. This is a lot of money you're spilling out here. Good way to have the Law sniffing around us again."

"Don't sweat it. Had Sharkey take care of it. It's all going through the club. The motor too. Don't worry. They can't touch us on it."

Johnny led him down the passageway and through the door, which led into a large, airy kitchen. It had all the usual things you'd expect to find – an enormous range, a sink, a couple of dressers – but was dominated by the enormous oak table in its centre. Standing at this now was Billie, cutting sandwiches and placing them in a wicker picnic basket. She beamed at Jack as he and Johnny entered.

"Morning, Jack. What do you think of the place?"

It was now a good three or four months since the night Jack had first met Billie at the club and she had become a definite fixture in Johnny's life. Johnny's assertion that he had found "the one" was apparently turning out to be true. Until now, none of Johnny's girls had lasted more three weeks before falling victim to his low boredom threshold. Not that Jack minded. He enjoyed Billie's company. She was funny and she was smart and he liked her a lot.

Jack could do little more than smile. This was the first time he'd really seen Billie outside of a club or pub, or even in daylight and the difference was marked. She was wearing a simple, floral summer frock, a far cry from the gowns and cocktail dresses he was used to seeing her in, and she was relatively unmade up. But the change suited her, as did the sunlight coming through the windows that caught the gold in her curls. She looked more beautiful than ever, thought Jack, not for the first time feeling a pang of jealousy.

Johnny nudged him in the ribs. "Come on. I'll show you the rest of the place."

All three of them walked back through the hallway to the front door. "Those will be where we'll put in the live-in muscle," said Johnny, hitching a thumb at the doors opposite the stairs. "We can live without a lounge for the moment."

"Live-in muscle?" said Jack.

"Yeah, I think two should be enough to have on duty at any time. What do you think?"

"I guess so. You think that's really necessary though?"

"Yeah, I think it might well be. In the short term anyway."

Johnny climbed the stairs, still talking as he went, and led them into the main bedroom, still stark and bare at the moment. "This will be ours. I was thinking about putting you in the one opposite."

"Wait a minute," said Jack. "Me?"

Johnny turned to face him. "Sure. You're my right hand, Jack. I'm going to need you here."

"And I can't just come and visit?"

"Nah. Better if you're here. Get things done quicker that way."

"I don't know, Johnny."

"Jack," said Billie, taking Johnny's arm to present themselves as a couple. "Johnny and I have talked about this and we both think it's a good idea. Please."

Jack shifted uncomfortably on his heels. "Am I to take it, with all this talk of domestic bliss, that there's going to be some wedding bells sounding soon?"

Johnny exchanged a glance with Billie and they both smiled enigmatically. "Possibly. In the future," said Johnny.

They were interrupted by a sharp knock on the still-open front door and a voice calling out: "Hullo! Anybody home?"

"Up here, Ferret," shouted Johnny.

Freddie's footsteps clumped up the bare, wooden stairs and he appeared in the doorway to the bedroom. One eye was closed, swollen and purple, his lower lip bruised and cut and one ear half-hidden in a grey bandage.

"Jesus Christ," said Jack. "What the hell happened to you?"

"Ain't you heard?" said Johnny. "He had a run-in with that Harry Blum bloke."

"What about?"

Johnny shrugged. "Blowed if I can tell. Said he was watching us. Said we should watch our step."

"Which is exactly what I've been saying, ain't it?"

"To hell with him," said Johnny. "He don't scare me."

"Which would be fine, Johnny," said Freddie. "Except you ain't the one getting pummelled."

Johnny raised an eyebrow at Freddie. "What have you got for us, Ferret?"

"It's all on…" said Freddie. His voice trailed off as he looked meaningfully at Billie.

"What?" said Johnny. "You can talk in front of Bil. We ain't got no secrets."

"Yeah, but all the same, Johnny."

Billie rolled her eyes. "It doesn't matter," she said, reaching up to give Johnny a peck on the cheek. "You boys have your shop talk. I'll be downstairs finishing the sandwiches."

When she had gone, Johnny turned back to Freddie. "Well?"

"Got it all, Johnny. Times and dates of all the pick-ups from the Danellis. We're ready to hit them whenever you say the word."

The Danellis were an Italian mob, based mostly around Soho, and with their fingers in just about every racket going. Racecourses. Clubs. Girls. Protection. It was in their protection game that Johnny was preparing to hit them.

"The word is said," said Johnny. "We'll start hitting them Friday."

"If we're going to do this," said Jack. "We should be smart about it. Hit them when they've made all their collections. Be safer to do it all in one big hit."

"No," said Johnny. "I don't want this done down some alley somewhere. It has to be public. People have to see the Danellis getting taken down. They have to know that it's not worth them paying up if the Danellis can't even protect themselves. And it's not enough to hit them just once. We have to keep hitting them until they can't take it no more. This is going to be a war, not a smash-and-grab."

"It's going to get bloody," said Jack. "We're going to need plenty of muscle."

"Whatever it takes," said Johnny, excitement in his voice now. "This is it now, boys."

"I better get going," said Jack. "Give Frankie and Sam and the others the SP on all this. We're going to have to be ready if we're going to start hitting them so soon."

"Leave it to Freddie," said Johnny. "You've got other duties today."

Jack looked at Johnny. He couldn't imagine what could be more pressing than an impending turf war. "Like what?"

Johnny grinned. "You'll find out." He turned back to Freddie. "Ferret, what the hell are you still here for? Get moving. Make sure everyone's ready to move when it's time."

Freddie sniffed and with a final glance at Johnny and Jack, he left.

When Johnny and Jack went downstairs themselves, they found Billie waiting at the foot of the stairs with the picnic basket in her arms. "Well, if you boys are quite finished, don't you think it's time we got moving?"

"Here, let me take that for you," said Jack and took the basket from her. At a nod from Johnny, he carried it out of the front door and put it in the back seat of the Bentley.

"Well, you two enjoy your picnic," he said. "And I'll see you both later."

"Where the hell do you think you're going?" said Johnny, joining Jack and Billie after locking up the house. "Get in the car."

"No, no, no," said Jack. "No fear. Do I look like some kind of gooseberry? I'll catch you both tomorrow."

"Please, Jack," said Billie, hooking her arm through his and leaning in so close to him that he could smell her perfume, feel her warmth. "It wouldn't be the same without you. Besides which, we ain't asking, we're telling."

"That's right," said Johnny. "You're needed."

"Really?" said Jack. "What for?"

"You'll find out," said Johnny. "Now will you get in, for Chrissake? We've got a long drive ahead of us. Like Bil said, this ain't open to negotiation."

Jack smiled and shrugged and got into the back seat. "Alright, you win."

"Course I win," said Johnny, sharing a grin with Billie as they both got in the front of the car. "I always win."

"So where on earth are we going anyway?" asked Jack, as Johnny steered the Bentley out of London, leaving the fog and traffic behind for clearer, open roads.

"The moon!" cooed Billie from the front seat, throwing her arms in the air and eliciting a chuckle from Johnny. It was clearly some private joke of theirs, thought Jack.

"I'm sure you two know what you're on about but I sure as blazes don't."

"Don't let it worry you, Jacky Boy," said Johnny. "All will be revealed soon."

And it was. Before long they were out of London and heading along the coastal road towards Sussex, green fields on one side of them, the brilliant blue of the Channel, twinkling in the sunlight on the other.

"So," said Jack. "Brighton, is it?"

"Yeah," said Johnny. "Nice day at the seaside. What could be wrong with that?"

"Absolutely nothing," said Jack. "Gets my vote."

Little over an hour later, they were driving along Brighton's Kingsway towards the Old Steine. It was still a glorious day and Jack felt cheerful and glad that they had strong-armed him into coming along.

"Here, Johnny," said Billie. "Let me off here and I can powder my nose." She nodded towards the public toilets at the head of the pier. "I'll see you boys up there."

"Sure you know where you're going?"

"Course I do. Not bloody stupid, am I?"

Johnny let her out and then swung the Bentley up the Old Steine. He didn't go far before parking. Johnny took his jacket from the back seat and straightened his tie. He took something from the pocket of the jacket and tossed it to Jack.

"Here, you're going to need this."

Jack opened the small, red box. Inside was a diamond-encrusted wedding ring. He looked at Johnny, who was beaming at him.

"Might not be any bells today," said Johnny. "But there is going to be a wedding. Congratulations, mate, you're my best man."

Jack laughed. "You bugger. Can't believe you didn't bloody well tell me till now. But Brighton?"

"Want to keep it low key, don't I? It's all going to kick off big time with the Danellis and the last thing I want to do is give them a big target. Keep it all quiet for now and we'll have a big blow-out once everything's more settled like."

Jack looked at the ring. "This is the one from that Glasgow job."

"I know, I know. I offered to buy her another one. Do it all proper like. But she wasn't having any of it. Nothing would do but that one."

"But if she gets nicked," Jack began, genuine worry in his voice.

"I know, it could get a bit hairy but it can't be helped. What the lady wants, the lady gets."

They both got out the car and started walking up through The Lanes towards the town hall. "I guess that's something you better get used to," said Jack.

"You got that right." Johnny stopped and turned to face his friend. "So, what do you think, Jack? I'm doing the right thing here, ain't I?"

"How can you even think otherwise?" said Jack. "She's a peach. You're a lucky sod and no mistake."

"I know it." They started walking again. "Born that way, I guess."

They arrived at the town hall and sat on the steps, waiting for Billie. Jack offered Johnny a cigarette and they smoked in silence. It was unseasonably warm for the time of year and Johnny, as in everything else, had even been lucky with that, Jack mused. They had started the trip with a sense of carnival, but now it had an added air of solemnity, of import. And Jack was surprised at just how happy he was. He felt like laughing. Anyone would think it was him that was getting married, that it was his special day, rather than the day that he saw the girl he'd just realised he'd fallen in love with slip through his fingers forever.

"Tell you what," said Johnny, shifting uncomfortably. "I think the Moon would be a bit bloody easier on your arse than this place is."

They were on the beach, staring out across the English Channel, and having their picnic. The deed was done. Johnny and Billie were man and wife.

"True," said Jack, kicking at the pebbles and shale they were sitting on. "Brighton does have the worst bloody beach in the world. Beats me why everyone continually goes on about it."

"God, listen to you two," snorted Billie. She was lying back in Johnny's lap, staring dreamily out at the water. "Moan. Moan. Moan. Good job you've got me now to keep you both right."

"Blimey," said Johnny. "That sounds ominous."

"I didn't think so," said Jack.

They were silent for a moment, enjoying the warmth of the sun, the tang of the sea air on their skin, the feeling of how all their lives had subtly changed in the last few hours. How they were all on the brink of something new.

"You think it's all going to go alright?" Johnny asked eventually.

"Why?" said Jack. "You think it won't? You want to call it off?"

Johnny thought for a moment. "Nah. We can do this. We have to. What choice do we have?"

"Plenty. I don't doubt we can do this. Easily, in fact. But a lot of people are going to get hurt in the process. Maybe even killed."

Johnny shook his head. "Not if we do it right. What it needs is the will, that's all. If people see that you're willing to take it all the way if you have to, they end up backing down. Because they can see the way it's going to go in the end."

"Even Aldo?"

"Especially Aldo. Aldo Danelli might be a lot of things but stupid ain't one of 'em."

Jack caught Billie's eye. She had turned round, propped up on her elbow, and had been following their conversation with interest.

"You sure you want to be talking about this now?" he asked. "On your wedding day and all?"

Johnny gave Billie's shoulder a squeeze. "Maybe you're right. Not exactly, what do you call it, decorous, is it?"

Billie sat up and turned to face them. "Hey, Jack," she said. "Show me your knife."

Jack raised an eyebrow archly, tempted to make a double-entendre of her request before realising that it might not be appropriate to do so with Johnny's new wife. He glanced at Johnny who shrugged, smiling.

He reached into the pocket of his jacket, which he had been using as a cushion against the unyielding pebbly beach, and took out his cat-stabber. It was his favourite knife and he never went anywhere without it. It had a long handle made out of carved, grooved, ebony and he'd spent many hours fine-tuning its spring-loaded mechanism so that using it felt like nothing more than having an empowering, formidable extension of his own hand. He held the knife in his open palm so that she could see, shielding the view from onlookers with his body as best he could.

"Open it," she said.

He did so, the blade springing free of its ebony prison with a smooth click. Jack took care of the metal, polishing and sharpening it daily, and it glinted in the sunlight with almost incandescent intensity. He looked around again, half expecting to find that some busybody had alerted a local bobby to come descending upon them. But no one else on the beach was paying them the slightest attention.

Billie reached out and took his hand in both of hers, moving the knife this way and that, fascinated with the play of the sunlight on the metal. She ran a finger along the flat of the blade.

"Careful," he said. "It's sharp."

She smirked and raised a mocking eyebrow at him. "Really? Because I hadn't realised that."

And then she released him, pushing his hand back towards him. "Thanks, Jack," she said.

He retracted the blade and put the knife back in his pocket, hoping that it wasn't obvious to either Johnny or Billie just how fast his heart was pounding in his chest.

"So, Billie, how's the singing game these days?" asked Jack.

They were walking slowly along the promenade. It was well into the evening now and they had watched the sun burn and fade over the horizon while they had had dinner in a small restaurant on the seafront. Now the Channel glinted under the light of the rising moon and Johnny and Billie walked arm in arm and they were all content and mellow under the satisfaction of a day spent well, and the soothing influence of a couple of bottles of good-quality Italian wine and after-dinner brandy.

"Wouldn't know," said Billie. "Retired now, ain't I, love? Married woman and all that."

"And how'd old Siddell take that?" Jack glanced from Billie to Johnny, assuming his responsibility for Billie's career change. But Johnny gave him a "hey, nothing to do with me" shrug.

"Don't know, pet. Told the old bastard to piss off a few weeks ago now. Ain't seen him since. He can go rot for all I care."

Jack smiled. He normally hated to hear a woman swear but Billie somehow managed to carry it off. As she did everything else.

They had stopped outside the entrance to the Grand Hotel. "Here we are," said Johnny. "We got you a room too."

"Do talk sense," said Jack. "I ain't staying with you guys on your bleedin' wedding night. I've been gooseberry enough for one day."

"Hey, we ain't asking you to share the bridal suite with us or nothing. Just to sleep in the same hotel, that's all," said Johnny, grinning.

"Jack, you know Johnny and I don't give a fig about all that crap," said Billie. "You know you're welcome. You ain't going to cramp our style in the slightest."

"It's not that I don't appreciate the thought," said Jack. "But it just ain't going to happen. I'm going to catch the last train home. If for no other reason than it's a big day tomorrow and I don't quite share your optimism that it's going to go off without a hitch. I should be there in case things turn ugly."

Johnny thought for a moment. "Alright, actually that's smart. But take the Bentley, at least." He cast a sly smile at Billie. "We ain't going to need it and I'd feel happier if you were looking after it."

"Alright," said Jack. "I'll take your motor. But don't blame me if I wrap it around a tree. You two kids have a swell honeymoon now." He began walking back along the promenade, before stopping and looking back at them.

"That house of yours, does it have an attic?"

"Yeah," said Johnny. "It does."

"Right then, here's the deal. I'll take the attic. I'll move in with you guys, fine, because I can see why it might make sense in terms of running the mob. But I'll only do it if you give me the attic. I don't want to be in the way."

"You wouldn't be in the way, Jack," said Billie.

"All the same, that's the deal. Take it or leave it."

Johnny shook his head, smiling. "Fine, have it your way. You can have the attic."

Jack smiled and bade them goodnight again. Johnny and Billie stood for a moment, arms around each other, watching him go.

"He's an odd fish, ain't he?" said Johnny, affectionately.

"He is," replied Billie. "But that's alright. We all are really. We're all odd fish."

FIVE

AS JACK had predicted, the onslaught on the Danellis' protection rackets stirred up hell. The first few attacks had the element of surprise, but after that the Danellis got wise and started sending more muscle to the pick-ups. The escalation started from there, with pitched battles taking place on streets that had until then been relatively peaceful.

The Black Mob realised that another tactic was required to avoid wholesale carnage which neither side could afford. Fast hit-and-run operations. They would scream in fast in their motors to corner the Danelli pick-up boys and only go toe-to-toe long enough to grab the takings before retreating quickly. If handled properly, they were done with the minimum of fuss, and with the minimum of bloodshed.

But the Danellis were not going to just lie back and take it. In fact, they were just getting started.

Jack now understood why Johnny had bought his house, had quickly married Billie, and brought all his lieutenants under one roof. He had realised the implications of a turf war with the Danellis and was operating under a siege mentality. He wanted one place that he could always defend and didn't want any flanks exposed.

But it was still a home and had to be furnished like one.

Jack didn't normally go on any of Johnny and Billie's shopping expeditions to kit out the house, having his hands full with the parry and thrust of the skirmishes with the Italian mob, but this time they had insisted. And by this time, he felt the campaign was all but over. The Danellis had been beaten back time and time again. Their men were battered and demoralised and a great many of them had deserted the Danellis to join Johnny's mob. As had most of the Danellis' clients for their 'protection'. Once they saw that the full might of the Danelli mob wasn't able to protect itself from Johnny's men, they quickly acquiesced to the newcomer's terms. The fact that these were, at least for the time being, more reasonable only made them more agreeable. The Danellis were all but beaten.

But Johnny disagreed when Jack had said as much.

"Aldo ain't that soft," he said. "He just knows when to pick his fights. Besides, we don't want him beaten. Take everything from a man and he's got no choice left but to go for your throat. We're just knocking him down a bit. Putting him in his place. Same as we'll do for the other mobs given time. We're pruning the garden here. We ain't digging the whole damn thing up."

They were in Regent's Street, choosing furniture for Jack's attic room. He had tried to insist on being happy with a few odds and ends – an old bunk, a few pieces of old furniture, but Billie wouldn't hear of it. "I'm having this house just the way I want it, thank you very much," she had said. "And I won't be having you making a mockery of the whole thing by filling my attic full of junk, Jack Spinks." And so, he had been dragged out on the town to kit out his new place.

Johnny and Jack stood outside the store having a smoke, while Billie was inside buying the place up, as she had been doing all over town most of the morning.

It was Jack, ever watchful, who noticed them first.

"Trouble," he said, nodding towards the two cars slowing to a halt on the other side of the traffic on Regent Street.

And trouble it was. Five men were getting out of the cars. Clearly Danelli boys. And leading them was Aldo Danelli's son himself.

Leo Danelli was not much more than 18, suited and coiffed as you'd expect the eldest boy of an Italian crime lord to be, and his face already scored and pocked by a dozen knife fights. He was handsome and mean and already known for his ruthlessness on the streets. A different proposition from the Danellis' usual muscle.

At that moment, Billie came out of the store, her arms full of brown-paper parcels.

"Stay back," said Johnny urgently. "Get back inside."

"You too," said Jack, his eyes fixed on Leo and the others who were still dancing between the traffic to get to them. "Make sure Billie's alright."

"You can't take them all. You'll need some back-up."

"So, I'll drop them. You just make sure they stay down."

Johnny took a step backward and ushered Billie back into the doorway of the shop. Jack, meanwhile, surged forward and hit the closest Italian hard on the jaw. As the man went down, Jack brought a knee up into the man's head, slamming it into the side of a parked car. He then whirled and set about the next man.

His hands went into his jacket and brought out a knife in each hand. Not for the first time, Johnny marvelled at his friend as he set to work, weaving lithely between his more lumbering opponents, slashing a blade here, thrusting with one there. It was almost balletic, he thought. Utterly controlled, completely masterful. By now, Jack had downed three of the men and none of them had got anywhere near them.

Johnny knelt beside the first man Jack had dropped. Ignoring the man's groggy threats and curses, Johnny grabbed the man's hand and broke his thumb and forefinger before doing the same on the other hand. As the man screamed and coiled on the ground, Johnny stood up again and was turning to do the next when he saw Leo weaving past Jack to head straight towards Billie.

Johnny grabbed him by the scruff of the neck and hauled him back towards the traffic. Leo spun and hit the side of a car but regained his balance and sprang forward once again. Jack had finished with the rest of Leo's team and placed himself between Leo and the others, while Johnny bent down to incapacitate more of the fallen Italians.

"You're done, kid," said Jack. "Go home, will you?"

"Not till I've cut me off a piece of that," sneered Leo, brandishing his own cat-stabber and nodding towards Billie. He sprang forward, but Jack sent him crashing sideways by scraping the side of his shoes roughly down Leo's shins. The boy screamed and fell.

Johnny stepped forward. "Give it," he said and Jack passed him his knife, handle-first. Jack stepped back and for the first time noticed the crowd that had formed – at a distance – to watch the fight.

"Better be quick," he said. "And don't cut him."

Johnny kneeled down beside Leo and put the blade to his cheek. "Tell Aldo it's done. Tell him he's lost and it's time he accepted that. If he keeps pushing then we'll have to do the same. You got me?"

Leo said nothing, but stared at Johnny with hatred. Jack could now definitely hear sirens in the distance. "Johnny," he said. "We gotta go."

Johnny didn't move for a moment and then he swung Jack's knife upwards in a smooth motion, leaving a small but perceptible cut on Leo's cheek. He passed the blade back to Jack.

"Come on," he said, also aware of the sirens getting closer. "We better get moving." He turned and offered his hand to Billie and all three danced quickly away over the prostrate bodies of the fallen Italians and away from the scene. They went quickly but without panic, and Billie felt a rush of pleasure, buttressed on each side by Jack and Johnny, as the crowd parted for them with sharp exhalations of breath and even little squeals of apprehension and fear.

"I told you not to cut him," said Jack reproachfully, as they went.

"I know, I know," said Johnny. "But what can I say? Sometimes I just like to improvise."

SIX

ALDO Danelli's business interests were many and varied. Publicly, he made his money from his stakes in bars, dance-halls, ice-cream parlours and restaurants, but much of his true wealth came from prostitution, extortion rackets and the occasional bit of bootlegging, not to mention track-side betting at most of the racecourses in the south of England. He tended to steer away from the armed robberies, the jump-up jobs and safe-cracking so beloved of the Black Mob because although the short-term rewards were greater, they tended to attract too much trouble and attention from the Law. And Aldo hated trouble. Which was why this current business with the Blacks was putting him in such a foul mood.

Danelli's empire stretched along the south-east coast, taking in the fleshpots from Brighton to Southend, the racetracks at Brighton and Lewes and several other hotspots where good money was to be made. But London was its heart. It was where Aldo had built it all up from nothing, with one ice-cream parlour in the heart of Soho after arriving in England at the turn of the century virtually penniless. And, although he would never have admitted it, Aldo

Danelli and Johnny Black shared a lot in common. Aside from raw ambition, they were both smart, understanding that a successful empire relied not on muscle, nor on money, but on people. On understanding how they worked, what they desired, and what they would and would not do to achieve those desires. Who could be an ally and who could only ever be an enemy. Success, Aldo knew, was built as much from talking to people as it was from damaging them.

Which was why he agreed to Harry Blum's request for an interview when he came to his main offices above his biggest dance-hall just off Piccadilly.

"Harry, come on in," said Aldo, rising from behind his desk, the very picture of delighted bonhomie. He had known Harry for a number of years, mostly from Harry's time on the Clubs squad and had a healthy respect for him. He had learned quickly that graft was not going to work on Harry and that he was one copper who could not be bought. But at the same time, he'd realised Harry operated on his own personal interpretation of the law and that if Aldo could master that, then he need never fear too much from the detective's interference.

"What can I get you?" he went on. "How about some good Italian coffee?" He nodded at the secretary who had led Harry into the expansive and opulently decorated offices and she left to fulfil the order.

"Take a seat, Harry," said Aldo, waving Harry towards a chair by the desk and pointedly pulling up one next to him on the same side. "It's been a while since we had the pleasure of your company."

"Well, you know how it is, Aldo," said Harry. "They like to keep me occupied. How's business, by the way?"

"Oh, you know, fine, fine," said Aldo. "It could be better. But what else is new, eh?"

"I heard you've been having a bit of trouble of late. With Johnny Black and his mob."

"Johnny Black?" said Aldo, his face essaying puzzlement. "I'm not sure I know the name."

The secretary returned with the coffee and a plate of Italian biscuits on a silver tray, which she laid on the edge of the desk. Aldo thanked her and set about pouring the coffee himself. Harry held his tongue until the secretary had departed and then said: "Come on, Aldo. We've known each other too long for you to try that one on. We both know who I'm talking about."

Aldo smiled. "Perhaps you are right. He's a teppista, Harry. A gangster. Nothing more. Why should we waste our lives talking of such trash?"

"Because it's my job. And your livelihood. The Blacks are trying to carve you, aren't they?"

"The key word there being 'trying', Harry. Believe me, they will not succeed. It is nothing. Pay it no mind."

"Come on, Aldo. We're talking pitched battles in Regent Street now. That's not something I can just ignore. You know that."

Aldo made a sour face. "My boy Leo. Always too hot-headed. I told him to let it lie, that I would deal with it in my own way. But, no, he has to go rushing in like the young fool he is. Believe me, I gave him a damned good roasting when he got back. You know I don't approve of that sort of rolling around in the street. It's undignified."

"And so, that's it? You're going to do nothing? You just let the Blacks roll right over you?"

"Harry, look at me. I'm an old man. Or getting that way anyway. I'm reaching the age where I'm starting to think about retiring. Not facing down some giovane toro in some alley or other."

"Perhaps that's the problem," said Harry. "Perhaps it's that weakness that Johnny's smelling now. Perhaps he's taking it all from you because you're not strong enough to hold onto it."

"Harry, what is this? You come into my world, take my hospitality and then you insult me?"

"Only because you have insulted me, Aldo. Your boy got carved. Johnny drew blood and in a very public way. You're telling me that Leo won't want an answer for that? And while we're at it, are you also trying to tell me that Aldo Danelli is just going to meekly walk away from this fight and into some retirement villa on the South Downs just like that?" Harry shook his head. "That's not the Aldo Danelli I know. Not by a long chalk. The Aldo I know would be preparing himself to put this upstart Black in his place. Which would be in the ground, more likely than not."

Aldo smiled again and replaced his now-empty coffee cup on the tray. "So, is this you telling me to think again? That I'm to keep the peace? Forget the slight to my son? To my business?"

"I wouldn't bother wasting my breath. But you're right, it's my job to make sure that the public doesn't get hurt." Harry was mindful of the talking-to Symons had given him. "These things escalate too easily. But as far as I'm concerned, I couldn't care less if you and the Blacks wipe each other out. Just so long as you don't start dragging civilians into your skirmishes."

"Harry, you offend me. I thought we were friends."

"Probably best not to make that mistake, Aldo. But I will say this, at least with you we all know where we stand. With Johnny Black, you never know what the hell the bugger's going to do next."

Aldo chuckled. "Better the devil you know, eh? You see how it is, Harry? Look at us. For you I am a necessary evil. Just the same as you are for me. We cannot realistically expect to ever live without each other and so we have reached a sense of balance, of understanding. With Johnny that will never happen. Because he's not interested in such things. He is more interested in the thrill that comes with chaos, with the chase. With change for change's sake. I am doing nothing but running a business while he is playing a game. That's what makes him so dangerous."

"You talk as if you know him," said Harry.

"I know his type," said Aldo dismissively. "I have seen it many times. Perhaps I was once the same myself."

"But not anymore?"

"One mellows with age. One has to. More coffee?"

Harry reached over and put his cup on the tray. "No thank you, Aldo. I think I've said all that I needed to say. And I must get on." He stood up, as did Aldo.

"No rest for the wicked, eh?" said the Italian.

"Nope," said Harry. "Not in this life anyway."

SEVEN

"I THINK," Johnny said over breakfast one morning, "that I quite fancy a day at the races this weekend."

Jack and Billie both looked at him. Normally, there would be at least a couple of the live-in muscle at the table with them, but as they had breakfasted late this morning it was only the three of them.

"That ain't like you," said Billie. "I've never heard you show the remotest interest in horses before."

But Jack knew where this new interest in the turf was coming from. "You think we're ready for that?" he asked.

"Yeah," said Johnny. "We've got the protection game sown up now. It's ours. But if we want to keep it, we're going to have to persuade Aldo to back off. For good. We can't keep having these skirmishes. And I'll be damned if I'll be having to keep one eye open for Leo Danelli every time I step out the front door. You know what those Eyeties are like. And eye for an eye and all that crap. Anyway, trackside betting is another big earner for the Danellis. If Aldo thought we might go after that too if he doesn't call truce, it might get his attention."

"And I'm sure that's occurred to him too. This isn't going to be just any old scuffle. It's going to be a war. He's going to have muscle. And I mean a lot of muscle."

"Then we're going to have more. Everyone we can get hold of. And war is the word, right enough. But we're going to win. I have no doubt about that."

"Well, I think it's all quite exciting," said Billie. "It's been ages since I've been to the races."

"And it's going to be a bit longer, I'm afraid, pet," said Johnny, lifting her hand to give it a kiss. "Because you ain't coming."

"Now, just you listen 'ere, Johnny Black—"

"No arguments. Not this time. You heard Jack. This is going to be a full-on bloody battle. I'm not having you in the middle of all that. No, you're going to be tucked up here on Saturday where I know you're going to be safe." He turned back to Jack. "I know I said I wanted everyone at the track, but I want a strong team here too. Just in case they try something while our backs are turned."

"Sure," said Jack. "But I don't think that's really Aldo's style. The bloke's got a sense of honour if nothing else."

"No, but I think it's probably Leo's and he might be harbouring a grudge of his own."

"I did say not to cut him."

"I know you did. But I just got caught up in the heat of the moment." He looked at Billie. "But you're staying here and that's final."

"Fine," Billie pouted. "But you get up to any hi-jinks out there with those Brighton tarts and you'll be in bloody trouble. Make no mistake about that, Johnny Black."

Jack had actually never been to the races before. He'd never really set a foot that far from London until Johnny had started his campaign of pulling jobs outside the capital. And he'd never been much of what you'd call a betting man so the racecourses held little appeal for him.

But unlike their previous, more carefree, jaunt to the South Coast, this trip had more of the atmosphere of a military operation to it. The Blacks had men heading to Lewes by the dozen, recruited from pubs and clubs all across London, some travelling by train, some by coach, some by car. They were all told to make their own way there and to have one expectation for the day – that they were there to fight.

Jack and Johnny drove up together, along with Sam Silk and Frankie Pliers who, together with another couple of key lieutenants, formed what was considered to be the Black Mob's inner circle. The mood inside the car was tense, in anticipation of the coming trouble.

"This won't be easy," Johnny said as he steered his Bentley along the Sussex coastal road. "Aldo ain't exactly fighting for his life here, but this is a battle he can't afford to lose. Which is why it's important we walk out of here with our heads held high."

"Don't worry, Johnny, we will," said Sam. "It ain't even a question."

"Frankie, I want a couple of our biggest bruisers to stick close to Johnny," said Jack. "Make sure he's kept out of the worst of the action."

"You got it," rumbled Frankie, almost invisible behind fugs of cigar smoke in the back seat.

"I can take care of myelf," said Johnny, almost sulkily.

"Yeah, but the Danellis will be looking to take you as their main scalp. Especially if Leo's in the mix, which he will be."

Johnny grinned, "You watch too many of them westerns, Jack."

It was a baking hot day at Lewes and it had brought the crowds out. It was difficult to move in the paddocks and between the trackside and the touts. But amid the summer frocks and sun hats of the regular punters, there were several grim, often scarred, masculine Latin faces in evidence. Aldo too had called in all his available muscle. There was an air of menace hanging over the whole track, of violence waiting to explode. As he wandered through the crowds, carefully placing his men, Jack wondered how oblivious the regular punters were to it all.

"We're pretty evenly matched, I'd say" he told Johnny when he reported back. "There's no telling which way this is going to go. Especially if the Law gets involved as well. If they steam in too then it could get brutal."

"You worry too much," said Johnny. "Besides, I've still got an ace up my sleeve."

He nodded towards a clearing in one of the paddocks. A roughly built lectern had been set up, upon which a man was speaking. Jack had seen him before, or at least his photograph. He was never out of the newspapers these days. But close up, the speaker didn't seem all that impressive. Lithe, with clipped and oiled hair and moustache and a dark, double-breasted suit, he could have passed for any toff on the omnibus. But he was attracting quite a crowd. There must have been at least three dozen men crowded around the lectern. Most were burly and thuggish-looking and all wore dark or black suits with a black armband on one sleeve, emblazoned with the same red and black insignia that adorned the front of the lectern.

"What the hell's this?" said Jack.

Johnny smiled. "Wait and see," he said.

The speaker had finished his address and Johnny stepped forward and pushed his way through the crowd to approach the speaker. The man smiled and shook Johnny's hand warmly. They both laughed, sharing a joke. Jack was mystified. He'd never heard of Johnny being remotely interested in politics before.

"Johnny," Jack murmured to himself, a nagging foreboding tugging at his insides. "What the bloody hell do you think you're playing at?"

The battle when it finally came was as brutal as Jack had anticipated. The Italians had been ready, had come in numbers and armed to the teeth, but so had the Black mob. The Blacks once again operated on a policy of hit-and-run, striking hard and fast at the biggest pockets of the Italian mob and then dispersing to regroup and then hit them elsewhere. This eventually had the desired effect of dispersing the Italians into smaller and smaller uncoordinated groups that were easy to pick off.

"That was a hell of a ruck," said Johnny on the drive back to London. Despite the livid bruise on the cheek and his bust lip, his face was a mask of elation. "But actually, I thought it ended up being a bit easier than we thought it was going to be."

"Thanks to your new friends," said Jack. He was the only one not sporting any obvious wounds from the day, largely down to his usual mix of skill and luck. "How come you didn't tell me you were bringing them along?"

The deciding factor in the fight had been Johnny's fascist friends. They had provided a second wave of fresh muscle who could steam in and keep the Danellis occupied while Johnny's men destabilised them from the rear. And the fascist mob fought with a brutal ferocity that took the Italians completely off-guard and even surprised the fascists' allies.

"What, and spoil the surprise? Besides, I didn't know for sure if they'd show up. They were something though, weren't they?"

That, at least, couldn't be denied, thought Jack. He couldn't recall ever seeing such savagery. And it wasn't the violence itself that had troubled him, it was the mania, the zeal, he'd seen in their eyes as they dished it out. He'd seen that kind of thing before, of course. They were the kind of men for whom the violence itself was the point, rather than merely an unpleasant means to an end. And bloodlust like that never failed to make Jack uncomfortable.

"Yes," he said. "They were something."

EIGHT

THE battle at Lewes attracted lots of attention. From the Press initially. Which meant the public, which meant the politicians, which in turn meant the brass at the Met. And at the end of this chain were the coppers on the ground who were expected to make the whole thing go away.

"They're doing their nut," said Symons when he briefed his squad. "People are jittery enough as it is. All this talk of another war. The last thing we want is people thinking that they can't go for a day at the races without walking into a turf war. Forty innocent bystanders injured or wounded. It's not on."

"I think it'll calm down now," said Harry. "Black's won essentially. The Danellis are a spent force. It'll be all Aldo can do to stop the smaller mobs sniffing around his carcass now. His blood's in the water."

"And what about Black?" asked Symons.

"Well, I'm guessing he'll be happy with what he's got. At least for a while. But I don't know. No one does. Probably best to keep an eye on him though."

"Well, let's see that we do." He raised his voice to include everyone in the briefing room. "And if Black shows the remotest sign of starting this nonsense up again I want him stomped on double-quick."

Harry smiled. Symons was finally getting into the game. Not before bloody time either.

"The other thing that's got them all riled upstairs is that these bloody blackshirts seem to be involved," Symons went on. "You can understand why. What with Chancellor Hitler's antics over in Germany, they don't want it getting out of hand over here. And they'll definitely want to know why they seem to be getting into bed with a no-mark hoodlum like Johnny Black."

Yes, thought Harry. I think I'd like to know that too.

Johnny entered the parlour, straightening his tie, and bringing with him the powerful aroma of freshly applied cologne. Billie exchanged a raised eyebrow with Jack, who was sitting at the table, drinking a cup of tea.

"Where the hell are you going all titivated up?" she asked.

Johnny put a badly printed flyer on the table. The dominant image on it was the same insignia that had been seen on the armbands of the thugs at the racecourse. Below it was a time, a date and an address.

"Meeting starts at seven," he said. "Got to get a move on."

"You're not serious?" Jack said.

"Course I'm serious. Going to be quite a big one this."

"What the hell are you playing at, Johnny? Getting mixed up with that bunch?"

Johnny grinned. "Am I to take it that you don't approve?"

"You take it right. I saw what they were like that day. There were nothing but thugs. We don't need thugs. We need blokes who can handle themselves without losing control. And there's a world of difference."

Johnny remained unperturbed by Jack's words. "Yeah, well they got us out of a jam that day. And I never welch on my debts."

"Jack's right," said Billie, nodding towards the paper on the table. "Those blackshirts, they're nothing but trouble. I don't want you getting mixed up with them."

"I'm going," said Johnny. "I said I would, so I'm going to."

"But why?" said Jack. "You don't hold with all that crap they spout. All that inferior races bullshit. Do you?"

"Course I bloody don't. What do you take me for, Jacky Boy?"

"These days," said Jack, "it's getting kind of hard to tell. So, why are you going then?"

"Aw, Jack, don't take that attitude. Look, why don't you two get your gladrags on and we'll all go. See what you think."

"I don't know," said Jack. "Think my jackboots are out getting repaired."

"And I think I'd rather stay in, if you don't mind," said Billie. "Spending my night with a load of blackshirt herberts isn't exactly my idea of a good time."

"Come on," said Johnny, bouncing childishly. "It'll be fun, I promise. And you both might learn something."

"You don't like 'em much, do you, Jack?" said Billie.

All three of them were walking away from the meeting hall. The evening was cold and crisp and they were all thoughtful, the sights and sounds of the meeting still percolating through their minds.

"Not much," replied Jack. He had been uncomfortable from the moment he had stepped into the hall, not much more than three hours previously. The meeting had been surprisingly packed, with an eclectic combination of both men and women from across the social spectrum. Jack had been expecting little more than the usual East End rabble-rousers, the type who were up for a bit of trouble and didn't much care about the reason behind it. But there had been more than a few well-heeled types that he would have described as middle class there too. Professional types, for want of a better word. It had made for an odd, uneasy rabble, but still a rabble nonetheless.

"You want to keep it down a bit?" said Johnny, looking over his shoulder at the pockets of burly, black-uniformed figures who were still drifting around the hall's entrance. "I don't fancy getting pummelled here."

Jack smiled, as if Johnny had just proved his point, and they walked on in silence for a moment. When he was happier that the fascists were out of earshot, Johnny asked, "So, what did you make of it then?"

"I think Jack's right," said Billie. "I think they're a bunch of loonies."

"Crazies," agreed Jack.

"Never mind about that," said Johnny. "No one's arguing about that. But what did you think about what they were saying?"

Jack had heard the fascists say a lot of things that evening, most of them pretty much a repeat of the nonsense you heard from them in the newspapers. The Jewish menace. The scourge of the idle, working classes. The dilution of the nation's lifeblood, *ad nauseum*. But he knew exactly what Johnny was driving at.

"I think I now know why you're so interested," he said.

The latter half of the fascists' meeting had been taken up with arrangements for a proposed demonstration and march which would take in many of the streets in east and central London before arriving at a wide and relatively well-to-do thoroughfare called Pringle Street. It was scheduled for the week after next.

"Nice part of town," said Johnny. "Lots of jewellers and other interesting places round there."

"Like Greene's?" asked Jack.

"Yeah, like Greene's."

Greene's was a jewellers just off Pringle Street itself. It was one of the most famous shops of its kind in London, and beyond, and Jack couldn't remember a time when Johnny hadn't been talking about doing a job on it. And now that he looked at him now, he could see the same gleam of zealous fanaticism that he'd seen in the blackshirts earlier, although it was for entirely different reasons. But that didn't mean it still didn't make Jack nervous.

"This march is going to be huge," said Johnny. "Wouldn't be at all surprised if things got out of control."

"It's possible," agreed Jack.

"Especially as I hear they're planning a big counter protest against it. There's a meeting tomorrow about it. Which you're going to, by the way."

"Could be interesting," said Jack, putting his misgivings aside. He knew Johnny well enough by now to know when he'd clearly set himself upon a course of action. "And I do like to meet new people."

"Yeah, I know you do. And the last you can do is give 'em a few pointers on the best way to conduct themselves. Only civil, ain't it?"

"I'll see what I can do."

"You boys," said Billie, beaming broadly, and hooking an arm through both Jack's and Johnny's to lead them up the street. "Always up to something."

NINE

COMPARED even to the savagery at Lewes, the disturbances on Pringle Street were brutal, ugly and utterly chaotic. But it was a slow burn. While the crowds, from both sides, had began assembling from mid morning, with the occasional tussle and exchange of angry words, it wasn't until well into the afternoon that the real trouble erupted.

No one was able to say for sure exactly what kicked it off, but it was clear to everyone present that violence of some kind was inevitable. The blackshirts, now no longer dressed purely in dark suits and armbands, but in a full militaristic uniform, dominated the streets, which had been closed off for the demonstration. The lines of people who had come to protest against the fascists' presence, galvanised by Jack and a few other undercover members of the Black Mob, were forced back onto the pavements by a cordon of police, hastily assembled by indecisive authorities, who emphatically did not want the march to go ahead but lacked the political courage to call it off entirely.

But what was not in doubt was that at some point just after two o'clock in the afternoon, the shouts and the jeers and the threats that had been simmering all day during the rallies and the speeches, erupted into something far more unpleasant. From there things could only escalate. The police were unable to hold back the crowds on the pavement and violent skirmishes quickly unfolded. And before long, the skirmishes developed into full-scale running battles. Cars and buses were attacked. A couple of them were set on fire and more were merely overturned to be used as cover for the missiles being thrown. Scuffles broke out everywhere, with the police being targeted for violence as much as both sides of the political debate.

It was in this chaos that the Black Mob made their move.

The plan was simple. Moving on from the tactics that had worked in both their campaigns against the Danellis, the Black Mob would conduct a series of fast, in-and-out operations – as many smash-and-grabs on the better-heeled shops in the area as they could before order was restored. They operated in small gangs of two or three which they hoped would escape attention under the cover of the larger, more violent mobs of the protesters. They would spend only a few minutes at each site, grabbing what they could through broken windows before moving on to the next one and making it difficult for the police to have time to react.

Johnny scooped another handful of pearls and silver from the window, shaking the booty free from the shards of broken glass that had fallen into the display. The gear on show in Greene's was everything he had expected it would be. Quality stuff. Distinctive. Hard to shift, admittedly, but that wasn't really the point for Johnny, not wholly anyway. To successfully hit this place was a statement of intent. It sent out the message that nothing was beyond Johnny Black now.

"Well, well. Hello, Johnny."

He turned at the window and looked down the narrow mews where Greene's was located. Blocking the entrance was a fearsome-looking, broad-shouldered man with a bullet-shaped bald head and a fierce, blue eyes burning out beneath a broad scowl. A copper evidently.

"Have we met?" he asked, trying to remain nonchalant. He was alone and he was unarmed. His jemmy was still wedged in the broken window, now too far to reach, or at least not before this scary-looking bloke had got a hold of him.

"Not exactly," said the man. "Ships passing in the night, you might say. We nearly ran into each other at the pictures. In Cardiff."

"Oh yeah." An old conversation with Jack was slowly nagging into life in Johnny's memory. "You're that Harry Blum, ain't ya? Heard about you."

Harry stepped forward, rolling up the sleeves of his shirt. "Can't tell you how gratified that makes me, Johnny. And it's reciprocal, believe me. I've been following your career with considerable interest."

Johnny took a step backward almost instinctively. It didn't take a genius to figure out what was going to happen next. He wondered whether lunging for that jemmy might not be such a bad idea.

"Now come on, Harry. Let's not do anything hasty here."

"Been busy, haven't you, Johnny?" said Harry. "Busy as a bloody bee. And you know what happens to bees sometimes?"

"They sting folk who annoy them?"

Harry smiled grimly. "They get swatted when they buzz around places they shouldn't."

Harry was moving slowly, maximising his threatening intent, but he was now almost upon Johnny. "Tell you what, Johnny. Why don't you let me show you what I mean?"

But Johnny had suddenly relaxed. "I don't think so, Harry." He nodded over the detective's shoulder. In the mouth of the mews were two enormous, burly male silhouettes, the insignia on their armbands just visible in the shadows.

"Everything alright, Mr Black?" said one. Johnny recognised the voice from one of the fascist meetings he'd forced himself to attend over the past few weeks. The bloke had been on the door at one of them and Johnny had shared a ciggie with him when he'd taken a breather from the endless ranting inside. He certainly didn't know the fellow's name but was nonetheless incredibly relieved to see him.

"Not really," he called out. "I seem to be in spot of trouble here."

"Police business," said Harry, barely giving the men a glance. "Move along."

One of the men hit Harry hard on the back of the head. The blow sent the detective reeling slightly, but he stayed on his feet. He turned around, with surprising swiftness for a man of his bulk and buried one of his enormous fists into his assailants' gut. The man folded, bent double, but before Harry could finish him off, the man's companion punched him hard on the side of the face. Harry rode the blow, stepping back to avoid the worst of the impact, but it gave the first man a chance to recover and he followed through with a furious head-first tackle that sent Harry crashing into one of the brick walls of the mews, winding him hard. After that, it was only a matter of time until he was on the ground, unable to completely fend off the onslaught of blows from both men.

Johnny watched all this with horrified fascination. He could hardly see Harry now, hidden as he was behind the legs of the two blackshirts. They were stamping on him now and even at his slight remove, Johnny could hear the dull thuds of their boots hitting muscle and bone. Harry made no more noise than the occasional grunt, but it was clear that he was in trouble.

Johnny felt revulsion rising within him. This was not the kind of violence he had ever had to rely on. This was savage, uncontrolled and he wanted to call out, to bring an end to it before they ended up killing the man on the ground.

But he did not.

Instead he crept past the two men who were still savagely kicking their now-helpless victim. Johnny saw Harry's chunky, blood-stained hand stretch out imploringly from between the legs of his attackers, but he ignored it, instead escaping back into the wider, but somehow less fearsome, madness of the street beyond.

TEN

IT TOOK several months to put Harry back together. For the first few weeks, he was unconscious, drifting in and out of wakefulness in a fug of morphine and pain and he had, at first, not been expected to survive. But, gradually, he spent more time awake than out cold, slowly becoming reborn into the world. Still here. Still living.

"There he is! Boris bloody Karloff."

Harry gave no reaction as Symons approached his bed. He couldn't, trussed up as he was in bandages from head to foot. Both legs and one arm were suspended in traction and he couldn't move his head more than a few inches. He felt more like a living – but fallen – statue than a man.

Symons pulled up a chair and looked at the wreck that was Harry Blum with some concern. All that was really visible were bruised, purple lips and one angry blue eye that glared out at the world, an ember of a constantly burning and barely tolerable agony within.

"How you feeling, Harry?"

"Just chipper," mumbled Harry through his bandages. He was

trying to sound cheerful, but his voice was cracked and broken with the effort of speaking through the pain. "I've got one toe that isn't feeling too bad today."

"Well, at least you're in the land of the living," said Symons. "Last few times we've been up to see you, we've just been sitting here watching you have a kip."

"Yes, well, you need a lot of sleep when you get to my age."

Symons chuckled, appreciating the effort that it no doubt took to get it out rather than the joke itself.

Both men were silent for a moment.

"Come on then," rasped Harry eventually. "Out with it. It's bad news. I can hear it in your voice."

"No flies on you, are there?" began Symons. "It's Johnny Black."

"Thought it might be."

"We've got nothing, Harry. Said he was with a load of those other fascist no-marks when the trouble went down. Got at least half a dozen of them who corroborate his story."

"Convenient."

"Well, they're closing ranks, yes. Not to mention the fact that more than a few of them have got friends in high places. We're not going to get anything out of them."

"I saw Black," said Harry, his voice hoarse with pain, effort and vehemence. "I can put him at that jeweller's."

"And it would be his word against yours. You know what will happen if they put you on the witness stand in the state you're in now. They'll say you're an unreliable witness. That your recollection can't be trusted."

"And it's just them that would be saying that?"

"Harry, that's hardly fair. If you say Black was there that's good enough for me. But it just isn't going to be enough to get him inside a courtroom. You know that as well as I do."

"So Black just gets away with it?"

"No, he doesn't just get away with it. His card is well and truly marked now. We'll get him. Black might think he's smart. But smart will only get you so far. Sooner or later he's going to slip up. And we'll be waiting for him when he does. He's going to pay for this, Harry, have no fear."

Harry didn't say anything. He was a difficult enough man to read at the best of times but swathed in bandages like this it was now impossible for Symons to even attempt it. But somehow he was aware of something going on behind that tortured, single, blue eye.

"You're kicking me out," said Harry quietly.

Symons took a deep breath. This was the portion of this visit that he had been least looking forward to. "Harry, you're lucky to be alive. Bloody lucky. But they tell me there's next to no chance of you walking again. What on earth did you think was going to happen? You should be counting your bloody blessings. They nearly killed you."

"Might have been better if they had. Murder charge would be a bit harder for you to brush off."

"For god's sake, Harry. What the hell are we supposed to do? You're just not going to be in any kind of shape where we can use you. But you'll be looked after, there's no question about that. We look after our own." Symons paused for a moment to get a grip on his own emotional discomfort. "Look, I know it's bloody, but you're just going to have to accept it." He stood up, eager to be away from the simmering rage hidden under those bandages. He had done this all wrong, he told himself. He should have waited, not kicked a man while he was still down. "Just you concentrate on getting well" he said, gripping the brim of his hat and edging away. "That's all you can do now. Let us worry about Johnny Black."

But Harry did not just accept it. It was not in his nature to do so. He slowly forced himself to walk again, dragging himself from one end of his ward to the other, bellowing curses and abusing the doctors and nurses trying to help him. And while his thoughts now started to burn with nothing but vengeance for Johnny Black, he had a more immediate, more prosaic, enemy. The metal and leather frame of the wheelchair that stood at one end of the ward. It waited there patiently for him, as if knowing that in time Harry would have no choice but to fall into it, and that when he did he would never get out of it again. That was something Harry was determined would never happen.

And it didn't. Harry did walk again but not without more or less constant pain and with a pronounced limp that grew worse as he tired throughout the day. His long-suffering doctors were not above describing his recovery as "a miracle" but Harry knew that was the last thing it was. A new force lived within him now, animating him, driving him on and there was nothing of the divine about it. It was hatred – pure and simple.

But his recovery didn't alter anything. He was still out of the Force, pensioned off and left to languish in impotent rage at the knowledge of his absolute defeat at the hands of Johnny Black. His grey, pointless, pain-filled recovery began to stretch from months into years. Black had taken everything from him and now all Harry could do was drag this broken, useless body around until it was finally time for him to die.

Or so he thought. It was not until the New Year of 1940 that Symons came to see him again, arriving at Harry's poky home with a bottle of Scotch and an apologetic, nervous look. Harry diffidently invited him in and poured them both a drink.

"How's the leg?" Symons asked, observing the limp and wince on Harry's face as he moved around the living room.

"Fine. Bit uncomfortable. But I get by." This was not strictly true. There was no moment of Harry's waking life now that did not involve some kind of pain. But he would be damned if he would admit that to Symons.

"I was having a chat with Phil the other day."

Harry dropped into his armchair, placing his stick carefully by its side. "Oh yes?" Illingworth had been the only one of the squad who had kept in touch with him. They went for a drink together every few weeks, keeping Harry abreast of what was going on inside the Force, and more specifically on the latest developments in the career of Johnny Black.

"He said you were getting about pretty well. That you'd jump at the chance to go back on active duty."

"Is that what he said?" A smile played around Harry's lips. He knew what was coming next.

"We'd like you back, Harry. We need you."

"I thought I wasn't needed. That there was no place for a lame old sod like me."

"Come on, that's hardly fair. What would you have done in my shoes? But things are different now. The war, well, it's pretty much sucked up most of the able-bodied coppers we had. The ones who are left, they're either too green or too bloody useless. It's a mess, Harry. And they're running rings round us. The game is changing beyond all recognition too. Rationing. Petrol. They've got all kinds of capers going on now that you wouldn't believe. And you wouldn't have to be on the streets. Not if you don't want to. It's your experience that we're after. What do you say?"

Harry got to his feet again and recharged both their glasses. "You already know what I'm going to say."

ELEVEN

"I'M not sure this is such a good idea."

Jack looked worriedly at Johnny as he slung his suitcase into the back of the Jaguar, the latest acquisition in the long line of ostentatious motors Johnny had gone through in the past few years.

"It'll be fine," said Johnny. "Besides, a change of scene will do us both good."

He looked up at the bedroom window of the house, where Billie was no doubt still fuming. That whole business with the coatcheck girl at the Tap Club had got way out of hand. How was he to know that, despite giving up the singing game, Billie had kept in touch with a lot of the girls at the club and that news of his little fling would inevitably filter back to her?

"I don't know what you thought you were playing at," said Jack, not for the first time.

"I know, I know," said Johnny. "You were right, alright? I guess I was just bored. You can hardly blame me."

This was a common refrain from Johnny these days. The heady days of '36 were long gone and now in 1939 the Black Mob had consolidated their position without any need for any further battles. The Danelli Mob had dwindled to almost nothing and the other outfits knew better than to try and take the Blacks on face to face. And yet, Johnny wasn't satisfied. Jack could see it in his eyes, in every restless sigh, in every frantic and ostentatious acquisition. Most of his time these days was spent talking Johnny out of reckless, suicidal capers – impossible safe jobs, foolhardy smash-and-grabs. They had to play it easy, he kept reminding Johnny. The Heavies still hadn't forgotten that whole business with Harry Blum and would jump at any opportunity to come down hard on them. It was essential they kept a low profile, at least for now. And Johnny would always grouse and grumble but then reluctantly agree in the end.

And then one morning, out of the blue, Johnny had proposed this trip to Jersey. Jack could actually see the sense of it. Until she calmed down over Johnny's little amorous adventure, there was a strong possibility of Billie tipping her husband down the stairs headfirst. If nothing else, Johnny taking himself off somewhere might give her a better chance to cool off.

"You want me to come with you?" he asked, as Johnny closed the boot of the Jaguar.

Johnny couldn't help but smile at the hopeful, yet expecting disappointment, expression on his friend's face. "Nah," he said. "I need you here, don't I? I need you to keep everything ticking over until I get back. And," he added, nodding up towards the bedroom window, "to see if you can calm her ladyship down before I get back."

"That could take some time," said Jack, with a smile.

Johnny chuckled. "Tell me about it. Look, stop looking so worried. I'll be back before you know it. You know me, a couple of days and I'll be sick to the back teeth of Jersey. Just keep an eye on everything until I get back."

"And what about this talk of a war? You sure it's a good idea to go gallivanting about at a time like this?"

"A war," scoffed Johnny. "There ain't going to be no war. And so what if there is? It's got nothing to do with the likes of us, has it? Life'll go on just the same for you and me. Really, Jacky Boy, you worry too much, you really do."

"Alright," said Jack, holding up his hands in defeat and stepping back to let Johnny into his motor. "Have it your own way. I'll see you when you get back."

And so in that sunny June of 1939, Johnny Black had got into his Jag and roared off towards the coast, blithely assuming that he'd enjoy a few carefree weeks of dalliance and freedom in the sunshine of the Channel Islands before sauntering back to resume his life.

He had seldom been more wrong about anything.

II. THE RULE OF THREE

ONE

JOHNNY strutted through the cavernous opulence of the lobby of the Excelsior Hotel, feeling exceptionally proud of himself. The fog of boredom that had once again been falling over him was lifted – largely because he'd just pulled off one of the smoothest solo jobs of his career. Admittedly, the safe was a 50-year-old Victorian number that you could probably have opened with a harsh word, but he'd popped the back with nothing more than a jemmy and a screwdriver and scooped out the cash, jewels and other valuables that now filled his bulging pockets – and all while the staff on the reception desk had never been more than fifteen feet away. It was a smooth bit of work, even if he did say so himself. Now all he had to do was get the hell out of there before they realised they'd been turned over.

"Johnny! Where on earth have you been?"

He was almost at the revolving door of the hotel's main entrance when the familiar voice rang out with nerve-jangling loudness. Greta Dinsdale, resplendent in evening gown and costume jewellery, was standing behind him, a pout of petulant displeasure on her face. The fiercely ambitious Greta had been clinging limpetlike to Johnny ever since she had caught wind of the rumours he'd carefully seeded about him being a movie producer on a location hunt. Not that Johnny had resisted too much. How could he object to having probably the most beautiful woman on the island, hanging on his arm, not to mention his every word? (Just so long as Billie never found out.) And over the last couple of weeks, he and Greta had become the 'It couple' of the Excelsior set, a status that Johnny revelled in just as much as Greta.

However, that was all very well when you didn't have pockets full of booty that felt as if it were glowing white hot and screaming out your larceny to the world. Johnny usually never had the slightest objection to being the centre of attention wherever he went, but he was aware that a number of the other hotel guests had turned to look at them now, sensing a drama brewing. His departure was not exactly going to be unnoticed.

"Greta, my dear," he beamed. "May I say you look positively radiant."

He embraced her and kissed her on both cheeks, but she still pouted at him like a sulky child, only partially mollified. "Johnny! You haven't forgotten about our dinner date?"

He had, of course. Much of what he said to and around Greta was done without much thought, as he created a wall of boast and empty promise to keep her rapacious ambition at bay. He'd found, in fact, that the appeal of her company had worn off rather quickly. While she was certainly pretty, beautiful even, she was also incredibly immature and shockingly self-centred, qualities which Johnny was only really willing to put up with in himself. Certainly, the more he got to know Greta, the more she paled beside Billie, who he was now missing more and more. His little holiday was definitely nearing its end, he thought, and he was looking forward to getting back to London, to Billie and Jack and the rest of the Firm as soon as possible.

"Of course not, my dear," he protested. "How could I forget something like that? I was just coming to find you, actually."

Greta smiled toothily, oblivious to his sarcasm, and held out her arm. "Quite. Well, then, shall we?"

Johnny glanced from Greta to the wide front doors of the hotel.

Common sense now dictated he make his excuses and get the hell out of there. Every second he lingered, he increased the chances of his being caught with the contents of the recently emptied safe on his person. In fact, he could almost hear Jack's doleful whisper in his ear to do the smart thing and leave. But then, common sense had never really been Johnny's strong point. To sit and have a leisurely dinner in the very hotel that he'd just fairly comprehensively robbed seemed not just foolhardy but also rather daring. And he could never resist daring.

"Yes, why not indeed?" he grinned, snuffing out the remaining voices of reason in his head. "After you, my dear."

He took Greta's arm and led her towards the dining room where the dinner-suited staff were already rushing to obsequiously attend to them. They were quickly installed at one of the best tables – Johnny's professed favourite – just next to a set of bay windows overlooking the restaurant's patio.

It was now that he was reminded of one of the pitfalls of spending another evening in Greta's company – the soporific experience of her extended monologues as she regaled him, not for the first time, with the minutest detail of the experience of Being Greta Dinsdale. There was no morsel of vacuous self-involvement or personal history that Greta did not find worthy of repeated and detailed analysis. It was, reflected Johnny, his own fault. Having introduced himself as a movie bigwig, he should have known that he was then going to be subjected to the longest and most interminable audition in the history of showbiz.

The upside to this was, of course, that Greta was far too involved in her solipsistic chatter to notice when his attention wandered to pretty much anywhere else in the dining room. But the other diners seemed, if anything, to be even more boring than Greta herself. A few holidaymakers here and there, but mostly moneyed retiree types. He found himself smiling at the thought of their spluttering outrage if they knew they were dining with someone who had just helped himself to their prized valuables, which were still burning hotly within the folds of his dinner suit.

And in due course, as Greta gabbled on, he found his attention turning to a growing commotion outside the glass-paned doors of the dining room in the hotel lobby itself. A rising amount of purposeful, slightly panicked rushing about, accompanied by hushed, urgent conversation told him that his raid on the hotel safe had by now been discovered.

He wasn't at this point overly concerned for his safety. He didn't expect that the local yokel constabulary would be up to much and would blunder around aimlessly for the first few hours, while the hotel staff would compound the disarray by flapping about, fretting over the hotel's reputation and the privacy of their guests. But if it did seem that they were getting a little too close for comfort, he figured he'd be able to slip away without too much trouble. It was one of the reasons why he always liked this window table. It combined impressive views with a ready-made escape route.

And it was at this precise moment that things started running away from him. He almost didn't notice to begin with. As the hubbub in the lobby became more heated and pronounced, he realised that he could recognise one voice over all the others. A low, rumbling baritone, with an edge of impatience and barely suppressed anger to it. He was certain he'd heard it before, but he couldn't quite place it.

The recollection of whose voice it was came at almost exactly the same time as its owner came into view. The pale, bullet-shaped head now sporting two snaking, jagged scars, which travelled more or less the entire length of his skull, lending it an even more fearsome air. It had been years since Johnny had last seen Harry Blum and while he was initially shocked by the detective's altered appearance, he could see from one look at the scowling rage on the detective's fact that the years had done nothing to mellow him.

"Fuck."

Johnny was barely even aware that he'd let the profanity cross his lips until he saw Greta's shocked face staring at him, her normally more-than-agile mouth locked for once into a scandalised 'o'.

"Johnny!"

He did his best to swallow his irritation at her and put on his best smile. "I'm terribly sorry, my dear. That was quite unforgivable of me."

"What on earth is the matter?" she demanded, still not quite mollified by his contrition.

"It's just that I remembered about a terribly important phone call that I completely forgot to make."

"I still don't think that's any kind of excuse for that sort of language." Johnny could see she was genuinely upset but suspected it was as much because he had interrupted her in full flow as the uncouth profanity he'd just used.

"I know, I know," he said, doing his best to suppress a smile as it occurred to him that if he had used that kind of language to Billie she would have just given him the same – and worse – right back. It was one of the reasons why he was starting to miss her so much. "Perhaps the best thing is if I go and see to that phone call before it slips my mind again," he said.

He stood up and left the table. He couldn't care less about Greta now. His only thought was getting out of that hotel before Harry Blum got hold of him. The local flatfoots were one thing but Harry was quite another. For one thing, he'd recognise Johnny on sight and for another, going by the wounds he was now sporting and indeed his very presence here, he was most likely looking for some kind of payback for '36.

Johnny crossed the dining room, doing his best to remain calm when every instinct was telling him to run. It occurred to him to make an exit directly through the patio but then decided there was no point calling attention to himself until he absolutely had to. He might still be able to slip out the front door of the hotel. Not for the first time, he found himself wishing that he'd listened to that little voice of common sense. He wondered if he was ever going to learn.

Johnny got to the door just in time to all but walk straight into Harry coming in the other direction. Yeah, he thought bitterly. My luck is really holding up tonight.

"Evening, Harry," he said, with a grin. "How you been?"

Harry was so dumbstruck by the sight of Johnny virtually walking into his arms that it took him a second or two to react and Johnny took advantage of this to push Harry roughly in the chest and then double back hurriedly into the dining room.

But by now, Harry had recovered his balance and was roaring orders at the hapless uniforms behind him. They all spilled into the room, trying to cut off Johnny as he danced between tables, baffled waiters and gabbling, shocked diners alike. The room was in uproar and it was becoming clear to everyone within it that Johnny's escape routes were becoming increasingly limited and that capture was imminent. Within a matter of moments he had ended up back where he had started, at his own table with Greta once again gawping at him in open-mouthed shock.

"Johnny!" she cried.

Johnny jumped onto the table, scattering drinks and what was left of his own main course in her lap. "Terribly sorry, my dear," he said, with a grin. "But something rather urgent has come up. Here, with my compliments." He fished a string of pearls from one pocket and tossed them into her lap. For all he knew, they were hers anyway.

He could see Harry and the other coppers barrelling their way across the dining room towards him and so he launched himself out of the bay window, just as Harry made an attempt to lunge at his ankles across the table, prompting fresh screams of outrage from Greta.

Swivelling to avoid Harry's grip, Johnny landed awkwardly on the parapet below just the window, and twisted on its edge before tumbling over the wall to the significant drop below. He plummeted through several feet of hedgerows and shrubberies until he landed heavily on the street below the hotel. The pain surging up his right leg told him that he had done himself some serious damage, if not out-and-out broken bones. But his immediate attention was taken up by the two uniformed policemen standing above him, and who seemed to be simultaneously bemused and gratified to find him drop right at their feet.

"Er, good evening, officers," he tried to say, but the pain now coursing up his leg meant that it came out as nothing more than a strangulated yelp.

He could already hear Harry's bellowing getting closer, as he limped down the hotel's drive as quickly as possible, eager to claim his prize. Johnny winced and sighed, telling himself to accept defeat with as much grace as he could muster, which wasn't much.

"Johnny bloody Black."

Johnny looked up from interrogation room table at which he

was seated and cuffed. He couldn't see too well out of one eye and he could feel the right side of his jaw stiffening. Harry had given him a brief going over on trip down to the station, but Johnny had a feeling that it had been a mere playful preamble to the proper beating that was no doubt to come.

"Alright, Harry," he said, doing his best to ignore the raw, bloody taste in his mouth. "Long time, no see. How've you been keeping?"

Harry stared down at him, the fury on his face plain to see. He did look a mess, thought Johnny. It looked almost as if Harry's head had been cracked open like an egg before being less than perfectly patched together again. Which Johnny supposed was more or less what had happened. That day had taught him the lesson that he should always leave the violent to stuff to Jack who had a knack for it and could control it. It had gone too far and Johnny was genuinely sorry for that. But he had a feeling that contrite apologies now would do nothing but enrage Harry even further and accelerate the onset of the violence that was surely imminent.

"So, what brings you down to Jersey anyway, Harry?" he asked. "Spot of sunbathing?"

"You bring me down here, Johnny, you do. I'd go to the ends of the earth to slap a pair of bracelets on you. You know that."

"Well, that's damned touching, Harry. It really is." He looked at Harry's eyes. One was still a clear, icy blue, but the other now had a slight milky sheen to it, giving it an uncanny, dead appearance. Harry had been scary enough in that alley back in '36 but now there was something new there, something manic and dangerously unpredictable. It was something Johnny wanted to have as little to do with as possible. Whatever we did that day, thought Johnny, we broke the poor bugger in some way. He felt a brief surge of raw fear as it occurred to him for the first time that he might not even make it out of this room alive.

And so he breathed a sigh of relief when the door of the interview room opened and a stocky, middle-aged man in a green, tweed suit strode in, a gawky, nervous-looking detective constable at his heels. This guy was much more like it. Your typical provincial CID copper and a far more manageable prospect than the implacable slab of human vengeance which Harry Blum seemed to have become.

"Right," barked DCI Gardiner. "Out."

It took a moment for both Johnny and Harry to realise that Gardiner was in fact speaking to Harry.

"Excuse me?" said Harry, turning his scowl towards the other detective.

"You heard me. Out. I don't want any out-of-towners lousing up my investigation."

"*Your* investigation?" growled Harry. "This is my collar."

"No. It. Isn't," said Gardiner, emphasising his words, as if speaking to a toddler. "It's mine." Gardiner's whiskery features had a piggish, stubborn quality to them that suggested their owner wasn't used to argument, far less to losing it. What was that thing, thought Johnny idly, about an immovable object meeting an unstoppable force?

"This man," said Harry, pointing to Johnny, "is wanted in connection with a list of offences as long as my bloody arm. Including a serious assault on a police officer."

"Not that you're holding a grudge or anything, eh, Harry?" added Johnny.

"In London," said Gardiner. "Not here."

"I'm talking him back to London," said Harry.

"No, you're not," said Gardiner. "He's just committed a major felony on this island. I fully expect to be in possession of a full confession by the end of the day. He'll be tried here by this island's judiciary and he'll serve his time here. And that's all there is to it."

Harry took a couple of steps forward and for a moment Johnny thought he was going to square up to Gardiner. Was there no one this mad bastard wouldn't put a beating on, he wondered? "This man is my collar," he said. "And there's no way in hell I'm going to let you take him from me."

"What are you going to do?" said Gardiner, with an unimpressed smile. "Give me a thumping too? That's not how we do things around here."

"'Ere, Harry," said Johnny. "I don't think he likes you too much."

Harry ignored him, focusing his attention on his new adversary. "You're not listening to me, are you, sunshine?"

"No," replied Gardiner. "It's you who's not listening. See, this isn't London. You're on my patch here. And you don't scare me. Not for an instant. Things get done my way down here or not at all. Now, I'm only going to say this one more time. I'm not having you interfering with my investigation. That means I want you out of this room and out of this nick. You can get the next boat back to the mainland. Or you can go and piss about in the rock pools for all I care. Just so long as I don't have to see or hear you. Now, hoppit."

For a moment, Johnny was sure Harry was going to hit Gardiner. He could see the jaw clenched with fury, a cable-like vein pulsing angrily on his temple. But in the end, Harry just stomped towards the door without another word.

"You can have him when we've finished with him," Gardiner called after him.

Harry didn't reply but slammed the door after him.

"Charming bloke, ain't he?" said Johnny. "Real, winning personality."

"Shut up, Black," said Gardiner. "You're going to start talking or I'm going to get him back in here and I'll let him tear you apart until you've told me everything I need to know. So start singing."

And Johnny did. They had him bang to rights after all, and a hotel full of furious witnesses ready to point the finger at him, not least of whom was Greta Dinsdale herself, happy to take whatever spotlight was left available to her. And so he quickly became reconciled to the fact that he was going to do some time, while taking what comfort he could in knowing that by doing it in Jersey, he was causing Harry Blum a not insignificant amount of frustration.

Aisde from his brief, he had only one visitor in all his time behind bars in Jersey and that was Jack. One afternoon, while glorious Jersey sunshine streamed through the single frosted glass transom of the grim meeting room of the local nick, he waited until Jack, immaculate as ever in black suit and Crombie, was led in by a warden.

Jack exchanged the briefest of glances with the guard who then retired to outside the room, while Jack took the seat opposite Johnny at the table.

"How much is that costing us?" asked Johnny, nodding to the

door, where the back of the guard's head was just visible through the glass partition.

"More than it should. But what the hell, you're worth it. Probably." Johnny grinned. "How's Bil? She didn't come?"

"No, but she did send a message. Something about me cutting off your bollocks and bringing them back to her tied to a stick of rock."

"Right. So, she's heard about Greta then?"

"It was all over the papers, wasn't it? As if you weren't in enough shit before. It's going to be some time before she cools off, let me tell you."

"Well, that at least isn't going to be a problem. Sharkey's been down. Tells me that there's no way around it. I'm doing my stir down here."

"Yeah, he told me." He gave Johnny a pitying look.

"I suppose you came all the way down here to tell me what a bloody idiot I am," said Johnny.

"Well, you are and I will. But what I really came to see about is what you want us to do while you're cooling your heels here."

"Business as usual, ain't it? It'll be down to you to keep things ticking over till I get out. Make sure none of the other Mobs try to take advantage."

"You mean like we would? I dunno, Johnny. You know me, I ain't cut out for all that head honcho crap. You know that."

"Yeah, I do," said Johnny. "But what the hell else choice is there? And you're more than up to it, Jacky Boy. But I know you don't like the limelight, so what I'm thinking is that Billie steps up to run the Mob for now."

"Billie? You sure about that?"

"Makes sense, don't it? That way it's still the Black Mob to all intents and purposes."

"Yeah, but still, that's a hell of a lot to lay on her shoulders."

"She'll be fine. Bil's as tough as they come. And she'll have you there to help her out. The rest of the Mob too."

Jack thought for a moment and then nodded. "Alright. Fine. I'll tell her."

"And it won't be for long neither," added Johnny. "Sharkey says I'll be out in a couple of years if I keep my nose clean. I'll be back before you know it."

"And how are you with that?" asked Jack. "Think you'll be alright?"

Johnny shrugged. "This place? No problem. Piece of piss."

"Have you even served time before?"

Johnny flashed him another grin. "Not a single day. But how hard can it be?"

"Can be for some. How are you finding it?"

"Alright so far. Got me an alright cellmate. Nice kid. Bloody awful burglar by all accounts but pleasant enough bloke. Look, I'll be fine. Just put me feet up for a couple of years, catch up on my reading and I'll be back in business before you know it."

Once again, Johnny couldn't have been more wrong. He was just beginning his sentence when war was declared and eight months later the Nazis marched into the Channel Islands. He watched with his fellow stunned inmates and warders alike as row upon row of striding, grey-clad German troops marched into main courtyard of the prison, under the ashen glare of the old Governor and the proud, triumphant smiles of his new triumphant overlords.

Johnny knew that day that his life had changed somehow, but it would not be for a great many months that he would realise by how much.

Johnny wrapped his fingers around the iron bars on the window and gave them a firm tug. Beyond the pocked and rusted rods and the grime-encrusted glass, he could see the flat, white rooftops of Jersey, twinkling in the sunlight, and the azure band of the English Channel. Aside from the bars, the only thing spoiling the vista was the ominous red and black of the swastika flying from Town Hall; an ever-present reminder of the islands' new masters.

He felt the bars give just slightly in their stone housing and a fine stream of crumbly, white dust rained down from the wall onto the flagstone floor. Not enough to make any difference to the solidity of the bars, or their ability to keep him confined there, but just enough to make him feel as if the walls of his prison themselves were mocking him.

"Jesus Christ," he said. "What a dump."

His cellmate Albie Fairchild, a skinny, 21-year-old serially inept burglar smiled up at him from his bunk. He knew what was coming next.

"It's embarrassing, that's what it is," said Johnny, adopting the tone of bravado he used when launching into one of his public performances. "I mean, doing time, it's an occupational hazard, ain't it? I accept that. But put me in a decent nick, for Christ's sake. Your Pentonville or your Scrubs. Not some yokel gaol in the middle of bloody nowhere. I mean, Jersey – it's not even Great Britain, is it? Not really."

Albie ignored the slight on his home island, recognising that while the barb was meant for him, there was no real malice behind it. He knew by now it was one of the methods Johnny used to create a sense of intimacy. The jokes and the jibes were meant to make you feel as if you had known each other for years, had grown up in each other's company. And despite the potential for it to go wrong, particularly with some of the short-fused maniacs you tended to meet inside, no one ever seemed to take real offence. Everything Johnny said or did was done with a kind of lop-sided charm that made it very hard to stay annoyed with him. Even the screws cut him more slack than they would anyone else. But that was Johnny all over, thought Albie. He could be picking your pocket and you'd find yourself laughing along with him as he did so.

"Johnny, what the hell do you think you're doing?"

Johnny could feel Albie hovering behind him somewhere, but he didn't take his eyes of the white-washed wall at the back of the Governor's private garden. Like his cell, the wall offended him. Its surface was rough, pocked and uneven and would be an easy climb. There hadn't even been any attempt made to render it off-limits with wire or broken glass – probably because the Governor would find this an aesthetically distasteful thing to have at the bottom of his garden.

Beyond the wall, there was a daunting but manageable climb to a grassy embankment and from there another to the road that would lead back to Jersey. That no one up to now had made a run for it by this method (at least as far as Johnny was aware) was more down to some kind of unspoken gentlemen's agreement between the warders and the prisoners than the remotest practical consideration of the possibility of doing so. Jersey wasn't like other jails. It was lazy and bucolic and operating on assumptions as archaic as its foundations.

"Just looking," said Johnny, softly.

"Well, don't. Come away before someone gets the wrong idea."

"Yeah, like who?"

"Well, like them for starters." Albie nodded towards two guards who were some distance away at the front of the Governor's little white-washed cottage, sharing a smoke as they gazed across the elevated view of Jersey and the Channel beyond.

But these weren't the plodding, ageing jobsworths of the regular wardens. These blokes were younger, leaner, uniformed in khaki, with red-and-black Nazi insignia on their sleeves. German soldiers who had been co-opted onto prison guard duty. Their arrival had unsettled everyone at the prison, from the Governor downwards, but so far they hadn't give anyone any real cause for apprehension.

Johnny gave the Germans an unconcerned glance. "They don't worry me."

"Well, don't you think they should?" Albie leaned closer to Johnny. "They've got guns."

"They ain't going to use them."

"You don't know that. Will you come away from there, for god's sake?" Albie had fear in his eyes and his brow was creased with concern. No one, it seemed, had become more disturbed by the arrival of the Nazis than Albie. "Before they bloody shoot you."

Johnny sighed and stepped away from the wall and both men began walked back through the garden. "Have to say I'm quite touched by your concern, Albie. Never knew you cared. Hope this doesn't mean you're going a bit fruity on me though or I'll be getting worried when they lock that cell door at night."

"Don't flatter yourself, mate. This is a cushy number and I don't want you arsing it up for the rest of us. Getting your brains spattered all over the Guv'nor's daffies or some bloody thing."

When the Nazis turned back towards the wall, all they now saw were two lags in gardeners' overalls ambling back towards the crumbling prison buildings, indistinguishable from every other prisoner in their charge, either outside or inside the walls. There was no cause for alarm.

TWO

JIM CLAY scuttled through the shadows towards the front gate of Brookfield Furriers. The street, slicked with a fresh rainfall, was deserted and in almost complete darkness thanks to the blackout, and he relied on the white sight lines as he picked his way towards the blue double-gates of the firm's goods entrance.

He could hear the distant wail of air-raid sirens and the whistle and low crump of bombs falling, buildings crumbling. Clay felt not a moment's guilt for his satisfaction at the destruction and chaos that was befalling his city. It meant the emergency services, the Law included, would be tied up for hours and far, far too busy to worry about what he and his pals were about to pull.

Once he reached the gates, he produced a crowbar from under his coat, forced it through the chain held together by a large padlock and gave it a determined and practiced push. Both chain and lock gave way on the second attempt and he deftly caught them before they had a chance to make a clattering fall to the ground. He then stowed them in the pocket of his overcoat and pushed open the gates.

Clay whistled and the ARP ambulance that had been waiting in the shadows glided forward and through the gates, guided by him. The ambulance was a stroke of genius, he thought as he followed the motor in and closed the gates behind him. It had been the Ferret's idea, which just went to show that while he might be an untrustworthy little shit, he still did come up with the goods when he had to. In the current state of emergency, an ARP ambo was the one vehicle that was guaranteed not be challenged on the streets. It was the perfect getaway.

The rest of the team were already clambering out of the ambulance and heading towards the main entrance of the warehouse. They made way for Clay who then forced the door. He pointed to two of the others.

"You two, out here. The rest inside."

He led them through a narrow, white-bricked passageway, all of them moving quickly but silently. There was another door at the opposite end of the passageway and Clay made short work of this too, working by the torchlight provided by his accomplices. Within moments they were inside what they'd been assured would be the main storage area of the warehouse. The demand for furs had slackened considerably because of the war, but they still fetched a tidy price on the black market. Tonight would be lucrative and easy work.

It was, if anything, even gloomier inside the warehouse and their torches fingered through the darkness as they tried to get their bearings but apart from the high stacks of crates and boxes, almost the first thing their beams alighted on was the towering figure of a lone man, standing in the darkness, shirt sleeves rolled up, truncheon in hand, ready to do some damage.

"Evening, boys," said Harry Blum, grinning evilly in the torchlight. "Let's be 'aving you."

Symons and his squad had been waiting patiently outside, giving their target a few minutes to get into place before going in after them. The two men who'd been left on watch didn't present anything of a challenge and after a brief tussle Tavener and Stott, two of the Heavy Mob's biggest bruisers, had them bent over and helpless across the hood of a car.

"Right, so far, so good," said Symons. "Now, where the hell's Harry?"

The rest of his men stared blankly at him and Symons didn't really need an answer. He already knew where Harry Blum would be. Right in the bloody middle of it.

"Typical," muttered Symons. "Right, come on. We better get in there before the silly bugger finds himself in traction again."

He left a couple of woodentops in charge of the two prisoners and led his team along the stone corridor to the warehouse. They could hear the sounds of a fight, cries of pain and alarm, the stamp of feet, the thud of bodies against hard surfaces, drifting along the stone passageway towards them. But when they got to the door at its end, all the sounds of commotion stopped abruptly and they were met with eerie silence. Symons glanced at his men before stepping, with some trepidation, through the doorway.

The darkness was absolute, without any other door or window to let in even the slightest light. But it was the relative quiet that was the strangest thing, thought Symons. Despite the sounds of hoarse, human breathing and the occasional low moan of pain, the place was eerily still. Certainly compared to the ruckus they'd heard moments before.

Symons fished in his pocket for his lighter and sparked it into life. For a moment, they could still make out very little as the flickering yellow flame danced quixotically across the walls of the room. But as the men's eyes become used to the jerky, uneven light, they began to see the full horror of what had just happened.

Sprawled across the stone floor and crates of what appeared to be some sort of stockroom were the prostrate bodies of maybe five or six men. Symons was relatively sure that none of them were actually dead, going by the groaning and twitching coming from them. He was equally certain, however, that they were all in a pretty bad way. But for him, the most shocking thing was the amount of blood on view. The white brick walls of the room were slathered thick with the stuff, as if bright red paint had been tossed with great abandon around the place by a hyperactive little child.

And standing in the middle of this carnage stood Harry Blum, sleeves rolled up, fists slick with the blood of the men on the ground.

His scowling face was a mask of primal vengeance, and seemed almost demonic in the light of the flickering flame. A colossus of implacable retribution.

"Jesus Christ," Symons heard Tavener murmur under his breath. And he had to agree. He couldn't remember the last he'd seen a sight remotely comparable in its casual brutality.

"Bloody hell, Harry," he said finally. "What the hell have you done?"

It was a bloody mess, literally. They used the crooks' own stolen ambulance to ferry two of the fallen to hospital but had to pull another one off air-raid duty – the docks had been getting badly pummelled that night – in order to transport the other two. There would be questions and then there would be bollockings and by the end of the evening Symons was in no mood to receive either, at least not without passing on some of the pain.

"What the hell got into you, Harry?" he demanded as they finished the clean-up in the warehouse courtyard. "As if I didn't know."

Harry said nothing. It was better to let Symons blow off steam at him. Speaking up now would only make matters worse.

"You're bloody lucky you didn't kill them."

"That's me all over," muttered Harry. "Lucky."

"There's going to be hell to pay for this. The brass are going to want to know why we're clogging up emergency beds with pummelled villains when they've already got their hands bloody full." He paused, having exhausted his exasperation. "Oh, just go home, will you? I've got no more time to waste on your bloody vendettas."

Symons watched Harry limp away without another word. It crossed his mind for a moment that Harry might be playing up his bad leg for sympathy but then dismissed the idea. Harry wasn't the sympathy type – either giving or receiving.

THREE

FREDDIE Winner's heart was pumping violently as he stepped across the threshold of the Black house. The gorillas on the door made a path for him, but their faces were tense, guarded, unreadable. Not that they were particularly friendly at the best of times, thought Freddie, but there was a definite edge to the place today. It was almost electric. Change was coming. He could feel it.

Freddie scanned the faces of the three minders, but even the new kid, Keith, was stoney-faced. "What's all the hullaballoo?" he said. He'd been summoned via a network of phone calls and runners at little past six in the morning. The call had been expected – so much so that he hadn't been able to sleep a wink, but that didn't mean it didn't still rankle to be expected to come running whenever they felt like it.

"You're wanted, Freddie," said Keith, nodding down the dark hallway towards the parlour. Freddie liked this kid. He was polite and at least showed him a bit more respect than the others. For now, anyway.

"Why? What's going on?" he asked with as much innocence as he could muster.

Keith shrugged. "Better ask them. Sounds like something went arse over tit with the Brookfields' job."

"Christ." He tried to assume an air of urgency as he hurried past the gorillas and down the passageway. But this play-acting was harder than he thought and it didn't come naturally to him. How would Johnny have reacted to a piece of news like that? he asked himself, and found that he didn't honestly know. That was one of the things about Johnny. You never knew from one moment to the next which way he was going to twist. Mind you, he couldn't recall Johnny ever having to deal with a piece of news like this. Jobs going pear-shaped – it just wasn't the kind of thing that happened to Johnny Black.

His apprehension increased with every step he took along the passageway. He tried to pull himself together. The quickest way to screw this up would be by being so bloody jittery. But he just couldn't rid himself of the feeling that he'd messed up, and messed up badly.

Billie herself was at her usual place behind the big table, hands folded demurely, tea cup and saucer in front of her. Her eyes never left him once as he entered the room.

Jack was leaning against the dresser behind Billie, immaculate in black suit, despite the earliness of the hour. He stared at Freddie with his sardonic, black eyes and looking for all the world like a malevolent, black crow. He too was drinking from a china cup and saucer. Right little tea party they'd got going here, thought Freddie.

"Alright, Ferret?" said Billie, with a smile that had neither warmth nor friendliness. "Come in and shut the door."

Freddie did so but still kept his distance from the table. His heart was thudding furiously in his chest, as if trying to burst free of its cage and throw itself on their mercy. He could feel sweat prickling the back of his neck and along his arms. He had to pull himself together. This was what he had wanted, what he had been manoeuvring for, but now that he'd managed it, he was scared shitless.

He wasn't going to be able to do this and had in fact called it all wrong. He realised that now. He didn't know how, but they were clearly on to him. Lord knows for how long. There was a definite atmosphere of confrontation, of menace, in the room, and far from being called here as the confidante he'd expected to be, Freddie increasingly had that sinking, fluttery feeling he would get whenever he found himself in the dock. His largely imagined control of the situation was seeping away with every passing moment and the extent of his delusion was making him feel sick.

"It's Freddie," he said, sullenly, hoping that by asserting himself, he could change the atmosphere in the room. He was damned if he'd let someone like Billie keep him on the back foot like this.

"Course it is," said Billie. "Cup of tea, love?"

"No, thanks. I'm fine."

For a moment there was silence, save for the sound of pouring tea as Billie served herself another cup, the clattering of the tea things, the oppressive, sonorous ticking of the clock on the kitchen wall. He'd always hated that damned clock.

"Something go wrong with the Brookfields job, then?" he asked, more to break the silence than anything else. This painful, accusatory quiet was making him uneasy, which, he supposed, was precisely its point.

Billie raised an eyebrow. "Oh, so you've heard then?"

"Only what they told me back there, which was sod all. So, what happened?"

"Well, Freddie," said Billie, "that's just what we're trying to find out. Ain't we, Jack?"

Jack didn't move from his spot at the dresser. He was still wearing that laconic smirk of his, but his dark eyes had a hardness, a contemptuous hostility, to them.

"Turns out Harry Blum is what happened," said Jack softly. Freddie didn't think he'd ever heard Jack raise his voice above a murmur in all the years that he'd known him, which he supposed was part of why he found him so unsettling. "Came down on the lot of them like a ton of bricks."

"Christ," said Freddie, trying to inject as much outrage into his voice as he could. "The Heavies? How the hell did they get to hear about it?"

"See, that's just what we've been wondering ourselves. Ain't we, Jack?" said Billie. Still with that icy non-smile.

"Thing is," added Jack, "the Heavies were there awful quick. The boys had barely begun when they showed up and started on them."

"So, you see what we're saying here, Freddie, love?" said Billie. "How'd they get in on it so quick?"

"Well, I don't know, do I?" said Freddie, perhaps a little more hurriedly than he would have liked. He definitely didn't like the way things seemed to be going. Didn't like it one bit. "I mean, how the hell would I know?"

"Well, you were one of the ones who came up with this little job, weren't you?" said Billie. "You were sitting right here when we dreamed up this caper. So, we were hoping that you might have some idea, some insight..."

"Weak link in the chain. That kind of thing," added Jack.

"Exactly, Jack. Nicely put," said Billie.

Freddie had been in enough interrogation rooms over the years to recognise Jack and Billie's little double-act for what it was. But that didn't alter the fact that they were still managing to rattle him. He'd known he'd have to face something like this, but he thought it would have been easier. Who'd ever heard of a mob like the Blacks being run by a woman anyway? It should have been simplicity itself to topple Billie and carve himself a cushy niche. It should have been as easy as bloody pie. But now it was clear that it simply wasn't going to happen.

"So, how about it, Freddie?" Billie was saying. "Who was the weak link in the chain?"

"Well, it certainly wasn't me, if that's what you're getting at," he blurted out. "This plan was perfect."

"Can't have been all that perfect, Freddie," said Billie. "Not from where I'm sitting."

"Well, I don't know, do I?" he protested. He could hear a note of pleading, of wheedling desperation, finding its way into his voice now, but there was bugger all he could do about it. He'd lost his little game. And he should have known better than to even have tried it. Now the best he could hope for was to get out in one piece. "It could've been anyone, couldn't it?" he said. "It could've been Johnny himself for all we know. I mean, he's inside already, ain't he? Maybe he gave this job up to earn a few Brownie points!"

Even as the words left his mouth, Freddie realised he'd made a mistake. He saw Billie's steely gaze spark with a momentary flash of anger. And even Jack's normally unreadable impassivity broke into a fleeting expression of incredulity, as if he couldn't quite believe Freddie's stupidity.

"Are you saying that my Johnny would have done us over like that?" said Billie, her voice little more than a whisper. "I mean, is that *really* what you're saying, Ferret?"

"No, of course not," he said hurriedly. "You know I wouldn't really think something like that, Billie. I was just thinking out loud, that's all. All's I'm saying is that anything might've happened. The last thing we want is to start getting all—"

"Start getting what, Freddie?" she broke in. "What don't we want to start getting?"

"Well, jumpy. Irrational, like."

"Ah. Irrational," Billie let the word roll around her tongue, coating it in undisguised contempt before spitting it back at him. "I see. And that's really the thing, isn't it, Freddie? That's what this is all about. That's what you think of me, ain't it? Because I'm a woman. Because we're all funny like that, ain't we, Freddie?"

"Now, hold on, I didn't say that," he protested. He looked pleadingly to Jack, hoping for at least some kind of sign of male solidarity against the capricious fantasies of women. But there was none forthcoming. Jack's expressionless veneer was back in place, and he left Freddie to twist under Billie's withering stare.

"See, I've been hearing rumours lately," said Billie, her tone returning to the almost conversational. "Quite distressing ones, I have to say. Lots of whispers below ranks, know what I mean? Seems like some might think I'm not up to the task of looking out for Johnny's interests while he's indisposed. No job for a woman an' all that."

Freddie said nothing, although he couldn't help but notice that Jack had straightened to his feet, his hand moving almost casually to his jacket pocket.

"And it seems it's actually a bit worse than that," Billie went on. "Seems that some have got it into their heads that with Johnny out of the picture now is the time to take a step up. Make a play, know what I mean, Freddie?"

And now Jack was slowly circling the table, making his way closer to Freddie. Freddie swallowed hard. If it hadn't been clear before, it was now quite obvious that things were about to get nasty.

"Not me, Billie," he said, taking an involuntary step backwards. "Not me."

"Well, one would 'ope not, wouldn't one, eh, Fred?" she said. "Take this Brookfields job, for instance. It was supposed to be sending out a message. That it was business as usual. That the Blacks were still in play even if Johnny was in the nick. That we were still on top of things. And now look at it. It's a bloody disaster, Freddie. I've got four of the boys in hospital with no good reason why and nothing to show for it either. That makes me look weak. Vulnerable."

"I'm telling you, I had nothing to do with it."

"It doesn't matter, Freddie. It really doesn't," she went on. "And it doesn't matter about Harry Blum either. He'll get his. Even if we have to put him back in bloody plaster again. But what we can't afford is to look weak, Freddie. Not right now."

Freddie took another step backwards, this time hitting the closed parlour door. Jack was a lot closer now, only a few feet away. It felt to him that things were happening in some kind of nightmarish slow motion. The inevitability of this moment from the second he'd stepped into the house now seemed obvious to him. He couldn't imagine why he hadn't seen it before. He'd seen Jack go to work on dozens of people over the years, but he'd never imagined, not even for a second, that he'd ever find himself on the wrong end of his blade.

"Billie, for the love of God…" he began. But his voice drifted away. It was no use, of that he was certain. He couldn't even see her now. His entire vision was filled with Jack – his white face, those curious, almost entirely black, glittering birds' eyes. He could smell the brilliantine in his hair, the stale smoke on his breath.

"Rule of three, Billie?" he heard Jack ask.

And then Billie's voice. "Yes, please, Jack, love. Rule of three." Her voice was light again, casual, as if he were offering her nothing more sinister than another cup of tea.

He felt Jack's long fingers clamp around his face, pushing his head firmly back against the door. Freddie found himself hoping that he wouldn't scream too much, but he knew that he would. They always did. Jack had a way of working that seemed to break the hardest of men and Freddie was a long way from being that.

Freddie winced, and waited for the blade.

The first scream almost made Keith jump as it drifted along the passageway from the behind the closed parlour door.

"Don't let it worry you, son," said one of the old-lag minders, without looking up from his cards. "It don't happen very often. Leastways, not to those that didn't have it coming."

FOUR

OF THEIR many regular watering holes around London, the Midnight Bell was probably the Heavies' favourite. There was no particular reason for this as it was neither the closest boozer to their HQ nor was it what you'd call the most salubrious. It was, in fact, your typical inner city pub, a cavernous sanctum of dark wood and brass, of frosted and stained glass, of bellowing, drunken masculinity. But over the years it was the one that they had tended to gravitate towards more than any other, to the point that it now felt like home.

And it was here that Alun Symons found himself one gloomy Friday evening, deftly manoeuvring a tin tray laden with pints towards the corner table currently occupied by half a dozen members of his squad.

"Here you go, Harry," said Symons, dishing out pints of bitter around the table. Harry did not react for a moment, staring blankly into space, only coming out of it when he realised several members of the squad were looking at him with silent amusement.

"Sorry. I was miles away."

"Evidently," said Symons, sliding Harry's pint across the table towards him. "I believe it is now customary to offer a penny for them."

"I would wager good money and more than a penny," said Illingworth, taking a deep draw of his own beer, "that they involve Johnny Black in some way. Am I right, Harry?"

A low ripple of masculine chuckling went around the table, not mocking, but not exactly empathetic either. Something in between. Harry's long-standing enmity with the Black Mob had now become a standard part of the squad's banter, although there wasn't one of them who didn't sympathise at least in part with Harry's feelings. Harry grinned sheepishly, forcing himself to be the butt of the joke.

"Alright, alright, knock it off, for Chrissake."

"I just don't get it, Harry," said Jim Stott, shaking his head. "They guy's in stir, ain't he? So, what's the problem?"

"Let it go, Harry," nodded Symons. "Johnny Black is not going anywhere, believe me. Don't worry, you'll get your crack at him once the yokels down there have done with him."

"If he gets back," said Illingworth. "Might be that we've all seen the last of Johnny Black if the Jerries have got their hands on him."

"That's true," agreed Symons. "Look on the bright side, Harry. Maybe old Adolf will do the job for you."

"Fat chance of that," said Harry. "Johnny Black has got more lives than a bloody cat."

"Well," said Symons. "Be that as it may, I have no doubt you'll be waiting at the pier to welcome him home with open arms once the war's over."

"Open handcuffs more like," said Stott.

"And in the meantime," said Symons. "We've still got plenty on our plates here."

"Like the rest of the Blacks," said Illingworth.

Symons groaned and rolled his eyes upwards. "Now, don't you bloody start, for god's sake, Phil."

"What?" said Illingworth, all innocence. "I'm just saying. Besides, I think they're starting to come apart at the seams anyway. Could be we might not have to do anything at all."

"How'd you mean?" asked Harry, interest piqued by his favourite topic of conversation.

Illingworth ignored the disapproving scowl coming from Symons and leaned forward conspiratorially. "Well, it's just that I hear Freddie Winner is walking around these days sporting a Rule of Three. And we both know what that means."

Illingworth drew his finger down his cheek in three perpendicular strokes to reinforce his point. A Rule of Three was a trio of deep, neat cuts, usually on the face or somewhere equally prominent, and close enough together that neat stitching would be impossible without tearing the skin between the cuts, thus guaranteeing a distinctive scar for life. It was widely recognised as the Blacks' 'signature' – a visible and permanent mark that you'd been 'spoken to' by the Blacks at some point in your career.

Harry took another sip of his pint, a thoughtful expression on his own scarred face. "Now I wonder what Freddie might have done to upset old Black Jack like that?"

"Harry, you're obsessed," said Symons. "It's not healthy. You're becoming our very own Inspector Javert."

"Who the hell's he when he's at home?" exclaimed Alfie Tavener, suddenly slurring into unexpected life at the end of the table.

"Beats me," said Stott. "I think he might work in Clubs."

"I suspect," said Illingworth, catching the look on Symons' and Harry's faces, "that it's a books thing. Am I right?"

Harry nodded. "Victor Hugo."

"Right, that's it," exclaimed Tavener, getting unsteadily to his feet. "If you lot are going to start with your bloody literary salon, then I'm off for a game of darts. Who's with me?"

Tavener took his pint and began weaving through the crowded pub, roughly in the direction of where he had vague recollections of there once being a dartboard. His departure sparked an exodus of the more sporting members of the Heavies, leaving just Symons, Harry and a couple of others at the table.

Symons chuckled as he watched his men go and patted his pockets, searching for his tobacco pouch and pipe. "We're surrounded by philistines, Harry," he said. "Philistines."

FIVE

FREDDIE knew he was in trouble when he saw Phil Illingworth weaving through the crowds on the Tottenham Court Road and obviously heading in his direction. There could only be one reason why the Heavy Mob would be looking for him and that little caper had already caused him more than enough trouble already. He turned sharply on his heels and began hurriedly retracing his steps, heading roughly in the direction of the Underground, where he felt certain that he'd be able to elude Illingworth if the detective proved to be persistent.

But he was so intent on plotting his escape from the detective behind him that he didn't realise he'd been caught in a pincer until was too late and he saw Harry Blum straight in his path and bearing down upon him.

The sight of Harry Blum coming straight for you in a public thoroughfare was very much one to cause alarm in your average villain and Freddie was no exception. He was instantly struck by a powerful memory of the first time he'd seen Harry bearing down on him on a public thoroughfare and he had no wish to repeat the experience. But on this occasion, Harry was even wearing a smile on his slab-like features – something that alarmed Freddie more than the prospect of a beating.

"Alright, there, Freddie?" said Harry, his considerable bulk effectively blocking any hope the smaller man might have had of slipping around him. "You seem to be in a hell of a hurry."

"Well, you know how it is, Mr Blum," said Freddie. He looked around nervously, partially to see if there were any escape routes that he hadn't yet thought of but also to make sure he hadn't been spotted by anyone he knew. But there was little hope of that. Freddie knew everybody. "Quite busy at the moment, ain't I? What with the war and everything, I've got a lot on."

And now Illingworth had caught up with them and was blocking any retreat Freddie might have made. He was hemmed in between the two of them.

"I don't doubt it, Freddie," said Harry with a grim smile. "I don't doubt it in the slightest." He clapped an enormous hand between the little man's shoulders with enough force to make Freddie wince. "How about a drink then?"

These were about the last words that Freddie had expected to come from Harry's lips. "A drink?" he repeated nervously. "Actually, it's a still a bit early for me, Mr Blum, so if you don't mind…"

He felt Illingworth catch him by the elbow. "Don't be like that, Freddie," he said. "No need to be all unsociable, like."

"Yeah, come on," said Harry with a sudden friendliness that was causing Freddie no end of alarm. "And you can tell us all about it."

"Take a seat, Freddie," said Harry. "Take a load off."

Harry and Illingworth had taken Freddie to a boozer in Fitzrovia. The lunchtime crowd hadn't started yet so the pub was still on the quiet side, but it was by no means deserted. While Illingworth, went to the bar, Harry led Freddie directly to a table more or less in the open centre of the pub.

Freddie took his seat gingerly. "Care to tell me what all this is about, Mr Blum?" he asked.

Harry looked at him blankly. "Whatever can you mean, Freddie?"

Nothing more was said by either man until Illingworth returned with the beers. The two detectives drank deep from theirs, each hoping to take the edge off the previous evening's hangover, while Freddie was content to sip at his with suspicion.

"Hits the spot, don't it?" said Illingworth.

"That it does, Phil. That it does," said Harry.

"Alright," said Freddie. "Enough's enough. You want to tell me what the hell we're all doing here?"

Illingworth looked at Freddie with surprise. "Just having a quiet pint, that's all, Freddie. Why, what's up?"

"What's up is the three of us sitting all cosy like this. I mean, what's the bloody occasion? What are you two after?"

"Just a chat, Freddie," said Illingworth, injecting a note of hurt into his voice. "Friendly little natter, that's all."

"Is that right?" said Freddie. "What about exactly?"

"Well," said Harry. "Off the top of my head, like, how about the Brookfields job?"

And here it comes, thought Freddie. Finally. "I don't know nothing whatsoever about it," he said.

"What? Nothing at all?" said Illingworth. "I find that rather hard to believe, Freddie. Chap who prides himself on his contacts like you?"

Freddie glared at the two detectives for a moment. Did they seriously expect him to start squealing, just like that? Well, they could go to hell. He was sick of people thinking they could just push him around whenever they bloody felt like it.

"Well, I did hear something," he said.

"And what's that, Freddie?" asked Illingworth.

"Well, I heard that you let this one," he said, nodding towards Harry, "off the leash. Put the lot of them in casualty from what I hear. Bloody horrific. He's the one that wants locking up, if you ask me."

Harry smiled. "What happened to your face, Freddie?"

Freddie had to make a conscious effort to stop his hand going up to his cheek. The three, deep scores on his face were on their way to healing as much as they were ever going to, but it was still throbbing like hell.

"Nothing," he said. "I fell, that's all."

"Fell?" said Harry, with a snort of disbelief. "Fell against what? Your dinner fork? Looks right nasty that does, doesn't it, Phil?"

"Very," said Illingworth, deadpan.

Freddie almost rolled his eyes. They were trying exactly the same routine that Billie and Jack had pulled on him only a few weeks before. Did they really think that he was going to fall for it? Mind you, he reflected, it didn't exactly work out brilliantly for him the last time either. He was beginning to wonder if he was doomed to be on the wrong end of everyone else's bull for the rest of his life.

"In fact," said Harry, now getting into the flow of their double act, "do you know what it reminds me of?"

"What's that then, Harry?" asked Illingworth innocently.

"That thing that Jack Spinks used to do with that little cat-stabber of his." He slashed the air with his hand by way of demonstration. "What was it he called it?"

"Rule of Three, Harry."

"That's it! The Rule of Three. Very nasty. I mean, you're never going to get a clean scar with that, are you, Freddie? Right bloody mess is what it is. You'll be carrying Jack's mark around with you for the rest of your days now. Now, what could you have done to upset Jack that he'd carve you up like that, eh?"

Freddie looked down at his barely touched pint. Harry's angry glare on his face felt as if it was going to make the cuts on his cheek open and bleed again all on their own. "I don't know what the hell you're talking about, Mr Blum. I really don't. Unless..." He let the word trail off into the air.

Harry raised an eyebrow. "Unless what, Freddie?"

"Unless that beating they put on you all those years ago has left you soft in the bloody head. Maybe it's time you gave up this game, eh? Early retirement maybe? Doesn't look like you can hack it anymore."

Even Illingworth didn't have time to react to the explosive force of Harry's response. The drinks on the table, ashtrays, the lot, suddenly went flying in all directions. Harry had Freddie pinned hard against the table's surface, his meaty hands clamping down hard and squeezing into his face. A couple of the patrons had stood up from their own places in alarm, but a warning glance from

Illingworth was enough to make them sit again. One thing the inhabitants of this particular boozer knew was when it was better to mind their own business.

Harry squeezed his fingers so hard into Freddie's face that the three weals on his cheek had started to weep and bleed again. "You think you're funny, you little cunt?" he hissed. "Do you want me to fucking go to work on you right here?"

Freddie's eyes bulged as Harry increased his grip. But there was still as much defiant contempt in them as there was fear.

"You don't frighten me, Harry," rasped Freddie through the constriction of Harry's other hand around his throat. "If you were planning to do some serious damage you wouldn't have brought me here, would you? I mean, what are you going to do? Give me a doing with all these nice people sitting here looking on? That ain't going to look too pretty, is it?"

Harry didn't look as if he would have had too much of a problem with that, but Illingworth recognised the truth of what Freddie was saying. So much so that he reached over and pulled gently on Harry's tensed, muscular arm.

"Come on now," he said. "Friendly chat is all this is. No need for anyone to get carried away now is there?"

Harry tightened his grip for an instant longer before releasing Freddie and taking his seat again. Freddie collapsed back into his own chair, gasping for breath and his hand going to the now weeping wound on his cheek. At a nod from Illingworth, a waiter approached them hesitantly and began clearing up the debris of Harry's outburst.

"You've got problems, Harry," croaked Freddie. "Definite bloody problems."

Harry glared at Freddie with contempt. All the play-acting and false bonhomie were now well and truly over. "Do we look like we're bloody stupid, Freddie?" he said. "Because we're not. I reckon you know as well as I do that someone's been feeding us some juicy titbits about the Blacks for quite some months now. More or less ever since Johnny got banged up, in fact."

"Is that right?" said Freddie.

"No names, no packdrill," Harry went on. "But good stuff. Reliable. And definitely coming from someone in the know."

"And you're pretty in there with the Blacks, ain't you, Freddie?" added Illingworth. "Any idea who it might be?"

"Can't say I do, Mr Illingworth."

"So, we've got this anonymous little bird singing its bloody heart out," said Harry. "And here's you walking about sporting a brand spanking new Rule of Three. I mean, you tell us, Freddie. Just what are we supposed to think?"

"I wouldn't dare presume, Harry," said Freddie, curling his lip just as far as could dare.

"Maybe it's a little, what do you call em ... a putsch," said Illingworth.

Harry nodded. "Good point, Phil. I mean, is that what you're at, Freddie? You can tell us. Because, you know, maybe we might be able to help. Isn't that right, Phil?"

"Absolutely, Harry. Always happy to be of service, we are. It's kind of our motto really."

"I have no idea what the two of you are going on about," said Freddie. "Bloody barmy the pair of you, if you ask me."

"We're just giving you the chance to come clean here, Freddie," said Harry. "I mean, all this sneaking around. Anonymous notes and what have you. It's no way for a grown men to behave now is it?"

"You ain't listening, are you?" said Freddie. "I don't know what the bloody hell you're talking about. And even if I did, and it was old Black Jack that did this to me, do you really think I'd be daft enough to tell your mob anything? He'd cut me a bloody Limehouse Grin if I did."

"That's a good point, Freddie," said Harry. "Very germane and all that. Let me answer it with another question. Why do you think we're all sitting here when, as you say, we might have got more out of you in a cosy little boiler room somewhere?"

Freddie shrugged.

"Well, it wasn't that we actually thought you'd start singing for us, nice as that would be. But not very likely given your previously intransigent nature. No, it was more to test this little theory of ours really."

Freddie said nothing, listening, and with a growing feeling that he wasn't going to like what he was about to hear.

"Well, we heard about your little accident," said Harry, once again gesturing to Freddie's wounded cheek. "So it seemed pretty clear to us that you've done something to upset Black Jack. And we were just wondering how he's going to take it when he hears you've sitting here chatting with us? Drinking our beer, all pals together?"

"They'll know that it is what it is," said Freddie without certainty or enthusiasm. "That you pigs pulled me in and that it was nothing to do with me. Yanking people's chains like this when there's bombs dropping all around us. It's a bloody disgrace."

"You sure about that, Freddie?" added Illingworth. "Because paranoia's a terrible thing. And what with your coat on a shaky peg with the Blacks anyway..."

Freddie glared at him. But he was right, he thought gloomily. His stock with the Blacks had plummeted dramatically since the Brookfields disaster. He could never quite tell what Jack was thinking at any given moment, not that he ever could. But it was quite clear to him that Billie hated his guts and that Jack hung on her every word. There was no guarantee whatsoever that they might not take this little encounter at face value, or even just use it as an excuse to hammer on him even further.

"Might be best to come clean, Freddie," said Harry. "That way we can offer you at least some protection if the Blacks do take a dim view."

"You really are a couple of bastards, aren't you?" said Freddie. "Well, get this through your thick bloody 'eads. I'm not scared of you. Either of you. And you can spread this horseshit any way you like but I'm not rolling over on the Blacks. It's more than my bloody life's worth and you know it as well as I do."

Harry sat back in his chair and folded his arms. Both he and Illingworth continued to stare at him for a moment, more like they were disappointed parents than anything else. And then Harry sighed and said, "alright, Freddie Sling your hook."

"Oh, I can go, can I?"

"Yes, you can go. Get your ratty little face out of my sight before I lose my patience."

Freddie didn't need to be told twice. He scurried out of the pub, ignoring the curious stares of the other patrons.

"Well, Harry," said Illingworth, when they were supping fresh pints to make up for the ones lost during Freddie's interrogation. "It was worth a try, I suppose."

Harry said nothing but drank in silence. He was sinking back into that dark place where there was nothing but him, Johnny Black and his unquenchable need for revenge.

SIX

JACK closed the front door, glad to be out of the bitingly cold morning air, which had been prickling at his skin and covering his Crombie in a sheen of misty water droplets. No sooner had he done so than he became aware of Keith hovering at his back, his open, blue-eyed expression making him resemble nothing more than an enormous, overgrown puppy.

"Christ, Keith. I'm going to have to stick a bell on you if you keep this up."

The boy took a swift step backwards. "Sorry, Mr Spinks."

"And call me Jack, for god's sake. How many times do I have to tell you? If you make it as far as getting a bed under this roof then you can pretty much consider yourself family."

"Right," said Keith, just managing to stop himself from an another spontaneous 'Mr Spinks' but its phantom still hung in the air between the two men.

"Was there something you wanted, son?" asked Jack, aware that the kid was still hanging about at his elbow.

"Yeah." Keith nodded down the hall in the direction of Billie's parlour. "You're wanted."

"That figures," said Jack. "Here," he added, handing the parcel under his arm to Keith. "Stick that in my room for me, will you. While I go and see what's what."

Billie wasn't alone in the parlour. Seated at the table were Frankie Pliers, who now ran the protection racket wrested from the Danellis, and Sam Silk, who looked after Johnny's clubs. Before them sat the remains of a plate of bacon and eggs. No one set foot in Billie's place without getting some kind of hospitality. But despite that, both men looked grim-faced as they nodded their taciturn greetings to Jack.

"What's all this?" he said. "War cabinet?"

No one smiled at the joke, although both Frankie and Sam nodded a respectful hello.

"It's Freddie," said Billie.

"And what's he been up to now?"

"I was talking to the barman at the Fitzrovia this morning," said Frankie, his voice nothing but a gravelly rumble. "And he said he had Freddie in there chatting away with Harry Blum and another one of the Heavies."

Jack raised an eyebrow. He was going to have to credit Freddie with a bravery – or stupidity – that he'd never previously realised he had. "You sure about that?" he asked.

Frankie nodded. "So he says."

"And when was this?"

"Last week he says."

"Boy doesn't take a telling, does he?" said Jack, unable to completely keep a tone of amused admiration out of his voice. "Friendly meeting, was it?"

Frankie shrugged. "He said there was some rough stuff to begin with but that they were all nice as pie after that."

"What's he up to, Jack?" said Billie. Her face was grim and she clearly found it a more serious situation than Jack appeared to.

"I've no idea," he admitted. "But I must admit I'd quite like to find out."

"So, what do you want us to do?" asked Sam.

"I don't trust him, Jack," said Billie. "I just don't. And I don't want him around 'ere no more."

"Well, that's easily fixed," said Jack. "Alright. Don't worry. I'll deal with it." He turned his attention to Frankie and Sam. "Alright, boys, thanks for bringing this to our attention. I'll be in touch once I know how we're going to play this."

"Yes," said Billie, flashing both men a brilliant, grateful smile. "Thanks, lads. It's much appreciated."

Frankie and Sam nodded and left. Billie started taking the breakfast things to the sink. There was something in the way she was moving that told Jack she was troubled in some way.

"Everything alright, Bil?"

She turned and looked at him. "Oh, I don't know, Jack. This... it's all too much. I feel like..." She paused, struggling for the words. "I feel like I don't know what the hell I'm doing. I wish... I just wish Johnny was here."

He reached out and put his hand on her shoulder. A brave move on his part. He wasn't sure how she would react. But she didn't seem to mind. For all he knew, she hadn't noticed at all.

"He'd know what to do," she went on.

"You know what to do," he said. "I keep telling you. This isn't Johnny's mob. It's yours. Or at least it is until Johnny comes back to us. And that means you've got to step up, pet. Take charge. So you just tell me what to do and I'll make sure it gets done. No problem."

She reached up and took Jack's hand. So, she had noticed. Her fingers felt firm and cool on his. "Thanks, Jack," she said.

"What for?"

"How about everything? You're a good one, Jack Spinks. I don't know what I'd do without you."

She held his hand for a second or two longer and then patted it lightly before releasing it and got on with filling the sink.

Jack withdrew to his room, disturbed at just how elated – and aroused – even that slight touch had left him. He felt a sudden need to escape to the cool solitude of his attic, to lie down and escape this new, growing, sense of confusion within him.

SEVEN

THE prison gates closed behind Johnny with a sonorous clang, as if announcing his release to the world at large.

But as he looked down the slight incline from the doors of the prison to the grey-green murk of Jersey, Johnny felt less than free, or indeed that he had very much to be cheerful about. The black, roiling clouds seemed oppressively low and not unlike the grubby walls of his old cell. Two equally grey-clad German soldiers were standing against one corner, smoking, eyeing him idly and without concern. In fact, the only source of cheer was the sight of Albie Fairchild climbing the hill to greet him. Albie was wearing an ill-fitting and patched up powder-blue suit that seemed to Johnny to be entirely inappropriate to the gloomy weather. But he reflected that his own attire was scarcely better. He was still clad in the same dinner suit he'd been arrested in, albeit now a lot shabbier, dustier and moth-eaten around the edges. He couldn't remember ever feeling quite as much the tramp as he did at present.

"So, they let you out, did they?" beamed Albie as he closed in on Johnny. "Wonders will never cease."

"Yeah," sniffed Johnny. "Standards are definitely slipping round here, ain't they?"

"How does it feel to be a free man?"

Johnny nodded down towards the two Germans on the corner. "This is free, is it?" He was surprised at just how morose he was feeling. He wanted to do nothing more than pound on the gates of the prison until they let him back inside, to crawl back to the safety of his cell and not have to worry about anything else.

"Christ," said Albie. "They've let you out in a good mood, ain't they? Snap out of it, for god's sake. At least you're out."

Johnny smiled reluctantly. "You're right. Don't worry, I'll whack on a sunny disposish in a second."

"Alright then. So, what's the plan?"

He clapped Albie on the back, willing himself into a better frame of mind. "The plan, my son, is for you to buy me a drink. Celebrate my newfound liberty and all that."

Johnny grimaced as he took his first sip of the beer Albie had just put in front of him.

"Christ, that's bloody awful."

Albie took a sip of his own pint. "What's the matter with it? Tastes alright to me."

"Nothing. I'm sure it's fine. I've just never really been able to get the hang of beer, that's all."

"Yeah, well, they were right out of Champagne cocktails, I'm afraid, so you'll just have to lump it."

They were in a poky little pub not that far from the jail. It was surprisingly busy, given that it was not yet midday. Johnny couldn't help but notice that there were also another couple of Germans here, drinking at the bar. No one seemed to be paying them much heed.

"Christ," he whispered. "They're everywhere."

"I guess that's why they call it an occupation."

"How's it been?" asked Johnny, his eyes still on the two soldiers.

"Not too bad actually," said Albie. "I expected it to be a whole lot worse, what with the stories you hear. But they've been nice as pie, more or less."

"Wonder how long that'll last."

"Well, that's the question, ain't it? But I'd say you'd better get used to it."

"Like I said," muttered Johnny gloomily. "I've just swapped one prison for a slightly bigger one."

"So, what are you going to do?"

Johnny took a thoughtful sip of his pint. "Dunno. Looks like I'm going to have to improvise, doesn't it?"

Johnny stood on the stone jetty, looking out over Jersey harbour. He lit a cigarette and stared at the moonlit Channel. Somewhere out there was home. London. Jack and the rest of the mob. And Billie. Not for the first time, he cursed himself as a bloody fool for running off here, getting himself stuck.

"Thought I'd find you out here."

He turned as Albie emerged from the back door of The Frigate, a seedy harbour-side pub where they'd both managed to find work. Albie had lucked out and got to work behind the bar whereas Johnny was left to humph crates around in the cellar. He couldn't help feel it should be the other way around. He was, after all, the one with the gift of the gab. He certainly couldn't see why he should have to be the one doing the grunt work.

Johnny offered Albie a cigarette and lit it for him. Albie nodded towards the row of tiny fishing boats moored below the wall upon which they were standing. "Thinking of making a break for it?"

Johnny smiled ruefully. It was something that crossed his mind every time he came out here. "Maybe," he said. "Think I'd make it?"

"Next to no chance," said Albie. "Remember Sid and Nancy Machon? They tried to make it to Blighty in a boat that wasn't much bigger than those and they didn't get five miles. You've got searchlights, machine gun posts on the coast here and patrol boats and mines out on the water. And then there's the question of what I'm guessing is your absolute lack of seafaring ability. Nah, I'd say forget it."

"Yeah," said Johnny. "I'd say you're probably right. But I've got to bloody do something. I can't just sit around here watching these clowns goosestep about all over the place."

"I'd be careful with chat like that," said Albie. "You never know who's listening."

"To hell with them. What are they going to do? Shoot me?"

"Yeah, maybe."

"I've got a mob to run. I've got a wife for Chrissakes. I got to do something."

"What the hell is this?" bellowed another voice from the doorway of The Frigate. This one belonged to Godfray, a burly Jerseyman who owned the pub. "Remind me what I'm paying you two deadbeats for? I've got tables needing cleaned and barrels needing changed. Get to it before I kick your arses into the bloody drink!"

Johnny rolled his eyes at Albie. "And sometimes the Jerries don't seem half bad, do they?"

They tossed their cigarettes into the water and returned inside under Godfray's scowling glare.

Johnny sat at the living room table in the crumbling lodging house he shared with Albie and a couple of other lags from the prison and scrawled furiously on his writing pad. Around him were the crumpled remains of nearly a dozen previous attempts at the letter he was writing and he still hadn't got it quite right.

Albie came into the room, still yawning and shaking off the hangover from the previous evening's lock-in, and looked with amusement at the debris of Johnny's efforts.

"What's all this?" he asked.

Johnny stopped writing and, after hesitating for a moment, passed the letter to Albie. The younger man's reading skills were not the best and it took him a few moments to get through the letter, with much befuddled scowling and mouthing of words.

When he had finished, he passed the letter back and said, "Are you out of your bloody mind?"

"I had a feeling you were going to take this attitude," said Johnny.

"Well, what do you expect, man? What you're talking about here, it's... it's treason."

"No, it ain't. Not from where I'm sitting anyway. I've got to get back to London, Albie. I'm sick of all this sitting around. I've got to get back to my life, mate. And as far as I can see, these buggers are the only ones who are going to be able to help me do that."

"Yeah, but this... when all's said and done, we're still British, ain't we?"

"Are we? Seems to me Churchill was pretty quick to give us up to the bloody Jerries. Don't recall seeing any Tommies storming the beaches to liberate us. As far as old Winnie's concerned, we're all Germans already. Why the hell should we owe them anything?"

The other man didn't reply, but his face had gone pale, a sign, Johnny knew, that he was as angry as Albie tended to get. "Look, I'm sorry," he said. "That was out of order."

Albie was silent for a moment longer and then he said, "I don't think you should do it."

"No," said Johnny, looking at his spidery writing on the paper. "No, I know you don't."

EIGHT

IT WAS a damp, cold winter's night several months after the argument about the letter and Johnny was lugging crates in the cellar of The Frigate. He was sweating, his bones were aching and all he was looking forward to was last orders so they could empty the pub and go home. He was even intending skipping the nightly lock-in that had by now become virtually mandatory but which for Johnny had just become tiresome.

The suddenly raised voices, some clearly in alarm, some in anger and some in command, accompanied by the thundering rumble of several pairs of boots on the wooden floorboards above him told Johnny that something was going on upstairs. Something very definitely out of the ordinary.

And sure enough, moments later, Albie appeared framed in the cellar's doorway. Johnny couldn't see his face against the buttery light from the pub, but he had no doubt that Albie's face would again be wearing its habitual creased mask of worried near-panic.

"Johnny, you better get up here."

There were Nazis in the bar, although this in itself was not unusual. They got quite a few off-duty soldiers in and for the most part Johnny was surprised at how decent a bunch they seemed to be – certainly less trouble than a great many of the locals. But these blokes were clearly here on business, unsmiling and hard-faced, and were in the process of hustling the patrons out of the bar, under the watchful eye of a single officer. The drinkers were going without any trouble, save for a subdued mumble of discontent, which was about as rebellious as your average islander tended to get with the Jerries.

Godfray stood behind the bar, his normally darkly scowling visage now etched with concern, and fear. Albie was hovering at the end of the bar, looking as if he might keel over with fright at any moment.

"What the hell's going on?" whispered Johnny. "A raid?"

"Dunno," replied Albie in a similarly hushed tone. "But I don't like it."

The locals had by now all left the bar and one of the soldiers bolted the pub's front doors. The officer turned towards the bar where the three remaining men exchanged worried glances.

"Is there something amiss, er…?" Godfray looked to the officer's uniform to get some idea of rank to address the officer, but gave up at a loss. "Perhaps a drink for your men?"

"Thank you, no," said the officer. "Regrettably, we are here on some official business."

"Nothing to do with us, I hope." Godfray was usually a blowhard and a bellowing unpleasant bully and Johnny had never seen him quite as supine as this. It was not pleasant to watch.

"I very much hope not," said the officer. "It concerns some sabotage against the interests and properties of the Reich."

"Sabotage?" said Albie. "We don't know nothing about that."

The officer turned his attention towards Albie and Johnny. "These men, they work for you?" he asked Godfray.

"Not as such," said Godfray, ignoring the glares of indignation from Albie and Johnny. "More casual, like. Strictly on an as-needed basis. I barely know them really."

The officer nodded. "I see. And can you account for their movements last evening?"

Godfray paused, contemplating washing his hands of them

completely, and then relented. "Well, I have to admit they were both here all last night."

The officer wrote something in his notebook. "All night? Very well. I feel perhaps we should continue this discussion elsewhere. If you'll come with us, please." He nodded to his men. "Take them."

"Hey, wait a minute," protested Albie. "You can't just hustle us away like this."

"I'm sorry," said the officer. "I was under the impression that you would be willing to help us with our enquiries into this very serious matter. Was I mistaken?"

Johnny couldn't help but notice that the soldiers' hands were now resting on the safeties of the MP40s. He couldn't imagine they would just gun them down here, but it was not a chance he was willing to take. He laid his own hand on Albie's arm. "I think perhaps it might be best if we do what they say. Just in case."

They were bundled into the back of a black Mercedes and driven at some speed through the blacked-out streets in the direction of the island's harbour. The air of anxiety inside the back of the car was palpable and was becoming increasingly shared by Johnny himself. He was beginning to fear that ending up in an unmarked grave somewhere was by no means an outlandish possibility.

They were certainly expected at the harbour. Another couple of officers and several soldiers were waiting around on the stone jetty for them to arrive and they were bundled out of the car at the point of several guns and towards a small fishing boat whose engine was chugging away patiently.

"Going on a trip, are we?" asked Johnny, with as much bonhomie as he could muster. He was sure now that all the stuff about sabotage was a crock, a piece of pure theatre on their part. Otherwise they'd have been dragged down to a cell somewhere to have confessions beaten out of them. No, the Nazis clearly had something else in mind. Purging the island of the criminal element maybe, he thought. That would chime with some of what he'd heard muttered darkly in some of the island's pubs. At the time, he'd just put it down to the usual doom-mongering and paranoia but now he wasn't so sure.

Or maybe his letter had just annoyed someone who mattered and they had decided to get him out of the way, although that didn't explain why they'd dragged his housemates along with him. Guilt by association maybe? Regardless, none of this boded well and he could feel a knot of fear growing within him at the expectation of getting a bullet in the head and dumped in the Channel. But he was damned if he was going to let these Krauts see his fear. The shivering, white-faces of Albie and Godfray seemed pathetic to him, badges of obvious and too easily adopted victimhood. They already look like ghosts, thought Johnny. But he wasn't going to go out like that.

After twenty minutes of hanging about on the freezing jetty, they were forced aboard the rickety-looking fishing boat at gunpoint. They were shoved aftwards and shackled to the bow before the officers and two of the guards retired to the wheelhouse. Johnny stared gloomily at the lapping, black water, rippling in the moonlight and the icy darkness stretching out beyond. Somewhere out there was France and it was almost certain that this was where they were heading. And even if the plan was for them to survive the journey, it was taking him in the wrong direction, further and further away from London and Billie.

A few moments later, the boat was tied off and, with much shouting in guttural German from the jetty, they were chugging away from the island and into murky darkness. The air was bitingly cold and Johnny reflected grimly that a bullet in the head might not even be necessary to kill them off. None of them had been allowed to stop long enough to pick up a coat and they were all in their shirtsleeves. He didn't suppose asking their captors for some oilskins or a sweater or two would have yielded much joy either.

As the boat picked up speed, they were soaked by sea spray and pole-axed by wind-chill and they shivered uncontrollably in the freezing cold. Johnny's fingers felt as if they were frozen to the bow rail he was clutching for support as the boat bucked and rolled under the choppy waves. Aside from what moonlight was managing to penetrate the clouds, the only illumination was the light from the wheelhouse, where the Germans were laughing and sharing hot drinks and hip flasks, their prisoners, for the moment at least, quite forgotten.

"Do you think we should try and make a jump for it?" whispered Godfray, his voice thick with cold and fear.

Johnny tested the shackles around his wrist. Steel handcuffs. And the wooden bow rail seemed sturdy enough too. He didn't see how they were going to get free, at least not without attracting the attention of those in the wheelhouse. "Good luck with that," he whispered. And where the hell would you jump to, he mused? The water looked bloody cold and he doubted that you'd be able to survive in it long enough to swim anywhere safe. And that was assuming you didn't end up with a bullet in the back the minute you jumped overboard anyway.

"This is all to do with that letter, isn't it?" said Albie in the darkness. There was no hint of accusation in his voice, just plaintive, matter-of-fact gloominess. But all the same, it made shards of guilt shoot through Johnny.

"I didn't send it," he lied and listened in the darkness to see if he could detect any hint of disbelief or accusation. But all he could hear was the rhythmic slapping of the water and the occasional Germanic guffaw from the wheelhouse and they passed the rest of the journey in gloomy silence, each man pondering on what the rest of the night might hold for them, and whether it was destined to be their last.

They very quickly lost track of how long they had been on the boat and Johnny had almost dozed off, in spite of the extreme cold and the nausea-inducing rocking of the little boat. But then one of the others had nudged him and he saw the spattering lines of lights of a rapidly approaching shoreline. The increased activity in the wheelhouse also told him that they were nearing their destination.

"Where do you think we are?" hissed Godfray in the darkness, his voice now almost unrecognisable, thickened as it was with cold and fear.

"France," said Johnny. "St Malo maybe. Somewhere like that anyway."

The port was looming up in sight now and they could just about make out the sight of buildings and vehicles and other boats, twinkling in the darkness. They were coming into a jetty not unlike the one they'd left on the other side of the Channel.

The Germans had now come out of the wheelhouse and were cursing at the cold and at each other. They started unshackling their prisoners from the bow line and dragging them roughly back up the boat, as the vessel made its final approach to the harbour.

Despite the lateness of the hour, the harbour on this side of the Channel seemed to be much busier, with the figures of several harbourmen working on and around the many boats that were tied up in the port. There also seemed to be far greater evidence of military presence than the low profile the Nazis seemed to be keeping in Jersey. There were ample displays of heavy guns, barbed wire, military vehicles and the like. There were also far more soldiers on show. It was perhaps Johnny's first view of what the war really looked like and it was a sobering one.

Their treatment by the Nazis was markedly different too. They were hustled off the boat with a greater emphasis on shouts, curses and aggressive shoves. Even the faces of these men were different, thought Johnny. Cold, inscrutable, and with something like rage, or perhaps even mania, flitting dangerously behind the eyes. And their hands never seemed to stray far too away from their rifles or their side-arms.

They were half-marched, half-dragged towards one of the waiting trucks and bundled into the back. The truck was already almost full of men as tired, beaten and bewildered as they were. The men on the truck stared dumbly at the newcomers for a moment but did not offer any words of comfort or even acknowledgement. Once they were aboard and had managed to squeeze themselves a place on the hard wooden benches that lined each side of the truck, the tailgate was raised and padlocked.

The truck drove for what felt like hours, first through the narrow streets of the harbour town, which quickly gave way to pitch-black country roads and then, gradually, to wider, better lit, more urban streets. Even in the middle of the night, there was a significant amount of traffic, although pretty much all of it was in the gunmetal grey and black of the German army. There were roadblocks and checkpoints, troops on foot and on motorcycles and they passed more than a few abandoned and burnt out homes and vehicles. At one point, they drove past a column of troops marching alongside the sinister grey form of a stationary German tank. And then the angular form of the Eiffel Tower, glinting blackly against the moonlight, confirmed Johnny's growing certainty that they were in Paris itself.

Eventually they reached their destination – a huge, forbidding-looking gaol. The multi-storeyed redbrick edifice, with its astounding array of Gothic turrets and crenelated walls, now topped with coils of barbed wire, seemed to Johnny like a fortress, almost designed to sap the remaining hope of anyone approaching it.

The truck roared through the open checkpoint at the imposing arched entrance to the building and into a wide open courtyard. It trundled to a halt and the truck's occupants were ushered out of the back with yet another series of shouts and curses. The cobbled surface of the courtyard was wet with the rain that had begun to fall during their drive to Paris and rang with the intimidating crump of marching boots. Albie's foot slipped on the wet surface as he jumped from the truck and Johnny stooped to help him back up.

"Christ," breathed Albie, his face ashen. "Look at this bloody place."

Johnny knew exactly what he meant. Neither he nor Albie were exactly strangers to the inside of a prison, but this place was something else entirely. This was the furthest thing you could get from the grey, jaded ennui of any civilian correctional institution. There were soldiers everywhere and they seemed to exude menacing, tightly coiled aggression. You could well believe that this was a place where you could be shot just on a whim and without anyone raising an eyebrow. Searchlights fingered the black skies and the jagged silhouettes of machine-gun nests were just visible at the top of the tower turrets. The red-bricked storeys of barred windows told them that this was a place it would be very difficult to leave once it had swallowed you up. It made the laidback atmosphere of the prison back in Jersey seem like a memory of an almost-forgotten holiday.

With more shouts, curses and shoves, they were harried onto the end of a long rank of shuffling, shambling figures that were slowly being marched towards the heavy double doors of the main entrance. The misty rain added to the general sense of defeat and loss and none of the men said anything or tried to make any kind of a protest as they were sloped inexorably towards the black, iron doors.

More prisoners from other identical trucks were also being filtered into the shuffling line. Johnny allowed himself to be dragged towards the gaping maw of the prison entrance by the flow of the crowd. For the first time in his life, he felt consumed by an absolute hopelessness.

And just as he was about to step through the darkness of the prison doors, Johnny caught from the corner of his eye two Nazi officers staring at him, with one pointing Johnny out to the other and then gesturing to a board in his hand. The other man nodded and the last thing that Johnny saw before being swallowed up by the darkness was the man's look of sardonic amusement and his curiously lop-sided smirk. He felt a flutter of panic go through him. He had been noticed. And it was becoming increasingly clear that this was a place where it was better not to be noticed.

NINE

THE place was called Le Cachot and despite having recently completed a spell in prison, Johnny still found the place to be something of a shock.

At first he'd been braced for a regime of extreme brutality and that he would now see the beatings, the cruelty, the torture that he'd heard whispers of on every street corner of occupied Jersey. But the Germans themselves didn't seem all that concerned with them. All the men were locked in one wing of the prison, all the women in another, but apart from the securely locked main door to each wing, no cell door was locked and they were all free to wander within these confines, with them only really seeing their German overseers when food was dished out. The true brutality would come from within the wing itself and was dealt by prisoner upon prisoner as the inevitable factions formed. To be alone or vulnerable meant to be preyed upon. Beatings, extortion, rape and even murder were commonplace with the guards doing nothing to stop it, beyond forcing a couple of the prisoners to carry out the corpses of any victims for burial. It was to them nothing but a source of entertainment, a macabre and brutal puppet show.

Johnny, Albie and the others survived by banding together, sticking with a few of the other English prisoners to find strength in numbers. Johnny made no attempt to assert himself here. In prison, you survived by remaining as anonymous and unnoticed as possible, and it was never truer than it was in Le Cachot. The Englishmen joined more refugees from Jersey and other fellow countrymen left stranded during the French Occupation in an enclave that took up three adjoining cells. This group looked out for each other, ensuring that no one member of their little group was ever left alone and vulnerable. They slept always with one eye on the open door of the cell, wary of any figure who crept too close to it, the sounds of the beatings, the attacks by the roaming rape gangs and the cries of those utterly broken individuals who screamed pointlessly and incoherently into the darkness ringing in their ears.

Albie was the one most shaken by life in Le Cachot. His only experience of prison had been the relatively easy life in the Jersey nick. "We're never going to get out of here," he would often moan when they were faced with the latest instance of the prison's casual brutality.

"Not if you keep thinking like that we won't," Johnny would say. "We'll get out. You've just got to think positively, that's all." But he could see that Albie was too mired in fear to really listen.

Godfray, on the other hand, took to life in Le Cachot surprisingly well. It gave full rein to his natural bullying tendencies and he soon became a feared and vindictive presence within the wing. Johnny, in fact, had to slap Godfray down when he tried to turn his intimidatory tactics on himself and Albie, but in general the Jerseyman proved a useful asset in keeping any other of the wing's predators at bay.

The Germans came into their wing, roughly at the same time the evening food (it could scarcely be described as a meal) was dished out. But this time they started picking and shoving men at random, forming them into a column, until they had selected maybe 15 or 16 of them. Johnny, Albie, Godfray and another couple of the

Englishmen were among those chosen. They were then marched through the gloomy, damp stone walls of the prison until they emerged in the courtyard where they had first arrived a number of weeks previously.

A similar number of prisoners from the female wing had also been selected and the two columns were lined up facing each other, as if in preparation for some sullen, macabre dance. A German officer then walked down the space between them, idly pointing to either one side or the other until six prisoners had been selected, three of each gender. Both Albie and Johnny were missed but the officer stopped at Godfray.

"Him."

Godfray stared at the officer dumbly for a moment but made no protest as he was dragged and pushed towards a wall that was already pocked with bullet-holes and dried, black bloodstains.

The six chosen prisoners were placed dispassionately against the wall while the rest of the prisoners were reformed into one column at the other end of the courtyard. They were then made to turn and face their isolated comrades.

No one said anything but it was quite clear what was going to happen next. They watched as six German soldiers were ordered into position facing the selected prisoners and raised their MP40s. None of the prisoners said anything, made any kind of plea for their lives, but each had a look of bleak, resigned acceptance on their faces. They were not the first to whom this had happened and they would not be the last. Godfray glanced for a moment over to his old comrades, but there was not a flicker of emotion upon his jowly features. No despair. No fear. Just blind acceptance.

The shots rang out in a strangely underwhelming burst of staccato and the bodies fell. But Johnny had not been looking at the bodies. He had been looking at the faces of the men who had done the shooting. Their faces had been blank, white masks, with their eyes as dead and glazed as the ones on the faces of those they'd just gunned down. He supposed this was necessary. In order to kill others in such a direct way as this, you needed to kill a part of yourself first. As far as he was aware, Johnny had never killed but he had ordered violence and retribution to be carried out against those who had threatened his interests. This had usually been carried out by Jack. He thought about Jack now. Had he turned the man who was probably his oldest friend into one of these blank-eyed half-men without even realising it? Or had the mere act of ordering violence upon another human being deadened himself in some way to which he'd remained completely oblivious?

And then it was over. They were ordered to pick up the bodies and take them to the burial pile before being shuffled back to their wing, reprieved for a while longer at least.

Albie became even more jittery after Godfray's execution, if such a thing were possible. He became convinced he was to become a victim in the lottery of the reprisal shooting squads and every time the Germans entered the wing his face would become pale and he would even begin to shiver uncontrollably. Johnny, too, had become far less confident of their chances of survival, but he did his best not to let it show, trying as much as possible to maintain his façade of unconcerned bravado.

And then the Germans came again. This time there were only two of them but Johnny recognised them as two of the men who had come to hustle them to the execution last time. They marched into the 'English' area of the cells and pointed directly at Johnny.

"You! You will come with us."

Johnny was aware of not just the Germans but of the other occupants of the cell staring at him – most with apprehensive curiosity, Albie with undisguised horror.

"Why's that then, chief?"

One of the Nazis stepped forward with a look that told Johnny he was clearly tempted to give him a rifle butt to the face and would do so if he received any more backchat.

"No questions. You will come with us. Now."

Johnny had no wish to get a busted mouth and there was no way of telling whether they might not take out any more insubordination on some of the others. Albie, for example, looked as if he was about to throw up with terror at any moment. But all the same he didn't want to allow himself to be merely led away meekly to get a bullet in his head. If this was where he was going to go out, he wanted to do so with at least some kind of a fight.

"Alright, chief. You're the boss. Just tell me where we're going, like."

The German took another step forward, this time raising the butt of this gun and Johnny held up a placatory hand.

"Alright. I'm coming. I'm coming."

"Where are you taking him?" stammered Albie from his bug-infested mattress. It was the first time, to Johnny's recollection, that he had spoken back to the guards at the prison. The guards ignored Albie, but Johnny looked down at his friend's pale, terrified face and gave him what he hoped was a reassuring wink.

"Don't worry, mate. I'll be back before you know it."

Albie looked less than convinced and Johnny didn't really believe it himself as they escorted him in silence through the stone corridors and out into the courtyard. Johnny couldn't help but glance at the killing wall, with its surface pocked with countless bullet-holes and stained with the blood of the long-dead. But the Germans continued to push him onwards, past the execution site and towards the main gate of the prison. He was led through the arched gateway to the prison and past the grim stare of several sentries before finding himself back on the street. For a brief moment, Johnny thought they were actually about to let him go and the whole thing had been the Germans' idea of a grim practical joke. But it didn't take him long to dismiss that idea. From what he'd experienced, he'd call the Jerries many things but humourists wasn't among them.

Parked in front of the prison was another shiny, black Mercedes and it was to this that the Germans now led him. One opened the back door like a hotel concierge and stood back slightly to let him enter.

"Inside."

Johnny looked from the soldier to the door and back. "Why?" he asked suspiciously. "Where are we going?"

The threatening glint had returned to the soldier's eye but before any further threats could be made, a German officer had leaned across from the back seat and was peering up at them. Johnny recognised him as the same sardonic-looking one who'd had Johnny pointed out to him on the night of his arrival at Le Cachot.

"I assure you there is no cause for concern, Herr Black," he said.

"Quite the opposite, in fact. Please, get in. We have much to talk about."

Johnny looked dubiously at the officer and then at the impassive face of his soldier escort. And then, realising that he really had very little choice, he shrugged and got into the car beside the officer.

The soldier slammed the car door closed and began stomping back towards the prison entrance. Before he'd got even halfway there, the Mercedes was already speeding off into the darkness.

TEN

FREDDIE Winner emerged from the seedy yet comforting fug of The Fox and Hounds into bitterly cold, blacked-out streets. The other patrons of the pub, now being kicked out by the no-nonsense barmaid, were slowly ambling their way home in the darkness. But Freddie wasn't moving. He was instead staring across the street to something that chilled him with apprehension.

Jack Spinks was leaning against the hood of Frankie Pliers's black Austin. Frankie himself was behind the wheel, tapping black-gloved fingers impatiently against it. Jack smiled thinly when he saw that Freddie had spotted him.

"Alright, Ferret?"

Despite his fear, Freddie approached Jack. "Alright, Jack? What you doing down here?"

"Heard this was where you were drinking these days. Thought we'd come down and offer you a lift. Just to show there's no hard feelings and all that."

There was no doubt in Freddie's mind that to get into the back of that car would be the last thing he'd ever do, just as he was certain that he probably wasn't going to have much choice in the matter. But still he said, "Nah, that's alright, Jack. Thanks all the same. Think I'll walk. Helps clear the head and that."

"Come on, Freddie," said Jack. "Don't be a dick. What's the point of making this harder than it has to be?"

Freddie considered running. But what would be the point? Even if Jack didn't catch him – and Freddie had seen for himself just how athletic Jack could be when he put his mind to it – Frankie would just mow him down before he'd got fifty yards up the road. And where was the dignity in that? Freddie realised that as far as the Blacks were concerned he didn't have much in the way of dignity anyway – to them he was just the Ferret – but if he could do nothing else now, he could at least prove them wrong on that.

"You do know she's playing you, right?" he said. "Making bloody monkeys of the lot of you. I mean, is this what the Black Mob is reduced to these days. Jumping to the tune of some bloody piece of skirt?"

"Just keep talking, Ferret," said Jack softly. "You're just going to make it easier."

"The name is Freddie. You can at least give me that. And I can't believe you're really going to do me like this. I've been with Johnny from the start. You too, Jack. Are you really going to throw all that over for some slut who's got ideas above her bloody station?"

Jack's lips thinned with anger. "Get in," he said. "Get in or we'll do you right here."

Freddie got into the car and Jack followed. Freddie revved up the Austin and it sped into the darkness.

Jack opened the front door as quietly as he could and closed it again gently, locking and bolting it in the practised way he knew would create the minimum of noise. This was not just to avoid alerting any wardens who might be lurking in the street outside – since the start of the war, the amount of busybodies who might poke their nose where it wasn't wanted had increased dramatically – but also to avoid disturbing any of the house's occupants who might already have retired for the evening.

But despite his care, Jack's arrival still managed to rouse Keith, who had been quietly dosing in his chair in the hall. He jumped, startled, but also embarrassed to have been caught napping on duty and tried to scramble to his feet. But Jack put a finger to his lips and silently waved him back into his chair.

He felt as if he'd brought the night fog in with him and that it was still hanging heavily around him, clinging to his face and the wool of his overcoat, making them both feel chill and damp. He shrugged himself out of the coat and hung it up in the hall, taking the cat-stabber from the pocket and slipping it into his trousers.

He was going to head straight up to his bedroom but was surprised to find see a light still burning in the parlour and so made a detour there. Billie smiled as she saw him enter.

"Alright, Jack? Fancy a cuppa?"

He pushed his fingers through his damp hair to flatten it into order and took a seat at the table. "Yeah, go on then," he said with a sigh. He suddenly felt incredibly heavy and weary. He always did after a job.

"Tough night, love?" asked Billie as she fussed over the tea things.

"Not the easiest," said Jack. "But I'll live. What are you doing still up anyway?"

"Not tired," said Billie. "Sometimes I just dread the idea of going to sleep. In case I don't want to wake up again, I suppose."

Jack was struck by the almost confessional frankness of her statement. It was unlike Billie to be that introspective but he didn't remark on it. Everyone was getting a little raw these days and besides he felt he'd understood what she had meant. He wondered if it might even have been meant for his benefit.

She brought the tea over to the table and took a seat beside him. For a moment, they drank their tea in silence. Finally, Billie asked, "What's it like out there tonight?"

Jack shrugged. "Same as usual. Cold. Wet. Black."

Billie had to suppress a smile. She'd seen Jack in this kind of gloomy mood before. Most people assumed he'd got the nickname 'Black Jack' because of his affiliation to Johnny's Mob, but Billie knew it was really because of his often morose disposition. She reached out and took his hands in hers. True enough, they were shockingly cold. She let her fingers run softly across his before enclosing his hands to warm them.

"You've got an artist's hands, Jack," she said softly. "I've always thought so."

"There's many out there who would disagree with you," he replied.

"Well, too bad they're not in any position to say any different then, ain't it?" she said.

"One less than there was this morning at any rate," he said.

She looked at him, still keeping hold of his cold fingers. "How was it?" she asked.

He lowered his gaze from hers. "Not the worst. Not the easiest. You know what he was like. Trouble to the end."

She kept her eyes on his until he felt obliged to look up at her again. "Thanks for doing that, Jack."

"That's what I'm here for."

She took his chin in her hand and smiled at him, almost with pity. "No, Jack, it's not. Not by a long chalk. Don't you ever forget that."

For a moment, nothing more was said. Jack was finding Billie's touch calming. He was usually jumpy after a killing, wired with a mixture of excitement and horror. But now he felt at peace. The madness and the blood finally at bay, at least for a while. He wanted to stay like this forever. It was perfect, he thought. The first sense of quiet he'd had in what felt like years.

And then she was moving away, heading towards the door, and taking that peace with her. "Don't you stay up till all hours now, do you hear me, Jack Spinks?"

He smiled at her. "I won't. Good night."

"G'night, Jack."

Jack listened to her shuffle along the passageway and pad up the stairs with a murmured goodnight to Keith. And then the house was silent again. He took a thoughtful sip of his tea, listening to all the usual sounds of the resting house, the ticking clock, the creaking woodwork, letting them fill his thoughts and using them to block out the memory of Freddie Winner's last whimpering, gurgling moments of life.

III. THE GOOD NAZI

ONE

FREDDIE'S body was found just before dawn by shift workers at one of the dockside warehouses. At first the corpse, floating face-down in the brown murk of the Thames, was assumed to be just another victim of the previous night's raids. The docks were still being hit pretty hard and stray corpses regularly turned up in the water, sometimes even days after the raids themselves. And although this body had only been in the water for what couldn't be more than five or six hours, it had already acquired the bloated, pasty pallor of all river cadavers. The rats, too, had been at it and the face, body and limbs showed signs of frenzied gnaw marks. One eye was already gone completely.

But all that was nothing to the grisly sight that lay just below the face. The throat had been slit from ear to ear in what was sometimes colloquially referred to as a 'Limehouse Grin'.

"Poor bastard," said Illingworth, staring down at Freddie's barely recognisable body.

Harry was standing some feet away with his back to Freddie's corpse and staring out at the devastation on the opposite bank of the river, most of the buildings nothing more than still-smoking shells from the previous night's raids. He could still just make out the bells of distant fire trucks, their night's work not quite yet over.

"How's that then?" he asked, turning back to face Illingworth.

"Well, you know," said Illingworth. "I know Freddie Winner was a wrong 'un and all but did he really deserve this?"

Harry scowled at him. "Yes, Phil, yes, he bloody did. He might never have picked up a knife, or pointed a gun, but Freddie Winner did as much damage as any other toe-rag we've banged up over the years. Remember that TB-infected meat on the black market last year? That was Freddie. How many did that put in the hospital? So, me," he directed his gaze at Freddie's mutilated corpse, half tempted for a moment to give it a kick, "me, I call this something like justice."

Illingworth shook his head and pointed to the body. "That's a Limehouse Grin he's sporting here. I don't need to tell you who likes to dish those out. This is down to us, Harry. At least partly."

"Bollocks," spat Harry. "If you think I'm going to shed any tears for a scumbag like Freddie Winner you've got another think coming. If he ended up here, like this, then no one did it to him but himself." He turned and began stomping back across the wasteground towards their car.

"Now where are you going?" Illingworth called after him.

"Got somebody I need to see."

Harry stared impassively at the solid wooden door to the Blacks' house and found himself hating it. It was odd to feel such animosity for an inanimate lump of wood and metal, but he did. He hated the dark green paint that was slightly streaked and bubbled from over-enthusiastic and amateurish application. He hated the burnished brass of the door knob and the letterbox and the nameplate with J.E. BLACK engraved upon it in pretentiously ornate lettering. He hated everything about this door, its indifferent solidity and its veneer of a suburban respectability that no one within had even the slightest claim to. But most of all, he hated the fact that Johnny wasn't actually behind it. That he couldn't just kick it down and drag him off to the prison cell where he belonged.

Eventually, he reached out and rapped sharply on the wood, ignoring the brass door-knocker and preferring to rely on his own meaty knuckles to announce his presence. Almost immediately the door was opened and he was faced with a broad-shouldered teenager. There were few men who could intimidate Harry in terms of physical presence but this youth could have managed it, if it hadn't been for the open, youthful, somehow not-yet-fully formed features below the sandy crewcut.

"Can I help you with something?" said Keith, a suspicious scowl across his brow.

"You're new," said Harry, making a mental note of the unknown face. Quite a fierce-looking kid, he thought. Bit of heft to him too. Looked as if he might be quite tasty in a scrap. But still a bit on the young side, still with a bit of softness to him. Not the kind of muscle that Harry would consider to be any kind of threat. At least, not yet. "Jack must be getting desperate if he's recruiting out of the kindergarten now."

Contrary to Harry's expectation, Keith's face relaxed slightly now that he had set the tone for the conversation. This was clearly someone he didn't have to pay any kind of deference to and that made things a lot easier.

"You Old Bill?" said Keith, more a statement than a question.

Harry produced his warrant card and held it up for a moment. "The lady of the house in, is she?" he asked.

"Got a warrant?" said Keith, folding his arms.

"Son," said Harry with a weary smile. "I don't need one. As you'd know if you had the slightest idea who I was."

Keith didn't budge. But Harry could see doubt and maybe even a little fear fluttering behind the kid's eyes. He wasn't half as confident in this encounter as he was making out. But still he held his ground. Harry wondered briefly if he'd be able to put the boy down if it came to it. The kid had both youth and bulk on his side and while Harry was still in pretty good nick for his age, he was by no means the man he once was.

And then a voice came from inside the house. "It's alright, Keithie. Let him through."

Keith glowered at Harry for a moment longer, but the relief on his face at no longer having responsibility for this confrontation was palpable. He stood aside and made room for Harry to walk past.

Harry had never been inside the Black house before. He was not sure what he'd been expecting but had assumed something more ostentatious, flashier, given the way Johnny presented himself to the world. The sunlight shining through the stained glass transom above the front door gave the dark hallway an almost tranquil, church-like aura as a smell of home-cooking wafted gently through the house. It felt truly like a home, thought Harry, and you'd have been hard-pressed to believe that this place housed some of the most ruthless gangsters in London. The only thing that gave it away were the two gorillas on duty, arms folded, and glaring at him with beetle-browed suspicion. Harry knew both of them by name, but he did not give them an instant of acknowledgement.

It was Jack Spinks who had issued the order to let Harry in. He stood framed in the rear passageway of the hall, a dark, angular silhouette, but one which Harry recognised immediately.

"Harry's as good as one of the family," Jack said. "Ain't you, Harry?"

Harry scowled at Jack, ignoring the smirks of the muscle in the hallway. He walked past Keith, heading for Jack, but then stopped as a thought struck him.

"What age are you, son?" he asked.

Keith looked at him mounting suspicion. "Why?"

"Well, I was just thinking that you must be getting close to call-up age, eh?" he said. "Looking forward to getting stuck into the Jerries, I'll bet."

Harry's hunch had been correct and he saw Keith blanch under his gaze. For all his bulk and menace, the kid was a white feather, hiding out here with scum like the Blacks rather than obeying the call-up. No doubt the Blacks had helped his papers to go 'missing', he thought. Filing this little nugget for future reference, he made his way along the passageway towards Jack.

"How you been, Harry? Been keeping out of trouble?" said Jack when he reached the doorway to the parlour. The mock joviality grated as it was intended to and Harry ignored it pointedly. Jack just grinned, enjoying seeing the detective bristle. But he stopped short of giving in to the temptation of giving Harry a matey pat on the back, for fear that he'd end up with a broken arm. Instead, he nodded towards the door and said, "Come on in."

Jack led him into the parlour. Billie was in her usual spot, at the middle of the huge, oak table.

Harry had never met Billie, although he had heard much about her. She was certainly attractive, he thought. All coiffed blonde curls, hourglass curves and elegant poise. Her eyes sparkled with quick intelligence under arched brows and her full lips were almost permanently set into a subtly contemptuous sneer, as if she found everything and everyone around her somehow lacking and even faintly absurd. The relative simplicity of her earlier nightclub glamour was now completely gone and had been replaced with something infinitely more complex, and more dangerous. Harry had been half-expecting to be dealing with some kind of dull-brained flapper but one look at Billie disabused him of that notion entirely.

Billie, for her part, was just as interested in her unexpected visitor. Harry's was a name she'd heard mentioned many times over the years by Johnny, Jack and many others in the Firm, and often with a mixture of exasperation and awe. Harry was almost the bogeyman that villains told their kids about to give them the shivers. She watched him coolly from behind her teacup, affecting nonchalance, while in fact sizing up this new adversary carefully. The long scars running almost the full length from his temples to his jaws lent him a fearsome air, but the knowledge that Johnny had been responsible for them also gave her a thrill of pleasure and pride.

But it was not the bulk, or the sense of grievance that made him so dangerous, she reflected. It was the fire of barely subdued rage and single-minded obsession that she could see sparking erratically behind his eyes. Yes, she could see why Harry Blum was so feared. He was like an old dog, just on the verge of madness after one beating too many. But while this unpredictability made him dangerous, she knew it was also something which could be exploited.

Jack busied himself at the range, pouring himself a cup of tea from the warming pot. "Take a seat, Harry," he said, still doing his all-pals-together act. "Fancy a cuppa?"

"I'm fine," said Harry, setting himself in an 'at ease' stance and locking his hands behind his back as he glared at the two of them.

Jack took his tea and took a position behind Billie. He didn't sit down, just in case things turned ugly. He didn't think that was likely, but he wanted to be ready just in case.

"I don't believe I've had the pleasure," said Harry finally, eyes fixed on Billie.

"And you never will, love, believe me," said Billie, also not taking her gaze off her uninvited guest.

"Sorry," said Jack. "I didn't realise that introductions were necessary."

"They're not, Jack, love," said Billie. "This, I take it, has to be the legendary Harry Blum? Couldn't be anyone else really, could it?"

"It's good to know that my reputation goes before me," said Harry.

"Oh, it does, love," said Billie. "Most famous cripple in London, ain't ya?"

Harry felt a little surge of rage but he suppressed it. To let her see his anger would be to surrender far too much so early in the interview. But part of him admired her for coming out on the attack straight off. She was definitely not someone to mess with lightly.

"And how is Johnny these days? Still having fun in Jersey, is he?" he said. It was not subtle, but it was the best he could muster. Already there was something about Billie that unsettled him. "But, of course, I guess you won't really know, will you? What with the Jerries having the whole island locked up tight. I suppose for all you know they might have shot him months ago."

Billie didn't have Harry's poker face and her eyes flashed with anger for a moment. He watched with satisfaction as she struggled to regain control.

"Was there something we can help you with, Harry?" she said. "Or are you just here to trade cheap shots?"

"Freddie Winner," said Harry.

The studiedly blank stares he was met with told Harry he'd definitely touched a nerve and that he was definitely in the right place. They'd put their wall up too quickly, and with just a bit too much perfection.

"What about him?" asked Jack.

"Fished him out of the river yesterday morning. Right bloody mess he was too. Somebody had given the poor sod a Limehouse

Grin." Harry ran a beefy finger along his throat to emphasise the point.

"Harry, please," said Jack, affecting a pained expression. "There are ladies present."

Harry shrugged. "Can't say I'd noticed." And lady or not, he *had* noticed that Billie was decidedly unmoved by the conversation. "So, you're saying that you two know nothing about it, then?"

Billie shook her head. "First I've heard of it. How about you, Jack?"

"Haven't seen the papers yet, have I?" he said. "Shocking though, isn't it?"

"Mind you," said Billie, smirking. "I did hear that Freddie did run around with some pretty rum characters."

"Yes, I'd heard something of the like too."

"Alright, alright," said Harry. "Spare me. But the fact remains that somebody did for Freddie. And somebody who knew what they were doing too. You're pretty handy with a blade, ain't you, Jack?"

"Am I, Harry? If you say so."

"That's just daft," said Billie. "I mean, why would Jack here want to do for Freddie? They were the best of mates. Weren't you, Jack?"

"Like brothers," said Jack, deadpan.

"Well," said Harry. "I did hear that Freddie might have been getting ideas above his station like. Maybe the kind of ideas that might make some people around here a little bit on the nervous side."

Billie shrugged. "Can't say I'd heard anything like that," she said. "What about you, Jack?"

"Nope. News to me."

"See, Harry?" said Billie. "Nothing doing. Freddie and us, we were all the best of friends. And there's nothing you can say otherwise. But, as I say, Freddie, he did run around all over London and with some right dodgy types and all. I'm sure you know what I mean. Black marketeers and the like. Any one of them might have had a good reason to do him in. Try the Eyeties. You might have more luck with them."

Harry placed his meaty fists on the table, pivoting his weight on them until his face was just inches from Billie's. "You think I won't put you down just because you're a woman?" he growled. "You're crediting me with a chivalry that I just don't have. I know that you've picked up all the little threads that your Johnny left dangling when he got put away. That puts you directly in my sights, love. Don't think for a moment that it doesn't."

Billie didn't flinch and kept her own flinty gaze fixed on Harry. "Am I supposed to be afraid of you, Harry?" she said. "Because I'm not. I mean, what is there to be afraid of? Just an over-the-hill cripple with a chip on his shoulder. You're nothing, Harry. Nothing worth bothering about anyway. Just a tired, old man with no guts left. And do you know why? Because my Johnny had them kicked right out of you years ago." Her sneer widened into a smile of icy sweetness. "Now, piss off."

Jack had watched this exchange with growing nervousness. He could see a thick artery throbbing on Harry's temple and was uncertain whether that meant he might lash out at Billie or even keel over of a heart attack. The latter would certainly have solved a lot of problems, he thought, and would even be slightly amusing. But failing that, it was clear that things could only get uglier from here.

"Come on, Harry," he said. "Time to go, don't you think?"

Harry didn't move for a moment and continued to eyeball Billie with undisguised fury. And then he straightened again. "Yes," he whispered, his voice still hoarse with anger. "I think you might be right."

He turned and walked out.

"Bye now, Harry," Billie called after him, mockingly. "Thanks for stopping by. But let's not make a habit of it, eh?"

They heard him thundering towards the front door and flinging it open. And then he was gone. The door was refastened far more gently and peace returned to the house.

From his position beside her, Jack couldn't actually see Billie's face. But he could see that she was shaking, somewhere between furious and tearful.

"Don't let him get to you," he said. "You were right. He's nothing." But even as he said it, he knew that it wasn't true. Harry Blum was something alright. And it wasn't anything good.

"He's a bastard," said Billie, her voice still trembling with emotion.

"My Johnny should have finished the job on him when he'd had the chance."

Jack let his hand fall to just beside her shoulder and he felt a little thrill of pleasure when her own sought it out, squeezing it strongly with gratitude.

TWO

FOR the first few minutes of the journey from Le Cachot, the officer didn't say anything and focused his attention on a bulging manila folder on his lap. Johnny noticed that on the top of it was his letter, now creased and worn, annotated in red ink in a German scrawl. It had been through many hands since he'd last seen it. He also caught a glimpse of several of the newspaper cuttings from the time of his trial, as well as pages of other official-looking forms and typewritten pages.

The officer himself looked to be somewhere in his early 40s, with neat, brilliantined hair and that lop-sided cynical smirk constantly playing around his lips. He eventually put the folder to one side and turned his attention to Johnny.

"Herr Black," he said, holding out his hand. "It is a pleasure to meet you at last. I am Herr Doktor Gert Weiler." He said the name with such a rehearsed confidence that Johnny immediately knew it was fake.

Johnny shook his hand warily. "Been reading up on me?" he asked, nodding towards the folder.

"Yes, indeed," said Weiler. "Your file makes for most colourful reading. We have been following your progress for some time now."

"Charmed, I'm sure."

"However, before we go any further, I have to ask you whether you are still of the same mind when you wrote this letter?"

"That all depends," said Johnny. "On what exactly you have in mind."

"I rather think ‚Herr Black, that," smiled Weiler, "that depends on you."

They drove for well over an hour. Darkened Paris streets gradually gave way to suburbs, which in turn were replaced by narrower country roads. Johnny was slightly surprised that Weiler didn't press the subject of his letter any further but was happy to sit back and peruse his folder in silence.

In truth, Johnny was somewhat relieved. As intrigued as he was by this latest turn of events, he was now dog-tired. Despite not having the remotest idea about what might happen to him next, he could feel the constant tension of life in Le Cachot seeping away from him, like poison being expunged from a wound. He was still slightly surprised that he had survived it without being shot and wasn't entirely convinced that it might not yet happen, but still he felt the most relaxed that he had in months. And by the time they reached their destination, a compact, walled country villa, he was ready to drop.

The car stopped in front of the main entrance to the house and Weiler led Johnny inside, past two saluting sentries and directly up the wide staircase to a second-floor bedroom. It was not large but was still probably the most comfortable room Johnny had seen since his arrest at the hotel in Jersey, which now felt as if it were several lifetimes ago.

"It's not much, Herr Black," said Weiler, almost apologetically. "But I trust it will suffice?"

Johnny didn't think he'd been so glad to see a bed in his life. "It'll do just grand," he said, already stumbling towards it.

"I'm so glad," said Weiler. "Now, get some rest. We'll talk in the morning." He retreated out the door and closed it gently behind him.

Johnny waited for a moment and then tried the door and was half surprised to find it was unlocked. He slid the door open a crack to find that there were no guards posted outside – just Weiler quietly slipping back downstairs.

He pondered whether it was worth making a run for it. But what would be the point? Even if he did get out the house, he was in the middle of the countryside in occupied France. Just how far was he likely to get? Besides, this was what he wanted, wasn't it? This was why he'd written that bloody letter in the first place.

But the most compelling reason for him to stay put was that he didn't think he was even capable of taking another step.

He all but collapsed on the bed and started fumbling with his bootlaces. He paused for a moment, the glaring eye in the framed picture of The Führer by his bedside catching his eye.

"Well, Adolf," he said. "What the hell have I got myself into now?"

There was no answer forthcoming and so instead he continued stripping out of his clothes and collapsed into a deep, dreamless sleep.

Sunlight streamed through the bedroom window as Johnny slowly struggled out of a deep, if all-too-brief night's sleep. The rainy gloom of the previous evening had evaporated and it was now a glorious morning, with every corner of his small, rustically furnished bedroom bathed in yellow sunlight. He dragged himself out of bed, already gasping and hacking for his first smoke of the day. He stretched and opened the little, lead-panelled window to let the morning in and was only slightly taken aback to find two German soldiers having an early-morning cigarette amidst a gaggle of chickens in the yard below.

"Guten Morgen," said one, as they looked up and noticed Johnny watching them.

Johnny smiled a wan, if slightly sheepish greeting before withdrawing back inside the bedroom.

He was vaguely at a loss as to how to proceed. The clock by his bedside told him it was now shortly after six. He hadn't had a long sleep but it had been the most easeful one he could remember having in long time and he no longer felt remotely fatigued. Rather he felt exhilarated, the fear and the apprehension of the previous evening gone. If they had intended to shoot him, they would have done it already, he was sure. What he'd been angling for all these months had now landed in his lap, so all he had to do was roll up his sleeves and get on with it.

He opened the wardrobe next to the bed to find a crisp, new, German Army uniform, complete with highly polished jackboots. Johnny stared at it for a moment. Was this meant for him or did it just happened to be stored in the room where he'd been sleeping? Would showing up downstairs wearing it be considered some kind of mockery? He had no idea of his place in this set-up yet and he didn't want to make any more of an ass of himself than was absolutely necessary.

He closed the wardrobe door again and turned to his own clothes that he'd left unceremoniously piled on the wicker chair next to the door. He had one leg in his old trousers, which were now stiff with grime and sweat, before he stopped himself.

"Fuck it," he said, tossing the trousers back on the chair and opening the wardrobe again.

He descended the wide, mahogany staircase, with more than a little apprehension. The staircase was lined with various stern-looking framed portraits, who seemed to be staring down at him with universal disapproval, no doubt because of his new outfit.

The uniform was slightly constricting and he'd never worn anything quite like it before. The boots, in particular, seemed to be incredibly uncomfortable and he imagined they would take some breaking in. But nonetheless he was still experiencing a vicarious thrill of guilty pleasure in wearing it. Putting on the costume of those who had, until just hours before, been his oppressors had a delicious air of transgression about it.

He followed the echoing of chattering male voices until he arrived at a long breakfast room. Several men, all dressed in German uniform of various rank, sat on each side of a narrow table upon which was spread more food than Johnny had seen in months. At the head of the table sat Weiler, looking indulgently down the table at his men, his trademark smirk still on his face. It was Weiler that first noticed Johnny enter the room and the smirk widened to a grin.

"Well, look at you," he said. "You look very…" He made a show of searching for the right word for a moment before settling on, "German." He let his men have their moment of quiet laughter, before adding, "I trust you are quite rested?"

"Much thanks," said Johnny. "Hungry now though." He made eagerly for the table. A couple of the men started shifting chairs to politely make room for him, but Weiler intervened by standing up, his chair screeching loudly on the parquet floor.

"Actually," he said politely, "I was wondering if you would mind breakfasting with me in my study just for this morning. I'd very much like to start getting you acquainted with what we do here. We can introduce you to the others later."

Johnny shrugged. "Whatever you like," he said. "You're the boss."

A couple of the men around the table gave him some rueful smiles of sympathy as he followed Weiler out of the dining room.

Weiler's study had clearly been someone's private library at some point. It was a comfortable, book-lined room which demonstrated the same cultured, educated style that seemed to characterise the rest of the house. Whoever had inhabited the house before the Nazis had taken possession clearly had good taste and serious money, thought Johnny. He also reflected that it didn't bear too much wondering what had happened to them, a brief image of Le Cachot, of the brutal, ugly life there and of the firing squads, briefly flashing to mind.

"Come in, come in," said Weiler, waving Johnny in the direction of a set of comfortable-looking armchairs and sofa by an as-yet unlit fireplace. Weiler himself busied himself at a cluttered but imposing desk, picking up the familiar buff folder that Johnny had seen the night before.

Johnny had barely settled himself in one of the armchairs when the door to the study opened again and another German officer entered. This one was younger than Weiler, with sandy hair and steel-rimmed spectacles. Despite his immaculate uniform, this man gave the impression of being somehow more of an academic than a strictly military man. He had wide, blue eyes that sparkled with curiosity and intelligence and a wide, sensuous mouth. He was carrying, rather incongruously, a tray loaded with what Johnny assumed must be his breakfast.

"Allow me to introduce Hauptmann Behrensdorff," said Weiler, as he took the opposite armchair to Johnny's.

Behrensdorff placed the tray on a low table in front of the fireplace and gave Johnny a perfunctory salute. "I am delighted to make your acquaintance, Herr Black," he said in clipped, German-inflected English. He gestured towards the food. "Please."

Johnny didn't need telling twice. He pulled the table as close to him as he could possibly manage and set about attacking the plate which was piled generously high with eggs, bacon, sausage and bread. Behrensdorff smiled indulgently but without warmth, and took a seat on the sofa.

Weiler, meanwhile, was once again flicking through Johnny's file. Eventually, he looked up, smiling with faintly mocking amusement at the sight of the Englishmen shovelling the food into his mouth as quickly as he could manage it.

"You'll forgive us if we talk while you eat, Herr Black," he said. "But there are a few formalities that we would like to get out of the way as quickly as possible so that we can commence your training."

Johnny shrugged. "Sure," he mumbled indistinctly, his mouth still full. "Be my guest."

Weiler lifted Johnny's letter from the file on his lap, peering at it through his spectacles. "'*I know London like the back of my hand*'," he read, "'*have an extensive network of underworld contacts and am easily the best safe-cracker in the British Isles. All skills which I believe would be of immense practical use to the Reich in an espionage capacity*'." He looked at Johnny. "You still consider this to be the case?"

"I do."

"You certainly seem to have a very high opinion of your abilities," observed Behrensdorff.

"Just because it happens to be true," sniffed Johnny. "I can't help that."

"Well," said Weiler. "First of all, I believe having an Englishman around would be too conspicuous for our purposes. From here on in you are Johann Schwartz, recently transferred here from Bonn. Your command of English can be explained by you having spent part of your childhood in the United States."

"Fine," said Johnny. "Suits me."

"How is your German?" asked Behrensdorff.

"Alright." This was an exaggeration. His German was limited to what he had started to teach himself from books when he'd first hatched his plan back in Jersey. "It could be better," he added, hastily, in case they suddenly asked for a demonstration.

"It will be by the time you leave."

"Behrensdorff here will be responsible for your training while you are here," explained Weiler.

Johnny smiled through another mouthful of egg and bacon. "Won't that be fun?" He was still not sure if he liked this Behrensdorff bloke. In fact, he wasn't sure if he'd come to any real conclusions about any of them, for that matter.

Behrensdorff returned with an equally diffident smile. "I am already looking forward to it," he said. "But, tell me, Herr Black, I am curious. What makes a man become a traitor? To turn against his own people?"

"I wouldn't say that's what I'm doing," said Johnny, softly but firmly. "Not at all."

Behrensdorff raised an eyebrow. "No? And what is it you think you're doing?"

"I've spent most of my life running from coppers and lawyers and judges. They'd already made me their enemy a long time ago without any help from me. The way I see it, I've been fighting the English a damn sight longer than you buggers have. Which is, by the by, because I'm in this for the money. I expect to be well paid."

Weiler chuckled. "Well, I'm satisfied by that. What about you, Karl?"

Behrensdorff was not smiling and, if anything, seemed more stiff than before. "Well, I think we shall have to see. Some things should be more important than money."

"True. But not many, eh, Schwarz?" agreed Weiler. "And please don't worry. There will be plenty of opportunities to make money. Serious money. Have no fear, you will emerge from this little arrangement a rich man."

Johnny didn't say anything but continued to eat. All three men were silent for a moment. And then Johnny could contain the question burning within him no longer.

"There is one thing," he ventured, with uncharacteristic hesitancy.

Weiler smiled at him indulgently. "And what would that be?"

"I left someone behind in that place. A friend. What are the chances of getting him out?"

The two Germans exchanged a glance. Behrensdorff said, "Who is he, this friend?"

Johnny shrugged. "Just what I say. We were together in Jersey. I just don't like the idea of leaving him there."

"Was he a criminal acquaintance this man?" asked Weiler.

"Yeah, he was a burglar."

"A good one?"

Johnny thought for a moment. Albie had, as far as he was aware, never successfully completed a burglary and had been collared on every attempt. But the kid kept trying, bless him, and kept getting banged up for his trouble. But Johnny had to admit it was unlikely that he'd ever have given Albie a job in his own Firm.

"No, not really," he admitted.

"Then, I'm afraid," said Behrensdorff, "that it is unlikely that we would have any use for him."

"It's just that he's not dealing with being in there very well," said Johnny. "I'd feel happier if you put him somewhere else at least."

"What is your friend's name?" asked Weiler.

Johnny told him.

"I'm afraid there's no question of relocating him," said Weiler. "Quite simply because there is nowhere to relocate him to. And to be quite honest, it was no small task getting you out of there, let alone anyone else. I'm afraid that he will have to stay where he is. For the time being, at least."

All three men were silent for a moment, but Johnny was aware how keenly Weiler and Behrensdorff were scrutinising him, analysing and noting his reaction. This was a test, he realised. No doubt the first of many.

"However," said Weiler. "I'll tell you what I'll do. I'll keep an eye on this fellow, see to it he's treated as well as possible, gets a bit more food, that kind of thing. He'll come to no harm, I assure you. And in the future, it may be possible to do more, perhaps even get him released. If we find ourselves in your debt, for example."

"Indeed," agreed Behrensdorff. "Never forget, the Reich rewards those who reward the Reich. A strong performance from you here could be your friend's salvation."

"In that case," said Johnny, pushing away his empty plate. "We'd better get on with it. When do we start?"

"Right now," said Behrensdorff, with just the faintest hint of human warmth creeping into his smile. "That is, if you've finally finished stuffing your face."

THREE

JOHNNY was surprised at just how quickly he began to enjoy life at his new home. They jokingly called the little three-storey villa The Chateau although it was really far too small to be really considered as such. But it was still more luxurious than anything he'd been used to for well over a year now and he adapted with alacrity to the new regime of comfortable beds, three decent meals a day and seemingly unlimited brandy and wine in the evenings.

Not that it was anything remotely resembling an easy life. The day started at seven and went on until late, and into each was packed a tight schedule of sabotage training, explosives manufacture, radio operation, cryptography and a dozen other disciplines. But there was still plenty of time off too and he had time to catch up on his reading, as well as for taking long, leisurely walks in the countryside, albeit on the proviso that he take one of the other 'boys' with him.

He really only saw Weiler at meal times and in the evenings, apart from the occasions he found himself summoned to his study on specific business, like a naughty schoolboy being sent before the headmaster. Training, for the most part, was supervised by

Behrensdorff but was frequently taken by his fellow 'agents', so that Johnny was often uncertain whether his companions were there in the capacity of instructors or students. This collegiate atmosphere was clearly deliberate, if slightly disconcerting, and towards the end of his time there, he too was asked to instruct some of his newer companions on basic explosives and safe-breaking, although he sometimes suspected it was actually his knowledge which was being tested rather than vice-versa.

His companions were an odd bunch, but on the whole likable enough. Aside from Behrensdorff and Weiler, he found he spent most of his time in the company of a reserved middle-aged man called Krause, a jovial, rotund joker called Fleischer and a fellow Londoner who introduced himself as Sidney Cook. At first, Johnny had assumed that Cook was a plant to make him feel more at home but, as he probed him on his background he found that he had a knowledge of London that could only come from someone who had spent a significant amount of time there. He found Cook's boasts of his underworld antics in the capital unconvincing, primarily because it was hard to believe he wouldn't have at least heard of him before now. But it wasn't clear to Johnny whether Cook was an adventurer doing his best to coast through the war on his own terms or was, in fact, in Weiler's employ to keep an eye on him.

They didn't trust him, of course. But why the hell should they? He certainly didn't trust them. And it didn't take much for the veneer of comradely affability to be replaced with frowning suspicion. For instance, one evening Johnny had been making what he thought was idle conversation with Krause as they all relaxed in the drawing room of the Chateau. Krause had been absent for a couple of weeks and had only just returned that day. This in itself was not unusual and most of the villa's inhabitants had been called away for an assignment or training elsewhere occasionally. These absences were seldom, if ever, commented upon.

"Good trip?" Johnny had asked.

Krause smiled thinly. "Yes, thank you."

"You look like you caught a bit of the sun. Been somewhere nice?"

The smile froze on Krause's lips. "Why do you have to ask such questions, Schwarz?" he asked.

Johnny just shrugged and grinned. "Just making conversation, aren't I? Don't worry, it's not like I was sitting here pining for you or anything."

And Krause laughed. A little too jovially, thought Johnny, for someone who was as normally as reserved as he was. And true enough, a day or two later, he was called into Weiler's study.

"I would be careful in the kind of questions you ask, Johann," he said. "Please don't forget that this is an Abwehr station, after all. And you wouldn't want people to get the wrong idea, would you?"

"And what wrong idea would that be?" asked Johnny.

Weiler smiled and held his hands open in a disarming shrug.

"Schwarz," he said, "if we truly thought you were spying for the British then we would not be having this conversation, would we? We would be watching the crows picking out your brains, yes? But all the same, we have to be careful. We have to produce results rather than just talk."

"And how am I supposed to do that? How am I supposed to make you buggers trust me?"

"I do trust you, Schwarz. And you will get your chance. More than one. But it is going to take time. And what's the sense of making this job more difficult for everyone than it already is? We are, I hope, friends. But we have to be more than that. We have to be comrades. You understand what I am saying, yes?"

"Yes, I understand."

"Good. Because at the end of the day, we are soldiers. All of us. And that means that we must always be prepared to do what must be done. That is the primary lesson we are learning here. All of us."

This conversation would trouble Johnny for months to come. What Weiler was saying to him was unambiguous; that they would quite happily put a bullet in Johnny's head if it became necessary. And Johnny couldn't really blame them if they did, because at the time he'd had that conversation with Weiler, he'd had a notebook burning a hole in his back pocket. A notebook in which he'd only that afternoon recorded the current transmission frequencies of the Abwehr unit in Nantes, joining the names and ranks of the occupants of the Chateau and the various explosive chemical formulae he'd been coached in over the last few months. It was the kind of thing that would almost certainly have got him killed if discovered and he wasn't even completely sure why he was taking such a risk.

He supposed it always paid to have some kind of insurance.

Johnny took a draw on his cigarette and squinted at the low, winter sun as he watched their instructor cross the grass to where he and his fellow 'students' were waiting. His name was Theiss and was a relatively new addition to the Chateau. He was ostensibly there to give them their explosives training but, it hadn't taken Johnny long to realise that he'd forgotten more about explosives than this weedy, self-important Kraut had ever known. And he had said as much to Weiler one evening, although, of course not in quite those terms. Weiler had merely given him a politic, lop-sided smile, neither agreeing nor disagreeing.

"Gather round, please," barked Theiss, clapping his hands effeminately. "I would like to continue your instruction on demolition methodology."

They were all assembled in the grounds at the back of the villa, which was where most of the 'practical' instruction, like hand-to-hand, weapons and explosives training was held. Theiss ushered them around a thick tree stump, which had had a thick hole drilled into it earlier in the day.

"If you'd like to gather round please," repeated Theiss. He was a reedy, stick-insect of a man with a twitchy, nervous demeanour who hadn't really managed to make many friends during his short time at the villa. He had been too standoffish with the men for that, only occasionally showing up at the evening (often rather drunken) soirées that even Weiler and Behrensdorff made a point of attending.

Theiss bent over and opened a battered old Gladstone bag that he'd placed on the ground next to the stump. From it, he produced three chemical vials.

"Now," he said, "moving on from our discussion of the composition of simple, easily available chemicals yesterday, we now see how, when combined, can create often devastating results in our sabotage work."

Johnny watched as Theiss gingerly began tipping the contents of the vials into the hole in the stump. "That's all wrong," he whispered to Krause, who was standing next to him. "He's buggered up the ratios."

Krause grinned and rolled his eyes. But Johnny found himself taking an involuntary step backwards as Theiss slipped a length of fuse into the hole and lit it. He took three steps back from the stump, motioning for the others to do the same. Not enough, thought Johnny, and took a further three.

The stump exploded in single flash of flame and a lot of smoke. But the attention from the actual pyrotechnics was almost immediately distracted by Krause falling to the ground and screaming in agony. All the men immediately rushed to him, but Johnny was the closest to him. Krause's face was ashen and he was gripping his right thigh tightly – where through his blood-soaked trousers a jagged lump of wood from the stump was clearly visible.

"Jesus Christ," said Johnny. "Don't move, mate." But Krause didn't even look as if he was listening, already succumbing to shock.

Johnny had only completed his first-aid training recently and this was the first time he'd had to put it into practice and so he began ransacking his memory trying to remember just what he should be doing next. At his back, he was dimly aware of Theiss trying to push through the crowd with vain cries of "let me through, let me through".

"You've had your chance," he heard Fleischer say. "And you've already done enough damage. Let Johnny get on with it."

"Right," hissed Johnny under his breath and set to work.

"May I come in?"

Johnny looked up from his bed to see Behrensdorff standing in the doorway to his room. This was so unusual to the point that Johnny couldn't remember it ever happening before and he half-wondered whether he should be leaping up from his bunk and standing to attention. Especially as the officer in question was really the only one among them who could be remotely described as a stickler for discipline. But there was something about the German's casual demeanour that told Johnny he was relaxing his usually strident views on protocol for the moment.

"Sure, come on in."

Behrensdorff even had the faintest hint of a smile on his face as he entered. As Johnny moved to stand up, he waved him back down good-humouredly.

"No, no, please don't get up. I just wanted to let you know that Krause is now out of hospital and will be rejoining us shortly."

"Good, I'm glad. Is he going to be alright?"

"Well, he'll still be limping around for a while but he will make a full recovery. I think he is more embarrassed to have been put in hospital by a tree trunk." This was about as close to humour that Behrensdorff got, so Johnny gave him the obligatory smile.

"And what about Theiss?"

Behrensdorff made a sour face. "He is gone and good riddance. I imagine he is now settling into his new life in the East."

The official line was that the campaign in the Eastern Front was going well and that victory for the Reich was all but assured but the whispers from the others, as well as some of the other German troops he bumped into now and again, told an entirely different story. It was certainly not the kind of place you would want to find yourself reassigned to, especially not after the cushy life of the Chateau. Johnny tried to muster up some sympathy for Theiss but found that he could not. He'd never really liked the bloke.

"What is it you're reading?" asked Behrensdorff, nodding politely towards the paperback folded over Johnny's chest.

Johnny held up his copy of H.G. Wells' *Shape of Things to Come*. He'd read it many times but this French copy that he'd managed to get Weiler to find for him was as much for practising the language as for leisure reading. He'd first asked for it as a minor act of rebellion, knowing the book had been on the Nazis' banned list, but Weiler had barely batted an eyelid at the request. Johnny now wondered how Behrensdorff would react to it.

But he too just nodded, and in a way that neither confirmed nor denied that he had read the book, or if he even approved or disapproved of it. "Good?" he asked.

"It is, actually," said Johnny. Wells was one of his favourite writers and he'd read this one several times. It had formed a large part of what was the closest Johnny ever came to having a political viewpoint.

"It is science fiction, yes?" asked Behrensdorff.

"Kind of. It's about there being an end to all this war bullshit, all these squabbling governments. Just one world government, so that everyone can get on with their lives in peace. Just be the best they can be without having some politician bastard telling them what they can and can't do, where they can and can't go."

For a moment he thought his little rant might offend Behrensdorff, maybe even get him into trouble. And, in truth, Johnny was surprised himself at the vehemence with which he'd made his little speech. But Behrensdorff just nodded once more. It seemed to Johnny that he seemed pleased with his reply more than anything else.

"Indeed," he said. "And that is exactly what we are fighting for here, you and I, are we not?"

"Yeah," said Johnny thoughtfully, "I suppose we are."

He was almost surprised to see the friendly smile on Behrensdorff's face as he turned to leave. He seemed to have inadvertently made an ally in the last place he might have expected. Of all the Germans at the Chateau, Behrensdorff was the one Johnny considered to really be a 'true Nazi' and the one to whom he had warmed the least. But maybe, he thought, it wouldn't hurt to have him think that he was more 'on side' than he actually was.

"Oh, by the way," said Behrensdorff, turning back at the door, "to celebrate Krause's return, we have decided to give you boys 48 hours' leave. I think they are planning to throw some kind of party for him. I feel certain your presence will be expected."

The festivities ended up being slightly wilder than even Johnny had expected. Although life at the villa was largely easy going, it was still work nonetheless, a 24-hour slog of training and instruction, broken only by meals and sleep, and even the most dedicated of them needed a break from it every once in a while.

For the first part of the evening at least, Johnny spent most of his time deflecting Krause's increasingly drunken and profuse thanks for "saving his life". The wounded German was the evening's guest of honour and was still hobbling around with the aid of a stick. But his Teutonic features, shining with sweating drunkenness, maintained a smile of beatific happiness for most of the night.

"This man," he said, clapping Johnny on the back heartily for about the hundredth time that evening, "this man saved my life."

"Forget it, mate," said Johnny, feeling awkward under the indulgently bemused smiles of his new comrades. "I didn't do anything. Nothing that anyone else wouldn't have done in my shoes."

"Look at them! It's true love, I tell you," roared Fleischer. Like the others, he'd been enjoying the opportunity to good-humouredly increase Johnny's discomfort at Krause's undying gratitude.

The evening was essentially on old-school pub crawl, a boisterous tour of most of the inns and hostelries of Nantes, with most of them taking the opportunity to down as much alcohol as possible, safe in the knowledge that for once they would be able to sleep it off the following day. Inevitably as the evening wore on, the group's thoughts turned to women, despite the fact that most of them could barely stand when Sidney Cook gathered them all in a conspiratorial huddle.

"Ere, boys," he whispered, "our luck's in. I've just been given a hot tip on where we can pick up some birds."

There were general boisterous whoops of approval, with Johnny being the only muted voice in the group.

"Nah," he said. "Think you better count me out of this one, lads."

There then followed the expected howls of outrage and disappointment. "What's the matter, Johnny boy?" Cook demanded. "Yer not going funny on us, are you?"

"Nah. It's just that the old lady will kill me if she finds out."

Cook snorted. "She's bloody miles away though, ain't she? And what she don't know can't hurt her, can it?"

"Yeah, well the last time I played away I ended up inside, didn't I? And then lumbered with you lot. I'm not making that bloody mistake again."

He got another round of drunken, roaring laughter for that one. But he was only half joking. The only woman on his mind these days was Billie and he was still kicking himself for his idiocy in Jersey. All he wanted to do was get home to her. And the longer he had to wait, the more insistent that feeling became. While being at The Chateau was a vast improvement on cooling his heels in Jersey, he was quickly becoming impatient with it. He wanted them to hurry up and send him back to England. Why the hell was it taking so long?

Krause slapped him heartily on the back. "Ach, leave Johann alone," he said. "If he does not wish to then that is his choice. And the fact that he has been much more sensible than any of us in his drinking suggests to me that he should be our driver."

There was a general hubbub of assent around the table and drinks were hurriedly downed in anticipation of the next portion of the night's adventure.

"Right," said Johnny, with a sigh. "Driving it is."

It felt almost like pulling a job, thought Johnny. He half expected some provincial French copper to appear out of nowhere and demand to know why he was lurking about at this hour. Across the road was the nightclub-cum-knocking shop that Sydney had insisted would be full of mademoiselles eager for their ardour and patronage. This had been the third place they'd been to and their attempts to find female company had been growing increasingly desperate. But this time it seemed they had met with success as he saw them come stumbling out of the club with several clearly equally drunk girls in tow.

Getting everyone squeezed into the back of the car was no easy task but somehow they managed it, albeit with much cursing, laughter and lewd commentary in a bizarre creole of German and French.

"Right," said Johnny. "Where to?"

This prompted further heated discussion and smutty giggling, both male and female. Eventually, Sidney suggested, "Why don't we all just head back to The Chateau and continue the party there?"

To Johnny this sounded like the worst idea possible and was about to say so when the back of the car once again erupted into drunken roars and cackles. And so he simply shrugged and started the car. They could worry about the surely inevitable fallout in the morning.

***

"What the hell were you thinking?" thundered Weiler.

And, as Johnny expected, they were all duly carpeted the next morning. He was glad that he had been taking it easy on booze. He had always been a lousy drunk and had never really enjoyed total out-of-control inebriation. That was how mistakes got made and he was often impetuous enough when he was sober. Even so, he felt nothing but empathy for the others who were having to undergo their roasting with full-on raging hangovers.

He didn't think that he'd ever seen Weiler so furious. Their commanding officer was normally the epitome of laconic good humour and always seemed to be at pains to appear to be "one of them". But now his face was crimson and every statement he made came flecked with spittle.

"This is meant to be an Abwehr training station," he growled. "Do you know what that means? It means that we are supposed to operate in absolute secrecy. Not bringing packs of whores through the fucking gates."

"It was my fault, sir," said Johnny. "I was driving. I should have known better than to let them bring the girls back here."

Weiler stopped and stared at him for a moment, as if weighing up whether he wanted to make Johnny the scapegoat for the whole situation.

"That isn't quite fair, sir," interrupted Krause. "Johann is the only one not to have been involved in this. We must take our share of the blame. Although it was, in fact, Sidney who originated the idea."

"Yeah," said Cook, with aggrieved indignation. "Thanks, mate."

"Enough!" bellowed Weiler, slamming his hand on his desk. "My own inclination would be to brush this whole thing under the carpet, but as you were all stupid enough to be spotted by the Gestapo I don't have that option. There's going to be hell to pay for this. Dismissed. Not you, Schwarz."

Johnny waited as the others shuffled contritely out of the office. For a moment, Weiler merely stood behind his desk, looking down at the papers strewn across it.

"Are we really in the shit here?" asked Johnny. For some reason, when they were alone the formality of rank had never seemed to apply to Weiler and himself. They had just never had that kind of relationship.

Weiler looked at him sourly. "The footballs will want somebody's head. And I'm going to give them Sidney's." 'Footballs' was the general nickname for the Gestapo, based on their preference for leather coats and the fact that they tended to be rather better fed than most other members of the German military machine.

"But why did you feel the need to cover for someone like Sydney? He would never have done the same for you." Weiler smiled thinly. "Surely you must realise by now that there is no room for sentimentality here?"

Johnny shrugged. "What can I say? I guess I just didn't want to point the finger at him. No one likes a squealer. Besides, he is a fellow countryman and all that."

Weiler chuckled and shook his head. "Don't be silly, Schwarz," he said. "You're a good German now."

FOUR

SYMONS emerged from his office, his face grimmer than usual. "Harry! With me."

Harry was at his desk, still ruminating over his morning's court appearance, where he rather satisfyingly helped send down an inept bunch of jump-up boys who'd tried to make off with a load of Army petrol. Small stuff, but every little helped.

"What is it?" he asked. He still wasn't convinced he was out of Symons's bad books over the Brookfields fiasco and was wary of stepping into another bollocking.

"Don't worry," said Symons. "It's nothing to be concerned about," before adding, worriedly, "I think."

They climbed the stairs to the station's fifth floor, traditionally the domain of the brass – something that didn't fill Harry with any more confidence. The difference up here was marked. Paper and fusty old portraits on the wall, carpet on the floors, an air of hushed silence. It was not Harry's natural environment and it made him edgy.

Symons knocked gently on one of the doors that lined the corridor and guided Harry inside.

Harry had half-expected to be faced with some whiskery example of the oft-invoked though seldom-seen bosses but instead standing by the window was a thin man in a well-cut three-piece, pin-striped suit. His dark hair, going to grey at the temples, was swept back from lined, aristocratic fine features. He could pass for a stockbroker or an MP but whoever he was, it was clear to Harry this man was not a member of the Yard.

"Take a seat, Harry," said Symons, taking one himself. "This is..."

The man turned from the window and beamed at Harry as he extended a hand. "Dominic Pickering. Delighted to make your acquaintance."

Harry shook the manicured hand and then took the chair beside Symons. Pickering gestured towards a tray on a mahogany sideboard. "Can I get you fellows anything? They've laid on some tea."

"No thanks, I'm fine," said Harry. Symons also demurred.

"Well," said Pickering, taking his place behind the enormous desk. "I suppose you chaps are wondering what all this is about."

"You're a spook," said Harry, bluntly.

Pickering shuddered and his smile froze. "Yes, I believe that is what the Yanks are calling us these days. Don't care for the expression myself. Bit disrespectful. But yes, I am with what we prefer to call the intelligence services."

"And what does a high-falutin' mystery man like yourself want with a humble flatfoot like me?" asked Harry.

"Johnny Black." Pickering sat back and smiled when he saw the expression on Harry's face. "Yes, I thought that might get your attention." He flicked a brief glance at Symons. "I've been told that he's quite the obsession of yours. What can you tell me about him?"

"Not much," said Harry. "Just that he's a sleazy little no-mark who should be decorating the inside of a cell. Which, if I'm not mistaken, he is right at this very moment."

"Well, this is where our interest lies," said Pickering. "And we're beginning to suspect you might well be mistaken. About his current whereabouts, at least.

"And where's that then?" asked Harry.

"First, tell me, where do you think Black's interests would lie? In terms of the war, I mean? Any Nazi sympathies, for example?"

"Well," said Harry. "He was mixed up with the BUF for a while back in '36."

Pickering nodded. "Yes, we know all about that. Bad business."

"I'm not sure how much you can read it into though," broke in Symons. "The Black Mob pulled a few jobs under the cover of the riots, but I've never seen anything since to suggest that Black had a genuine inclination towards Fascism."

Harry gritted his teeth. Symons's dismissiveness rankled, largely because he thought he'd be more sensitive to events which had changed Harry's life forever. "No smoke without fire, is there? Besides, I wouldn't put anything past Johnny Black."

"No, you wouldn't," said Symons. "But with respect, Harry, some of us have to remain a bit more objective."

"All the same," said Pickering. "It's useful to know."

"What is all this about anyway?" asked Harry.

Pickering took a deep breath, weighing up just how much he should share. "I hope it's clear that anything discussed in this room cannot go any further. It's not an exaggeration to say that it could directly affect the war effort if you do."

Both men nodded.

"We've been intercepting some Nazi radio traffic. North of France, pretty innocuous stuff – mostly Abwehr training transmissions. Our sources suggest they have an outpost in Nantes somewhere. But some of the messages are, well, they're a little on the odd side."

"Odd how?" asked Harry.

"Snatches of bawdy routines. Music Hall ditties, off-colour jokes, that kind of thing. Enough to suggest that their author could well be English. And we keep getting a name. Schwarz."

"Blackie," explained Symons.

"Thanks," said Harry. "I got that. And you think it could be Black?"

"You don't think it might be possible?"

"It might be. But it could be anything, couldn't it? It might just be the Jerries pulling your chain."

"Quite possibly," agreed Pickering. "And it could indeed be anyone. But consider, Black would already be in German hands in

Jersey. It would be simplicity itself to ship him across the Channel. If they thought him to be useful. Don't you think it might be likely that they would?"

"Black is a slippery little no-mark," said Harry. "But he's good, organisationally speaking. There's at least half a dozen jobs he's pulled here that we haven't been able to finger him for. Yet. And he's one of the best safe-breakers in the business. I'd say the Krauts might be interested, yes."

"That's all very well," said Symons. "But safe-breaking and put-up jobs are one thing. Are you really saying that Johnny Black would turn traitor though? That's a whole different thing altogether and I'm not sure I see it, personally."

"Patriotic type, is he?"

"Like blazes he is," said Harry. "His only loyalty is to himself. I'd say he would have no trouble throwing his lot in with the Germans. Not if the price is right."

"Mercenary fellow, eh? Yes, those are often the worst. But the Nazis like them because they know how to control them, being little more than gangsters themselves, I suppose," said Pickering. "Well, alright. Thanks awfully, gentlemen. You've been most instructive."

Symons rose to leave. "And that's it, is it?" demanded Harry.

Pickering looked at him quizzically. "I'm not sure I follow."

"I mean, what happens now. With Black, I mean."

"Well, nothing really. If this in fact turns out to be true then he's in occupied France and well beyond our reach."

"And if he comes back?"

"Well, that would be a different matter, of course. It would be incredibly useful if you could pass on anything you hear from your, ah, underworld contacts or whatever you call them."

"And that's it? We're your messenger boys now?"

"Harry, enough," said Symons. "Come on."

Harry stood up.

"Thank you again, gentlemen," said Pickering, a little more firmly this time. He was clearly anxious to be rid of them now that he'd got what he wanted.

"What the hell was that?" said Harry as they both descended the stair to their floor again.

Symons shrugged. "Don't ask me, Harry. I only work here."

FIVE

"HERE," said Weiler. "I think you're going to need this."

Johnny looked down at the automatic pistol Weiler was holding out towards him, butt first. He took it gingerly. It was not the first time he'd seen a gun, of course, even since the war started, but it was the first time that he could ever remember actually handling one. He'd always had someone else to do that kind of dirty work for him.

"Sure you trust me?" he asked, hefting the heavy pistol in his hand.

Weiler snorted. "What are you going to do? Shoot your way out of France with one round of ammunition? I think we're past all that now, don't you?"

"I reckon we are. Does this mean that I'm finally about to see some action?"

Weiler smiled. He had been becoming increasingly aware of Johnny's restlessness, but he was equally not prepared to let one of his most promising protégés out of his sight until he was absolutely certain that he was ready to be deployed in the field. It was a realisation he'd reached not without regret as he'd become used to the Englishman's company and knew he would miss him.

"Not in the way that you think, I suspect," he said. "The Führer has decided to intensify our presence within Vichy France, but with the Eastern campaign not going as well as expected, all operational units in the area have been pressed into service. That, unfortunately, means us too. We'll be taking part in a series of raids on suspected insurrectionists and to seize any intelligence materials we might come across. That will mean us all going back into regular uniform and it also means us all being armed. Including you. I'm even going to let you have some bullets."

He gave Johnny one of his lop-sided, sardonic smiles. "Try not to shoot yourself with it."

Johnny kicked the front door of the house with as much savagery as he could muster. With the first blow the door held, but he could hear the creak and splinter of the wood, which suggested that it would not resist him for long. On the second kick, the hinges parted from the frame slightly and on the third the door gave way completely.

He shouted loudly in German to the occupants who he could hear scurrying about in the darkness beyond. He could hear scuffling and panicked, urgent chattering and he felt a brief flicker of slightly guilty pleasure that he was the cause of this alarm. He called to the troops at his back in hoarse German and they clambered through the hallway of the house, their boots clattering on the dusty wooden floorboards.

He found he was enjoying himself enormously.

Johnny stepped out into the sunshine, feeling awkward in his new uniform. This was the first time since his first day at the villa that he'd been expected to be in full military dress and, with the peaked cap and M40 slung across his chest, it was also the first time it had been truly brought home to him that he was now essentially part of the Nazi war machine.

The others too were dressed in full uniform, many for the first time as far as Johnny knew. But there was no consistency to the uniforms and they looked like a decidedly mismatched bunch to Johnny's eyes. There had been no stipulation on what uniform they could wear, so long as it didn't exceed their current rank. So for most of them that meant the garb of the rank and file. Behrensdorff, however, had rather predictably chosen the uniform of the SS and Weiler himself the florid and slightly dated ostentation of a cavalry officer, with fart-catcher trousers and a ridiculous helmet.

Now they all stood outside the front of the villa where several cars had been requisitioned to take them on their mission.

Weiler beamed as he looked up and down his rather motley garbed unit. "Are we all here?" he asked, like an avuncular uncle ready to embark on a day trip. "Then let's be on our way."

"Care to tell us where we're going, sir?" asked Fleischer.

Johnny saw Behrensdorff stiffen. Clearly getting into the SS uniform was going to his head. He looked at Fleischer coldly. "That is on a need-to-know basis only."

But Fleischer only grinned and cast a look in Weiler's direction. Weiler laughed too and Johnny saw Behrensdorff blush slightly.

"Don't worry," said Weiler. "We're not going far. And all will be revealed soon."

Weiler, Behrensdorff and the other more senior officers all piled into the one of the cars, while Johnny and the rest of the more rank-and-file trainee agents got into the other two and all three vehicles glided out of the villa's driveway.

Despite the reticence of Weiler and Behrensdorff, they hadn't been on the road for much than forty-five minutes, following the officers' car in convoy, when their destination became apparent.

"Limoges looks like," said Fleischer who was driving the car Johnny was riding in.

"Good hour or so yet then," said Johnny, taking a swig of the half-bottle of brandy that was getting circulated around the car and lighting up another cigarette. It was turning into a beautiful day and he was determined to enjoy the drive through the French countryside, regardless of what would be waiting for them at the other end.

They arrived at Limoges shortly after midday and were all feeling just slightly woozy from the booze as they clambered out of the car.

While the city was not exactly in chaos when they arrived, there was still a discernible air of panic in the air. The streets were full of trucks, motorcycles and German troops. The city's inhabitants looked on fearfully, realising more with resignation than anything that the days of the Vichy regime were at an end and that the Nazi Occupation had finally caught up with them.

"Right," said Weiler, as his men assembled in front of him. "We are here today to help the regular forces in an operation to round up suspected insurgents. To do this we will divide into two teams and each will take half the list of addresses we have been issued with. I shall lead the first team while Behrensdorff will lead the second."

Johnny was relieved to find himself in Weiler's group. Since they had left The Chateau that morning, Behrensdorff had been in increasingly exuberant spirits, his eyes glittering with an almost manic fanaticism. He was clearly in his element and their mission, to spread oppression and terror was one that enthused him much more than it did any of the others.

And yet, it struck him that he was experiencing similar emotions himself. As he kicked in doors and stormed into the homes of terrified people, he wasn't feeling shame or disgust as much as an adrenaline rush. He remembered the Nazis that night in the pub when they came to take him away and thought how restrained they had been compared to how he was behaving now. And then he thought of the men who had gunned down Godfray and wondered briefly where he fitted along that spectrum of duty.

Johnny kicked open the door to a back parlour, raising a cloud of dust and plaster as it slammed back against the wall. There was very little evidence that this house was actually lived in, with not much in the way of usable furniture or the other effects of day-to-day living. And yet it clearly had several occupants who, it seemed to Johnny, must either be refugees or resistance fighters. As far as his superiors would be concerned, these people were just the types they were looking for.

He was now staring at an old man who was kneeling by a fireplace and shovelling papers of some kind into the feebly flickering flames in the grate. The look of sheer terror and guilt on the old man's face as he stared down the barrel of Johnny's submachine gun told him the bloke was clearly up to no good. But there was a fatalism in the man's eyes too, as if he would be unsurprised if Johnny now shot him on the spot. Johnny again thought of the dead, unfeeling, almost bored, expressions of the firing squad in Le Cachot and it was with something like shock that he realised that in the eyes of this old man, he was now one of those men.

They remained frozen like that for a moment. It would be almost comical, thought Johnny, if it hadn't been for the atmosphere of absolute terror between the two of them. This was not the first time he had held someone's life in the balance, but it did seem to him to be the first time he'd been so nakedly aware of it.

"Go on, hoppit," he said in English eventually. "Get the bloody hell out of here."

The old man looked at him distrustfully, clearly understanding him but still expecting some kind of a trick – as if expecting to be shot in the back the moment he turned to leave. And then he stood up and started shuffling towards the door where Johnny stood.

"Not that way, you bloody idiot," he hissed, aware of the violent sounds of commotion throughout the house behind him. "You'll have to find some other way."

The old man nodded. "Merci," he whispered and turned back into the room. He lifted the window quietly, taking care to make as little noise as possible and then disappeared through it with surprising dexterity of a man of his years.

Once he was gone, Johnny knelt by the fireplace, picking some of the still unburnt papers from the flames. He couldn't really make head or tail of them. They were mostly handwritten notes, some with dates or places names, and some were crudely drawn maps. The only thing that he could be sure of was that the old man hadn't wanted them falling into Nazi hands. He wondered for a moment if he shouldn't keep them to add to the dossier he'd been compiling but then decided against it. It was too risky if he were suddenly subjected to a random search. For all Weiler's protestations, he still didn't know just how much they trusted him or whether, for that matter, this whole little trip wasn't just another test of his loyalty. And he was damned if he'd let himself end up facing a firing squad over a few probably meaningless scribbles of paper. Not after all the effort he'd put into getting this far. And so he put his lighter to the lot, making sure they were burned beyond recognition in the grate.

When Johnny emerged from the last house on their 'hit list', he found Weiler and the rest of his team rounding up a ragged collection of prisoners. It was getting dark now and piles of furniture were being dragged from the houses and tossed onto bonfires, finally giving the whole operation the hellish glow that Johnny had initially feared it would have. When he looked at the prisoners, all he could see were tired, frightened human faces, with little sign of defiance or rebellion about them. Johnny looked around for the old man he'd let escape that afternoon, but there was no sign of him. There were more women and children and old men among them than anything else, with expressions varying from tear-stained distress to bleak, despairing acceptance. The whole thing seemed to him to be pretty far removed from his own admittedly limited understanding of war.

There must have been something of this in his expression because Weiler turned to him with a look of grim understanding. "Look at them," he said. "They might be guilty. They might not be. But why the hell should I be the one to send them to a concentration camp?"

He turned to one of the other men. "Let them go," he said. The soldier's eyes flickered with a moment's doubt for a second before he saluted and turned on his heel. Minutes later the whole crowd were being ushered away by the soldiers, wandering away bewilderedly away into the darkness.

"What about Behrensdorff?" asked Johnny as they watched them go. He could imagine Behrensdorff, still striding around somewhere in his SS uniform, being outraged at seeing the tangible results of their contribution to the operation dispersed back into the streets.

"To hell with Behrensdorff," muttered Weiler, in a way that suggested that he wanted to add "and to hell with the rest of them too". He spat into the fire closest to them and they listened to its hissing combustion for a moment. Then he gave Johnny a crooked grin.

"Come on, Schwarz," he said. "Let's find ourselves a bloody drink."

SIX

IT TOOK Jack a surprisingly long time to realise that the sound he was hearing as he lay sleeplessly on his attic bunk was the sound of Billie crying. It wasn't that he lacked sensitivity. It was impossible to even take a walk outside without seeing the pain that was all around them now. Bombs were falling and people were scared. Many of them were lonely, missing loved ones, grieving for the ones who were already dead, or as good as. They were all walking around in an increasing state of shock. And, of course, this applied to Billie as much as anyone else. He knew Billie was hurting, that she felt Johnny's absence more keenly than anyone but all the same, to hear her sobbing like this was somehow as shocking to him as if he had caught her naked.

At first he tried to ignore it. It wasn't, after all, the first sound emanating from Johnny and Billie's bedroom that had troubled him over the years. The sounds of their love-making had often been embarrassingly clear to Jack lying alone more or less directly above them. So much so that he'd bought a box of wadding that he could use as earplugs to drown out the sound of it. Not out of anything remotely resembling prudishness or embarrassment, but out of respect for Johnny and Billie. He didn't want to feel like some kind of intruder, an interloper on their intimacy.

It crossed his mind to reach for that box now. It was within arm's reach, just under his bed. To leave Billie to the privacy of her sorrow. But, no, it was too late. He'd heard it now. The soft, feminine sobs, not just of distress, but of something close to absolute despair drifted through the floor. They were not loud but they still cut at him, deeply and mercilessly, drawing blood with ruthless, precise strokes. To ignore it, to try to blot it out, would just be cowardice.

Yet still he waited, part of him hoping the sounds would stop on their own and solve the problem for him. But they did not so he reluctantly got off his bed and pulled on his trousers and shirt. He descended the narrow wooden ladder that led from his attic to the top floor of the house.

The place was in darkness and he stopped and listened for a moment to the varying creaks and ticks and echoes of the slumbering house. From the ground floor, the low rumble of the male grunts and snores of the boys was just audible. But closer, louder and more discernible were the sounds of Billie's gentler sobs on the upper landing. Steeling himself, Jack crept towards the bedroom door, remonstrating with himself at every step for his presumption. But still he kept going, seemingly unable to stop himself.

The crying stopped immediately the moment he rapped softly upon the door. He heard some frenetic snuffling, rustling and fumbling. And then a series of light footsteps, approached the other side of the door.

"Yes? Who is it?" Her voice still sounded small, vulnerable. He knew she would hate someone, even him, hearing her like that and every instinct in him told him to turn around and head back up the stairs, to save her embarrassment. But it was way too late for that now.

"Billie?" he whispered into the door. "It's Jack."

The door opened slowly and just wide enough for Billie to peer out at him. Her hair was tousled and her eyes ringed with red from the tears and she was wrapped in her dressing gown. Despite the obvious attempts to make herself presentable, Jack could still see the haunted vulnerability in her eyes and it pained him.

"Hi, Jack," she said softly. "Everything alright, love?"

"I was just about to ask you the same thing," he whispered. "You OK?"

"Yeah, fine," she said, less than convincingly. "Bad night, you know?" She smiled weakly at him. It struck him then that this was the first time that he'd ever seen her looking so defenceless. He felt as if he were seeing her, the real her, for the first time. The face she put on for the others in her parlour den was really as much of a performance as when she had been singing in the clubs. To see this new, achingly fragile side of her made his heart burn with even more intense longing for her.

But despite the turmoil within him, all he did was nod. "Yes, I know," he said. "Is there anything I can do?"

She shook her head, still smiling softly. "No, Jack, love. I don't think there is. Do you?" She suddenly raised her gaze to look at him, as if to emphasise those last two words.

Her gaze discomfited him somewhat and he was by no means unaware of the obvious potential of the two of them standing here like this in the middle of the night. The air between them seemed charged with possibility. "Well, if there is," he said, "just let me know. I mean it. Anything at all."

Reluctantly he moved to turn away, but Billie reached out her hand to stop him, her smooth fingers caressing his cheek. Her touch felt searingly warm. Almost breathtakingly so. "You're a good man, Jack," she said quietly. "Don't let anyone ever tell you different."

He raised his own hand to hers, uncertain whether this was to prevent her intoxicating touch or as proof that they really were standing here like this. Could it actually mean what it seemed to? Her fingertips were still wet with her own tears and he felt somehow that she had marked him with them, that he had taken them into himself through her touch, and mixed them with his own. Her fingers continued to move across his cheek and now curled around his neck.

And then, suddenly, her other hand was on his cheek, framing his face and pulling him down towards her. Their lips locked together, their hands pressing each other's faces together with an almost violent urgency. He coiled his arm around her waist, feeling her yield beneath his touch, allowing herself to fold into him. They fell back into the bedroom, swaying in a strange, semi-coordinated dance across the floor, navigating their way towards the bed, their lips still locked to each other, their tongues flicking at each other hungrily. Jack was sure he could feel fresh, hot tears against his cheek but he could not tell whether they were hers or his own.

They fell upon the bed, still locked together. The raw energy of their need coiled around their bodies, sparking and lashing between them. He could feel that he was hard now and he arched his back to drive himself insistently against her. Her dressing gown had fallen open now and his hands caressed the taut curves of her body through the smooth silk of her nightclothes. Her body felt soft, yielding, beneath him and she opened herself to him, her calves pressing against his back, pushing him more strongly against her. He felt completely enveloped by her, surrounded by a warm, intoxicating sense of purpose and need, the thousand insecurities and doubts of the world at large falling away like a shed skin.

And then she was stiffening beneath him. Her knees wedged between them and her hands were on his chest, gently, reluctantly, but insistently pushing him away. Her breathing, at first shallow and urgent, regained its sense of silent control. The rhythm of need that had been leading both their bodies now faltered and sputtered to an end and they were just themselves again.

"Stop," she whispered hoarsely. "We can't."

"Can't we?" It was not really a question, nor was it anything like a challenge but neither was it petulance. He knew the answer just as well as she did, although it did little to stop him feeling the unfairness of it. And it did not stop him making that final, plaintive appeal for something that he already knew he could not have.

She increased the pressure on his chest, forcing him upwards further still, until she could slide from under him, removing herself to safety. She sat upright at the side of the bed, closing her robe tightly around her before taking his hand, guiding him to sit down beside her. He did so, guiltily aware of his still raging erection.

"You know we can't," she said. She pressed his hand between both of hers, caressing it urgently, as if seeking to impress upon him the strength of the desire that she still felt but was unable to act upon.

She looked at him now and there was a sadness there, a definite sense of regret, but there was also the steely determination of old. This was the Billie he recognised. The pragmatic, business-like Billie. The decision-maker. That moment of vulnerability, of raw, human need, had vanished as quickly as it had come, leaving, if anything, a greater sense of desolation within him.

He felt unable to look Billie in the eye now. The self-pity that had gripped him a moment ago was fading but it was being replaced with something even worse – shame. He felt sick with himself. He had been ready to betray Johnny, betray himself and all he'd ever been, and all in the name of lust. For an instant, he'd forgotten why he was here, what was at stake, and in doing so, had nearly destroyed it all.

Jack stood up to go. He suddenly felt that he had to get out of there, while he still had the strength to do so. He wanted to get back to the safety of his little attic room, to lie down in the cool darkness, to hide. He found himself suddenly thinking of the blades he kept neatly stored and oiled under his bed. For the first time, the idea of carving himself, creating a physical manifestation of this more elusive internal pain suddenly seemed overwhelmingly attractive. And logical somehow. After all, hadn't that been what he'd dished out to Freddie for a far less blatant act of betrayal?

He felt Billie's grip on his hand tighten, resisting his attempts to break away. "Don't go," she said. "Not yet."

"I should."

"I know. But don't. Stay. Just for a while." Once again her eyes caught his, full of quiet, almost desperate, entreaty. "Please."

She slid up to the head of the bed, gently, but insistently, dragging him with her. Once he was settled, she lay her head upon his chest and gently draped his arm around her. They lay like that for a moment, both silently willing the awkwardness and guilt that still hung in the air to leave them for at least a while.

Eventually he felt obliged to break this weird, almost accusatory, silence. "You do know that Johnny's not exactly been faithful to you over the years?" he asked gently, hating himself for saying it, while simultaneously unable to stop himself. It felt like an even greater betrayal than the frenzied but abortive animal lust of a few moments previously. That, at least, hadn't used words, and therefore had no thought, behind it. He wondered whether with that one, stupid, question he wasn't in danger of breaking what connection he had with Billie, of making her hate him just as much as she had hated Freddie, and with similar reason.

"I'm not stupid, Jack," she said quietly, but without remonstrance or accusation. Her voice vibrated against his chest, as if she were trying to speak directly to his heart, rather than his face. "I know all about his wandering eyes. His wandering everything, in fact. And I knew perfectly well what he was up to down in Jersey. But that doesn't mean he wouldn't take a pretty dim view if he thought we were up to anything. You know him, Jack. You know what he would do."

"I could take care of Johnny." He said the words with neither passion nor conviction.

"Could you, Jack? And more to the point, would you really want to? I mean, really? Look how far the two of you go back. Further than Johnny and me do. A lot further. Would you really be able to tear all that up? Because I know I couldn't."

He was sure she was crying again and could feel the warm dampness of fresh tears wetting the fabric of his shirt beneath her cheek. He wished he could cry himself but it had all gone now. He was empty again. The cold matter-of-fact truth of her words had hollowed him out once more.

"Besides," she went on, "this isn't just about you. Or me. Or Johnny, for that matter. It's bigger than all that. We've got the business to think of as well, the whole sodding family. There's too much at stake, Jack. I mean, we can't really let all that go to hell in a handcart just because we've gone a little sweet on each other. You know that as well as I do."

Jack didn't say anything. Again, she'd unleashed another little blade that had cut him with unerring, if unintentional, precision. This felt like a lot more than "going a little sweet" to him. In fact, he thought, there seemed very little "sweet' about it. More like aching torment. He loved her, he knew. Probably from the first moment that Johnny had introduced them all those years ago. But that didn't mean that she wasn't right.

He looked down at her. She had closed her eyes now and her head was resting on his chest. She seemed to him curiously relaxed, serene almost. He supposed that there was nothing more to be said and she was just enjoying this moment of peace for as long as it could last. Jack realised he had no choice but to do the same. This was it, he thought. The one night he would spend with her. He would never again feel this close to her.

And she was beautiful, he thought. You'd have to be crazy not to see that. Yet even in repose, you could see her strength. Her full lips still had their slight curl of a sneer and her slightly scowling eyebrows seemed to make her aware and in control, even when she was at rest like this. Some people, thought Jack, are attractive because you can still see the child they once were within their features. But Billie wasn't like that. He just couldn't imagine what she would have been like as a child. There was no evidence of it anywhere in her appearance. It seemed to him that she had been born fully grown, never been anything else other than the near perfect example of matured womanhood he now held in his arms.

He closed his eyes also. It would be morning soon and the real world of sacrifice and denial, of unfulfilment and of dissatisfaction and unhappiness would soon burst in on them once more. But right at this moment he felt drowsy and accepting and as at peace as he supposed he ever had a right to expect. He relinquished his lust, his quiet rage and his thwarted desire, and allowed himself to drift back to darkness, and the few hours of peace that he had left.

SEVEN

THE following morning, Billie called a meeting of the Mob. It was only the second time she had ever done so, the first being when she'd first taken over running the outfit after Johnny's conviction. She had preferred until now to deal with the various senior members on a more personal one-to-one basis, much in the same way that Johnny had. So the early morning dispatch of various runners across the city with this new summons caused something of a stir and by 11am, there were a dozen or more of the Firm's most trusted lieutenants crammed into the kitchen, waiting to hear her speak.

It was unusual for the kitchen to be so full of animated life and chatter, especially at that time of day. Billie had been cooking since dawn and the table groaned with food and drink. Crates of beer had been brought in and there was an air of excitement, almost of celebration, as if the gathering was for something as innocent as a family wedding or a christening.

"Right," she said, once everyone had been fed and watered to her satisfaction. The chatter around the room died down and every eye in the parlour turned towards her. "By now you'll all have heard about Freddie. First up, I want to make sure no one's got a problem with it. Because if you do, now's the time to speak up."

A few faces flickered in Jack's direction, where he was seated by Billie's side but, predictably, no one said anything.

"Good," said Billie. "Because I'm sure you'll all agree it was a situation that had to be dealt with. But now that it has, I think the time has come for us to start taking the initiative again."

"Begging your pardon, Billie, love," said Sam Silk. "But what exactly do you mean by that?"

"What I mean, Sam, is that the war could be good for us. It could be real lucrative. Really help us consolidate our position. But it seems to me that we've been a bit distracted. Letting it all slip away from us. And it ain't just us. A lot of the old Firms are losing their grip. All these new mobs, the Poles and what have you, they're muscling in, carving it up for themselves. Well, that ain't going to happen to us. We ain't going nowhere. Not when we all worked so hard to get here."

"And what about the Heavies?" asked Sam. "Heard you had a visit from Harry Blum the other week."

"I don't give a fuck about Harry Blum," said Billie, matter-of-factly. "He sticks his nose in and we'll finish what my Johnny started on him. I'll put that bastard in the ground if I have to. Now, what I want from you boys is ideas. Jobs. The bigger, the messier the better. We're going to let everyone know that this is our town and it's going stay that way. Is everyone understanding me?"

There was a general murmur of assent from around the table. Several of the men exchanged glances with each other, raised eyebrows, silently daring each other to speak, but none did. Billie was the boss and the boss had spoken. It was now their job to make what she wanted happen.

"Right then," she said. "Get to it."

When they had slowly filtered out of the kitchen in a hubbub of chatter, Jack said to her, "Well, that was a hell of a speech. Worthy of old Winnie himself, that was."

"Well, you did say it was my mob," she replied. "Just figured it was time I took charge, that's all."

"Well, you did that, I reckon."

"We've got to do something, Jack," she said. "We can't just sit here and twiddle our thumbs till Johnny gets back. Things are changing too much out there. New mobs, new capers. If we just sit back, this outfit will be history. And I ain't gonna let that happen."

"No, you're right," he said. "But you sure you're up to this though? What it might mean?"

She looked at him fiercely. "Why, Jack, you think I ain't?"

"I didn't say that. It's just. Well, it could be war we're talking about here. It could get ugly is all I'm saying." He suddenly felt as if he were back in 1936 again and could remember saying exactly the same things to Johnny.

"We're already at war," she said. "How's a bit more going to make any difference?"

EIGHT

JOHNNY hit the ground with a thud he felt sure had knocked some of his teeth looser. His head rang with the impact and both the glaring blue sky ahead and the sun burning within it seemed to be reproaching him for the sheer idiocy of what he was now attempting.

His senses were still slowly settling back towards normalcy when he became aware of Behrensdorff's polished boots striding across the grass towards him.

"No, no, no," the German's clipped tones seemed to be a lot further away than the boots now in front of his face and Johnny wondered if he hadn't done himself some permanent mental damage. "That is no good at all. All this will achieve is a dead agent. And we have no use for one of those."

A ripple of laughter erupted somewhere above him. His parachute training lessons had recently begun attracting an audience, so useless was he at it. He'd tended to land flat on his face, Buster Keaton-style, every time and it was only by some kind of miracle that he hadn't actually broken any bones yet.

"Up, please," said Behrensdorff, clapping his hands impatiently. "Again."

Johnny groaned and got to his feet painfully. The turf around the tree had been softened with water but you wouldn't know it when you hit it. This was his fifth jump of the morning and he seemed to ache from every muscle. He stared at the thick oak tree with the rope ladder hanging down from its topmost bough, where a makeshift, and decidedly rickety, platform had been constructed. The distance from the platform must be over 30 feet at least, he thought. To jump from it was insanity and yet this was what Behrensdorff had been having him do repeatedly for the past two days.

"Right," Johnny muttered. "Let's do this."

"It's time," said Weiler. "I have received confirmation that Operation Broken Wing has been approved."

Johnny was relieved. Since the operation in Limoges, he had become increasingly impatient for training to be over and to be on his way back to England. The novelty of his time at The Chateau had all but completely worn off and he was once again feeling restless and jumpy. And so he was incredibly happy as he stood in Weiler's study with Weiler and Behrensdorff beaming at him like a couple of school masters seeing their head boy graduate with full honours.

Yet something still made him affect an air of indifference. "That's nice," he said, with as much casualness as he could muster. "And what's that when it's at home?"

Weiler smiled, not fooled for an instant by Johnny's nonchalance. He gestured to the series of maps and plans laid out across his desk. "A sabotage mission. You are to travel back to London and assemble a small demolition team. This, as we know, is one of your specialities. Your target is the De Havilland aeroplane factory in Hertfordshire. We want it out of action. Once our reconnaissance planes have confirmed that you have successfully carried out your mission, you will be paid the sum of 15,000 Reichsmarks."

Johnny was unable to completely conceal his pleasure at both the mention of the money and just the mere prospect of finally being in action. "Sounds good to me," he said.

"You think you will be able to accomplish this?" asked Weiler.

"Yeah, I don't see why not. Money for old rope, ain't it?"

"Remember, you must pick your team with extreme care," said Behrensdorff. "There can be no mistakes."

"Don't worry," said Johnny. "I know some people who are perfect for this kind of job."

"Ah," said Behrensdorff. "But can you trust them?"

"Some of them I can. And as for the others, I can trust them to the trust the money. But I'll need some slush cash up front, obviously."

Weiler nodded. "You'll get five thousand to take with you to cover expenses and the rest upon your return to the Reich."

"Fair enough."

Weiler slid a sheet of typewritten paper across the desk towards Johnny. "Here, sign this."

"What is it?"

"A contract between you and the Reich for the proposed operation. Nothing to be alarmed about, I assure you."

Johnny glanced through the document. It seemed to be all the usual lawyerly guff – in the event of this, in the event of that – but he wasn't overly concerned about it. It didn't strike him as being a particularly enforceable document. A bit like a bank getting a Mob to sign a contract to promise not to turn them over. Just how would you even begin to enforce such a thing? He picked up a pen from the desk and scrawled a large, florid signature across the bottom of the document.

"There you go," he said, quietly slipping the pen into the pocket of his tunic.

"Excellent," beamed Weiler. "Now we can get moving, yes?"

Johnny nodded. "No objections from me. What's next?"

"Next," said Behrensdorff. "Is that we finally get you to learn how to jump out of a plane properly. Until you can manage to do that, you will be going nowhere, my friend."

The painful climb up the rope ladder to the rickety platform seemed to be taking longer and longer with each attempt, as his aching muscles intensified their protests. And this, it seemed, was not lost on Behrensdorff.

"Faster please," he barked, in his controlled, clipped tone. "Time is also a concern here."

"You're enjoying this," Johnny shouted back down to the group below. "I can tell."

"There is a certain degree of humorous value to your efforts," admitted Behrensdorff. "But I have no wish to be delayed while we wait for your broken bones to heal. So, concentrate please."

Johnny muttered a few choice curses under his breath and continued his climb. Below him, he could still hear Behrensdorff's nasally tones rising towards him.

"You must give way to the ground, not resist it. It is, after all, a fight you have no hope of winning. It is much bigger than you are, yes?"

This got another ripple of laughter from the others. Christ, Johnny thought. Behrensdorff managing to raise a laugh. Who'd have thought it? And just when he thought that he'd seen everything there was to see at The Chateau.

He was nearing the platform at the top of the tree now and so he forced himself to concentrate. He wasn't sure if he could handle many more of these jumps today. His arms and legs were beginning to feel shaky and weak. And it was annoying him that he hadn't been able to master this as quickly as would have liked. Most of the other disciplines he'd picked up pretty quickly but this one had eluded him. The fact that it was the one that was also the most bloody painful to practice didn't help matters. And it was the one thing holding him back from getting home to England.

He was on the platform now. Below him, Behrensdorff and the others looked alarmingly small. There was no getting away from the fact that it was a long way down. Every instinct in him was insistently telling him to step further away from the edge, not go closer towards it.

But even at this height, Behrensdorff's didactic tones still managed to drift upwards to him. "Remember, please. Be pliable. Be loose. Give way to the ground. No stiffness whatsoever. No tension."

"Easy for you to say, mate," muttered Johnny, allowing himself to slip back into English for a moment. He tensed himself, fondly imagining that he was about to dive into a pool of water, rather than onto hard turf.

He jumped.

Out of a Focke-Wulff bomber and into bitterly cold night air.

The wind rushed past him, stinging his face. Below him lay England, a patchwork of deep blues and subtle blacks and purples under clouded, sparse moonlight. And it was getting closer. Behind him, the once-deafening roar of his plane's engines had receded to be replaced with the sound of the wind rushing past his ears.

He was being buffeted a bit too heavily by the wind currents and allowing himself to drift. He didn't want to land too far from the planned drop zone and so he turned his attention to trying to control his descent. It was proving more difficult than it had seemed in his practice jumps and he could almost imagine Behrensdorff's brusque, impatient voice in his ear berating him for making a mess of it. He felt something warm on his upper lip and became aware of droplets of hot liquid rushing past his face. He was bleeding. His nose most probably, he thought. He was forever having nosebleeds when he was a kid.

But it was the looming, rushing, blue-black ground before him that was occupying his attention. He fumbled and reached for his ripcord and was immeasurably relieved to feel the sharp jerk and whoosh as his parachute was released and unfolded rapidly above him. The tension of the straps against his body made him gasp and his sharp descent now slowed to something altogether much more sedate. Not that Johnny felt particularly relieved by this. He had always hated heights, as his falteringly inept parachute training had shown, and to be slowly floating thousands of feet above the ground was only marginally better than rushing to meet it at speed. He would only be truly happy when the whole horrendous business was over with altogether.

Eventually the ground started to loom larger, completely filling his field of vision and he began to feel less like something that was floating freely in the air than something which had temporarily slipped free of the ground and was now faced with the imminent prospect of rejoining it, hopefully with as little complication as possible.

What happened next did so without any conscious agency on his part. He rolled, and performed a combination of perfect landing manoeuvres that allowed him to land lightly on the freshly ploughed field without even a stumble. Behrensdorff would have been proud, Johnny thought to himself.

As he started gathering in his still slowly descending parachute, he reflected wryly that the one time he'd been able to perform a perfect, textbook landing there had been no one there to see it.

Once he'd gathered up the silks in his arms, he took a more detailed look around to get his bearings. He was definitely on farmland somewhere, which was par for the plan, so he'd no real idea of how far he had drifted from the drop zone or if he had landed more or less on target.

He could just make out the inky silhouette of a farmhouse against the horizon. It was a darkish night and the house was some distance away, but he couldn't be totally sure that there was no possibility of being spotted from one of its windows and so he decided it would be prudent to find cover as quickly as possible. The field he'd landed in was bordered on one side with what looked to be fairly dense woodland and it was to here that he made for.

He moved slowly, partly because of the weight of the enormous pack on his back, and partly to minimise the tracks he made on the ground. There was no way to avoid this completely, of course, but he didn't think it was sensible to advertise his arrival any more than he absolutely had to. And, besides, he could once again hear Behrensdorff's nagging voice in his ear urging him to do the job properly.

Once he'd made it to the safety of the woods, he shrugged out of his backpack and propped it up against a tree trunk. The pack contained, among other things, a radio set with which to contact the Abwehr once he'd completed his mission, but it was the small entrenching tool that he now removed from the bag. With it, he dug a sizable hole in the undergrowth and into this he stuffed the folded parachute silks. He then pulled off his jump overalls and also stuffed them into the hole. Beneath them he was wearing the uniform of a British Army private. There had been some debate between Weiler, Behrensdorff and himself as to whether this was would, in fact, be a good disguise or whether a lone private might end up attracting more attention than a civilian would. But in the end Johnny had insisted upon the uniform, more because he fancied trying it out than anything else.

He fished into the pack again and produced an envelope stuffed with British currency, stowing it carefully in one of the pockets of his tunic. He then unfolded the flaps on the pack to expose the controls of the radio set and hurriedly checked them to ensure the radio hadn't been damaged during the fall. When he was satisfied that it had not, he redid the cloth seals and made sure it was safely stored in the pack. He then took the entire backpack and wedged it into the hole before using the entrenching tool and scattering some scrub to disguise the disturbed soil. It was too risky to drag this around with him while he was trying to get set up and so he would have to return for it when he had done so, and hopefully had some transport. When he was satisfied that the pack was sufficiently hidden from view and wouldn't be discovered unless someone went out of their way to look for it, he stood up, stowed the entrenching tool in his knapsack and with a sigh set off through the woods, hoping that he didn't have too long a walk before he chanced upon a town or village.

It took him just over two hours to arrive at Elsham, a small market town that was still defiantly asleep when he arrived at what must have been just after 4am. He settled down to wait at the railway station for the first train to London.

At shortly after five, a portly and bad-tempered station master made an appearance, clearly surprised to find a soldier sprawled against the wall of the closed waiting room at this early hour. He was obviously even less impressed when Johnny failed to stand up as he approached.

"When's the next train to London then?" asked Johnny as the station master fished on his ring of keys for the one to the waiting room.

"Why'd you want to know?" asked the station master. He'd clearly taken an instant dislike to this stranger, but he seemed to Johnny to be the type who would take an instant dislike to just about anybody who crossed his path.

"Because I want to get back up to London, don't I?" said Johnny, lighting up a fresh cigarette and pointedly not offering the stationmaster one. He'd quickly sized him up as officious, pompous and generally your typical provincial pain in the arse. To try and ingratiate himself would be pointless, he decided. He would have to use another tack.

"What you doing down here anyway, soldier?" asked the station master. "Where's the rest of your regiment?"

"On a two-day pass, ain't I?" said Johnny, getting to his feet. "Got lucky with a land girl up here." He gave the station master a conspiratorial nudge in the ribs. "They're not half up for it those birds, are they? You blokes must be doing alright out here."

Johnny saw the station master bristle visibly. He had called it right. The man was a prude on top of everything else. When Johnny had left him, all the man would remember him for was his licentiousness and alley-cat morals – an example of the degeneracy of the modern city-dweller rather than a potential German spy.

"Anyway," continued Johnny breezily. "That was all very well and nice an' all, but I don't want to waste *all* my leave on her, do I? Want to get back up to London and see my old lady for a spell too, don't I?"

The station master averted Johnny's intense, matey gaze by consulting his pocket watch. "The first train to Paddington is at quarter past," he said icily. And with that, he moved off up the platform, desiring to have nothing more to do with this dissolute young soldier.

"Thanks very much, I'm sure, chief," called Johnny after him, relishing his performance. "Much obliged."

The train to Paddington must have been a Funk Express because Johnny found it to be more full of stuffed shirts and bowlers than he'd have expected at that hour. But they left him to himself for pretty much the entire journey with no one so much as giving him a second look.

He found the reason for this once he'd got off the train at Paddington. There were uniforms everywhere – and not just the ones that he'd been used to, the police and the various civilian services, but military uniforms of all kinds, as well as various auxiliaries. It seemed to Johnny that everyone was in uniform these days – with even the office workers and other civilians clutching tin hats and gas-mask bags as they went about their daily life. He supposed it must have been similar in Jersey but, aside from the Germans on every street corner, he just hadn't noticed it being as pronounced there. And what with prison and then The Chateau, he hadn't really been exposed to what the war was really doing to people. All these months he'd been dreaming of being back in London, but now that he was here he found that London had gone and changed on him. It was only vaguely like what he remembered, half buried behind sandbags and blimps and a sense of urgent, frightened urgency.

But it was still London! And he felt a buzz, a charge of happiness, as he all but skipped down the platform, surrounded by the crush of the crowds and the chattering preoccupation of life in the city. He felt like laughing out loud or hugging everyone he bumped into. It had taken him forever, but he was finally back in the one place he truly belonged. He almost danced along the platform, a sense of victory springing through his steps.

The first thing he did was head to a Lyons and ordered himself a pot of tea and some breakfast. The thick wad of notes in the envelope that Weiler had given him was burning a hole in his pocket and he had had to resist the temptation to head straight for the Ritz and start spending in style. That would hardly have been covert, he thought. It had occurred to him more than once over the past months that there was probably no one less suited to the life of a spy than he was. Keeping a low profile had just never been his style. But now it had to be.

The question was, he mused as he finished off his tea, was, now that he was back, what was he going to do next?

He'd lost his house key months ago, but he wasn't too bothered by that. One of the boys would let him in he was sure. He was already smiling at the thought of the commotion his unexpected arrival was going to cause as he strutted across the street to the front door he knew so well.

He'd not even finished his jaunty knock when the door was flung open and he was faced with a thick-set, sandy-haired young man with a brow furrowed with suspicion and hostility.

"Can I help you?" growled Keith, glaring at the newcomer, his eyes flickering momentarily with what Johnny sensed was mild alarm at the sight of his uniform.

Johnny gave him his best grin. "You're new." He was initially surprised at being presented with a new face in his own home. It had used to be the case that you'd have to serve with the Firm for quite some time before you got house duty, which was, after all, a pretty cushy number and required sustained proof of absolute loyalty and reliability. But he'd been gone for quite some time now, and he supposed that the war had dwindled the mob's ranks as much as it had everyone else's. Johnny had no doubt that if this kid had been considered good enough for the job by Jack or Billie then he was more than up to it.

"Yeah," said Keith. "I'm getting that a lot lately." He folded his arms pointedly. "Something I can be helping you with?"

Johnny peered over his shoulder to see if he could spot Billie or Jack or one of the more familiar minders. "Yeah," he said. "Billie or Jack about?"

"Who wants to know?"

While Johnny was, to some extent, pleased that Jack had hired such a truculent watchdog for the house, he had never imagined that he'd find it this hard to gain entry to his own house. Nevertheless, he gave Keith another of what he considered to be his most charming grins.

"Well," said Johnny. "If you don't know then it's probably not my place to tell you. Besides, I wouldn't want to spoil the surprise."

Keith scowled at him. "What the bleedin' hell are you on about, mate?" he demanded. A fresh thought passed, visibly, across his face. "Here," he said. "You ain't anything to do with that copper, are you? That Harry Blum toe-rag?"

Johnny almost broke into a laugh. He gestured to his uniform. "Me? Do I look like one of the Heavy Mob to you, son?" He was about to put Keith out of his misery when he stopped dead, his heart plummeting. The implications of what he was doing had only just struck him.

"Well?" growled Keith impatiently, arms still folded.

Johnny shook himself out of his reverie and replaced the smile on his face. "Nothing, mate," he said. "Nothing at all."

"I should say so," said Keith. "So why don't you do one? And tell your pal Harry to stop moping around here. Or sending his cuthberts to do it for him. You got me?"

Johnny smiled. Despite his bulk, the kid just wasn't really threatening at all. He couldn't help but like him and he could see why Jack had put him on house duty. "Right you are, son," he said. "I'll do that."

He started walking up the street, aware of Keith's glare still on his back. Talk about bearing a grudge, he thought. But it put the mockers on coming home, at least until this job was out of the way. He wouldn't be able to do sod all if he had the Heavies taking a personal interest every bloody time he broke wind. Johnny had always prided himself on his reputation for keeping his cool, but he experienced a brief surge of unreasoning anger now. To get so close and then once again have it snatched away from him... Fuck you, Harry Blum, he thought. Fuck you to hell.

NINE

JOHNNY didn't actually leave after his encounter with Keith but instead waited around for a couple of hours, lurking out of sight in an alley between the houses on the opposite side of the road. He didn't exactly have a plan; he only knew that he didn't want to give up that easily. Not after all the effort he'd put into getting this far.

More than once he considered just marching across the road and trying again, asking to see Jack or one of the other boys if he didn't get any joy with the kid. But each time he stopped himself. Even if he got inside, there was no question that once word got around – and he had no doubt it would – one of his first visitors would be Harry Blum. And although he'd done his time in Jersey and as far as he knew there was nothing that Harry could out-and-out nick him for, the last thing he wanted was for the Heavies to be constantly sniffing around. It was going to be tricky enough without the Old Bill breathing down his neck.

But he wasn't even going to go through with that now, was he? He was home now and he could forget all about that business, couldn't he? Well, for one thing from the way that Weiler and Behrensdorff went on, he wasn't the only German agent operating in the UK. And he didn't think they'd take too kindly to being double-crossed. He wasn't sure that he wanted to invoke the fury of the Abwehr and have the threat of assassination to deal with on top of keeping the Heavies at bay. And then there was Albie. It was pretty much certain that the first thing the Germans would do if Johnny didn't return was put a bullet in Albie's brain. And Johnny wasn't sure he would be able to live with that. Albie's white, terrified face on that last night in Le Cachot haunted him enough as it was. Turning his back on him would be no better than pulling the trigger himself and contrary to what the likes of Harry Blum thought of him, Johnny didn't consider himself to be a killer. Not for the first time, he found himself marvelling at how he managed to constantly make his life so complicated.

He was torn from his thoughts by the sound of the front door opening and closing across the street. It was a sound that took Johnny back years and it somehow couldn't be mistaken for any other door. It had its own cadence and signature, a jangling reminder of happier times.

And there was Jack. He hadn't changed a bit, thought Johnny. Black hair, already receding into a widow's peak, the dark, almost inscrutable, features. The suit in undertaker black and the immaculately brushed Crombie. Johnnie grinned at seeing his old pal again, feeling the years of separation melt away. Without thinking, he let out a piercing whistle at Jack's retreating back.

It was a very particular whistle, one which they had specifically come up with to give an early warning of approaching danger while out on a job. Sure enough, Jack stopped in his tracks and began looking around the street, eyes narrowed, scanning for trouble, hand slowly but instinctively going for the coat pocket where he had his everyday blade. Still beaming, Johnnie popped his head out from his hiding place.

"Oi. Over 'ere!" Johnnie popped his head out from the darkness of the alley, waving discreetly once, before disappearing back into cover. You couldn't be too careful and for all he knew the Heavies were having his place watched.

Jack looked dumbfounded and even a little pale as he crossed the street to the alley and Johnny couldn't help but chuckle at the shock on his friend's face.

"Jesus Christ, Johnny," said Jack after several moments of staring at his friend. "What the hell are you doing here? Christ, it is you, isn't it?"

"Well, it ain't bloody Marley's ghost, is it? Who the hell do you think it is? Course it's me."

"But what the hell are you doing here? How did you get off Jersey?"

"With great bloody difficulty, let me tell you, son. With great bloody difficulty."

Jack laughed in slightly nervous disbelief. "I can hardly bloody believe it. When did you get back?"

"Just now. Tried to get in but that nursery-age bulldog you've got on the door wasn't having it. He's a bit bloody keen, ain't he?"

Jack grinned. "Yeah, that'll be Keith. Good kid. Takes his job very seriously, it has to be said. Well, you're here now. Come on, let's get you inside." He took Johnny's arm, as if to lead him across the road to the house.

"Nah, wait a minute," said Johnny, holding his ground. "The kid told me that you've still got Harry Blum sniffing around something terrible. That true?"

Jack nodded. "Yeah. Had a right go at Billie too. I thought I was going to have to pull them off each other the last time he came to call."

Johnny chuckled. "I'd have liked to have seen that. Still, it does bollocks up things a bit." He paused, biting his lip in thought. "Christ," he said. "What a mess."

"Well, I hate to say it, Johnny..." Jack began.

"I know, I know, that it's all my fault. Things just got out of hand, OK?"

"Well, things tend to do that. Especially if you're involved. Look, you coming in or not?"

Johnny didn't answer. There was nothing he'd love more than to cross that road and walk into that house and back into his old life, but it just wasn't going to be that easy. He could see that now. "I can't," he said. "At least, not yet. I've got a few things that I've got to sort out first."

"Is that right?" said Jack. "Such as?"

Johnny thought for a moment. Could he really just blurt out to Jack what he was planning? He'd known Jack for years and they'd followed each other into dozens of scrapes and the craziness he'd got himself caught up in would undoubtedly go a whole lot smoother if he had Jack by his side. But despite his nonchalance with a blade, Jack had always lived by a usually unshakeable personal code in which he divided the world into those who 'had it coming' and those who did not. He remembered Jack's disapproval of their dealings with the blackshirts way back in '36. How would he take the news of Johnny working for full-blown Nazis, especially with the war on? Something told Johnny it wouldn't be well.

Besides which, there was something slightly off about the way that Jack was looking at him now. There was a reserve, an edginess there. Something was wrong, something that Johnny just couldn't quite put his finger on.

"It's complicated, Jacky-Boy," he said, cagily. "I'll tell you once I've got it all straight in my own head."

Jack's eyes narrowed. And there it was again, thought Johnny. There was definitely something different about Jack alright. Something he wasn't telling him. But then again, maybe it was just the shock of seeing him, he told himself. He'd been gone a while now. Perhaps it would just take time for things to settle down again.

"Alright," said Jack. "And in the meantime just what am I supposed to tell Billie?"

"I don't know. Nothing, I guess. Let it be a surprise, eh?"

"Come on, Johnny. She's been worried sick about you."

"Yeah, but like I say I've got stuff to do. Low-profile stuff. Can't do that if Billie is tearing around London looking for me, can I? And she will if she knows I'm back."

"It's up to you," said Jack with a sigh. "But you should give her more credit. You should see the way she's held everything together here."

"Yeah, I know. But it's only for a few days. And then I'll be back properly. Promise. Till then let's keep schtum, eh?"

Jack shrugged. "You're the boss."

"That's good to know. Anything could have happened while I was gone," said Johnny, and then he added, not without concern, "It hasn't, has it? Everything's still alright, innit? Billie's still OK?"

If the light had been better in the alley, Johnny would have just been able to make out a momentary flicker of guilt behind Jack's eyes. "Yeah, she's fine," Jack said. "You know, bearing up. We all are. But everything's fine. Just the same as before."

"She still pissed off with me, is she?"

"Nah, she's fine," said Jack. "Water under the bridge, ain't it? I think getting occupied by the Jerries got you off the hook there."

"Knew they had to be good for something," muttered Johnny. "Listen, Jack. If I needed to pull a job and I couldn't use my own team – you know, for fear of the Heavies sticking their big nose in – who would you suggest?"

Jack thought for a moment. "Difficult to say. Things are all royally messed up at the moment like. New mobs and the Heavies still breathing down everybody's necks. The Danellis maybe. They're in a right state. Could be they might welcome a bit of work, even if it does come from an unlikely source."

"The Danellis," repeated Johnny, without enthusiasm. "Christ, changed days, eh Jack?"

"It is at that. But they've locked up Aldo though," added Jack. "So you're going to have to go further down the food chain."

"Like who?"

"I hear Leo is still wandering around these days like a spare prick at an orgy. Might be your best bet."

"Leo Danelli," repeated Johnny. "It just gets better and better, don't it? I'm guessing I'll find him in the usual places?"

"Most likely. Neapolitan is probably your best bet." Jack shook his head. "Johnny, what the hell is going on?" There was exasperation in his voice but also genuine concern.

"Nothing. A job. It ain't something I can get into now, Jacky boy. Give me some time. Just a couple more weeks and we can all get on with things being the way they were before."

Jack looked doubtful. "But where the hell are you even going to stay? Let us help you, for Chrissake."

Johnny shook his head. "You can't. At least not right now. Not if you've got Harry Blum hanging on your bloody coat-tails. You know that. Just let me do this, alright, Jack? Then I'll be back and I'll tell you about the whole bloody crazy thing."

He began moving off up the alley.

"Wait a minute," said Jack. "Where are you off to?"

"Got to get going," said Johnny. "The sooner I get this out of the way, the sooner I can come back. And remember, mum's the word till I get back."

And with that, he disappeared into the shadows. Jack listened to his footsteps fade as Johnny picked his way through the back alleys that the two of them used to haunt as kids. And for a moment Jack was a kid again too, blithely following Johnny on whatever damn fool idea he'd come up with that day. But then it was gone and he was back in the darkness, wondering if it wasn't long gone time that they both did some growing up.

IV. ALLIANCES

ONE

HARRY pulled the ancient, juddering heap of the squad Invicta up to the curb. The motor chattered and shook as it came to a halt and was still growling into silence as Harry and Illingworth got out and climbed the stairs to the derelict offices.

The building had once belonged to an insurance company but the 50-pound UXB that had sheared off the roof had meant they'd had to find alternative premises several months previously. It looked like they'd left in a hurry, too. Numerous desks and chairs and filing cabinets were stacked against the walls, some with in-trays, blotters and piles of paper still on them. A coat-stand by the door had a couple of old garments hanging from it. Dust motes danced through the disturbed air.

Laid out across the empty floor were eight male bodies, each surrounded by its own spreading halo of coagulated blood. At the far end of the room was the remains of a safe that had clearly been blown with gelignite. Inexpertly by the look of it, thought Harry, judging by the charred appearance of the stack of banknotes lying next to it.

"Christ," said Harry. "What a mess."

Symons and the rest of the squad were already there, separated into small clumps of two or three, trying to make sense of the scene, co-ordinating the woodentops doing the grunt work. "Really, Harry?" muttered Symons. "A mess. Is that what you call it?"

Harry did his best to ignore his Guv'nor's obvious displeasure. "Do we know who these blokes are?"

"They are, or rather were, a jump-up team for the Dubanowski Mob. New crew from Poland. Just here a few months and starting to make waves. I've had Alfie keeping tabs on them."

"Reckon they're going to be pretty pissed off now," observed Illingworth.

"Unlikely," said Symons. "Because we've just received word that what's left of the Dubanowskis has just been found down Bethnal Green way with a bullet each in the brainpan. Alfie's down there now seeing what's what."

"A turf war," said Harry.

"Thank you, again, Harry," said Symons. "Heaven knows what we would do if you weren't here to tell us what's what. Have you ever considered doing this for a living? This lot were spotted by an ARP warden huckling that safe into the back of a van. Came here to blow it most likely and divvy up the loot. Looks like someone else had other plans though."

Harry glanced towards the safe and the pile of cash. Aside from being slightly charred from the amateur attempt to blow the safe, it had been sprayed with the blood of god knows how many of the dead men. "They didn't even take the money."

"It's a message, pure and simple," said Symons. "And one that's not exactly hard to misinterpret."

Illingworth nodded towards the men on the floor. As well as a single bullet-hole to the temple, each of them had their throats gashed from ear to ear. "More Limehouse Grins," he said. "I guess we know what that means. But I don't get it. Johnny Black is still tucked up down in Jersey, ain't he?"

Harry exchanged a glance with Symons. "But the rest of his Mob isn't."

Illingworth nodded. "And what with poor old Freddie Winner

getting done over too, it does sound like they're up to their old tricks again. But why now?"

"Well, that is the question, isn't it?" said Symons. "Couldn't be that somebody might have been rattling their cage, eh, Harry?"

Harry stared down at the pasty, blood-stained corpses. "It looks like the Black Mob had a hand in this but I've never heard of them pulling anything on this scale. Full-blown massacres like this, that just isn't Johnny's style. Or Jack's."

"Yeah," said Illingworth. "But they're operating under new management, ain't they? Though it is hard to believe that a woman could order something like this."

Symons leaned in close to Harry, an uncharacteristic scowl on his face. "I told you not to shake things up, Harry. But, no, one war's not good enough for you, is it. You far prefer to have two or three on the go at the same time."

"We'll sort it out," said Harry.

"With what? I've got no more men. Certainly not enough to start coping with pitched battles on the bloody streets. Not now. This crap was bad enough to deal with back in '36, but we just don't have the wherewithal to deal with it while we're stretched as thin as this. The best we can hope for now is that they all bloody kill each other – and don't take too many civilians out in the process. But just so we're clear, Harry, you have incurred my most profound – *most profound* – displeasure. Now get this mess, as you most succinctly put it, cleaned up. And do it quickly."

Symons stepped daintily over the corpses and strode out of the offices. Harry continued to stare at the blasted safe and did his best to ignore the 'I told you so' look he knew would be on Illingworth's face. He was thinking of what had just been said and whether Billie Black could be capable of instigating something like this. He had no problem believing it. There was a look that you learned to discern in the face of those who would go on to kill, often growing to enjoy it in the process, and Billie definitely had it.

"Vendettas, Harry," he heard Symons' voice float up from the office stairs. "They never end well. Read the Jacobeans and you'll find out what I mean."

TWO

JOHNNY rapped smartly on the house's front door and took an expectant step backwards. He almost burst into a grin when the door was opened by Sydney Cook but stopped himself when he saw Cook regard him with an impassive lack of recognition.

"Yes?"

"Excuse me, mate. This isn't Collins Street is it by any chance?"

"No, I'm afraid not," said Cook, with very little trace of the Cockney accent he had affected in Nantes. In fact, thought Johnny, there seemed to be little of the Cook he'd known in France here. He seemed, leaner, colder, and more serious. "Collins Street is another two streets along."

"Right, my mistake. Look, mate, don't suppose I could trouble you for a glass of water, could I? Been on me pins all day and I'm absolutely parched."

"Of course." Cook held the door open wider. "Please do come in."

It was only once they were safely inside, with all the codewords and double-blinds completed, that they laughed and embraced in recognition.

"What the hell are you doing here, you old bugger?" chuckled Johnny. "Ain't you meant to be on the Eastern Front somewhere?"

Cook led Johnny into the living room and produced a bottle of whisky from a sideboard. He poured out two glasses.

"Yeah, like that was ever going to happen," he said. "They needed me here, didn't they?"

"Doing what?"

"I'm your point man, ain't I? I'm here to make sure you've got everything you need."

"Keep an eye on me you mean."

Cook grinned. "Well, that too. But don't be so suspicious, mate. Those Krauts think the bloody world of you. Believe me, I know."

Johnny took a seat in one of Cook's armchairs and sipped his whisky. "So, all that business with the tarts in Nantes, that was all set up, was it?"

"Nah, of course it wasn't. Weiler was still proper pissed off about that. He just took advantage of it to get me away unnoticed, like."

"So, the others don't know you're here either?"

"Well, Weiler and Behrensdorff do obviously. But nobody else. Need to know, ain't it? The Abwehr's as leaky as a bloody sieve and they love their checks and balances do the Krauts. Don't trust nobody, they don't. Probably wise too. Anyway, what's the state of play with your own op?"

"Well, we got complications already," admitted Johnny. He told Cook about his encounter with Keith and the probability of interest from the Heavies.

"Yeah, that is a bugger, ain't it?" said Cook. "You probably did the right thing there. So what's the plan?"

"I've got a few ideas. It's not ideal, but I think I know someone who might help."

"Well, don't look at me. I don't do field work. I'm strictly a liaison. I keep well out of operational harm's way. Me getting collared could bollocks up half a dozen different ops. So, you're on your own I'm afraid, mate."

Once again with Cook, Johnny got the impression that his every utterance was shrouded in exaggeration and self-aggrandisement, but he merely smiled and said: "Understood."

"So, what do you need then?"

"Place to stay might be nice."

Cook shook his head. "Well, you can't stay here, mate. Too bloody risky. You got this address written down anywhere?"

Johnny held up the slip of paper he'd been carrying in his pocket. "Yeah."

"Well, burn it double-quick. Ain't you got anywhere else you can bunk down?"

"There's probably an old safe house somewhere I can put up in. I'll take a nosey around."

"Fine. Anything else you need?"

"Yeah, there's a radio still buried in a field in Kent that'll need digging up pretty sharpish."

"That's no problem. We can sort that out. You'll need that to keep Nantes up to speed. They get really jittery, really quickly. And if there's anything you think you'll need, then let me know. And I'll help sort out your passage back once the deed is done."

"Right," said Johnny, finishing his whisky. "Best get started then."

The Neapolitan, as its name suggested, was an Italian place deep in the heart of Soho. It was a long, narrow watering hole with pretensions to Continental chic – all clean lines, high stools, leather booths and chrome facings – and attracted a mixed clientele of deadbeat artists and writers sloping across from Fitzrovia, slumming socialites and the more presentable end of London's underworld. It was the type of place that Johnny used to love before the war, but this was one bar that had usually remained off-limits and that was because it had been one of the main concerns of his bitterest enemies. To have shown his face here would have meant introducing it to the wrong end of a razor. But times change and it was now precisely those old enemies that Johnny was looking for.

It was early in the day when he walked in, a time that he'd chosen with the utmost of care – still quiet enough that he'd have room for manoeuvre if things turned ugly but late enough that there would be at least a few witnesses around to prevent the Danellis from cutting his throat solely on principle. But that didn't stop him from feeling somewhat nervous and more than a little exposed as he entered the bar. The afternoon sun gleamed off the polished wooden floor and the chrome, giving the whole place a lazy, summer feeling, somehow too woozy and indolent to be the scene of any sudden violence and Johnny hoped he was right in that assumption.

The barman, a greasy-looking Eye-tie with lazy, hooded eyes, black, wiry hair slicked into a ridged corkscrew arrangement and a mouth crammed full of broken, ill-fitting teeth, grinned in recognition and mock amazement as Johnny approached the counter. Johnny knew his face as a 'go-to' man from way back but couldn't recall ever having spoken to him face-to-face. In the old days he would always have left that to Jack or one of the other boys. But now he had to do his own running about.

"Blow me," said the barman, accentuating his already-thick accent for effect. "Johnny Black as I live and breathe."

"Alright, Giuseppe?" said Johnny as he perched himself on one of the high barstools, relieved that he'd managed to pluck the barman's name – which was as phoney as his accent – from his memory. "How's tricks?"

Giuseppe shrugged. "You know," he said. "Been a while since we've seen you in here."

"Don't be bloody daft, Giuseppe. You've never seen me in here."

Giuseppe gave him a grin that looked like a bombed graveyard. "True enough. So, what's the occasion?"

"Looking for someone. One of your old pals. Leo Danelli."

"Ain't seen him around, Johnny. Not for a good while now."

"Don't come the cod, Giuseppe. You know as well as I do that he practically used to live in this bloody place. No way in hell you don't know where he's at."

Giuseppe shrugged and smirked again. "Even if what you say was true, Johnny, I don't think Leo would thank me too kindly for dishing out his whereabouts to the head of the Black mob, do you?"

"He might do when he finds out the reason I'm looking for him."

Giuseppe propped his elbows on the zinc-topped bar and leaned in confidentially. "Well, if you tell me what it is then I'll be sure to mention it to him if he ever does pop in."

"Stop pissing about, Giuseppe and just bloody tell me where he is, will you? I'm looking to help him not bloody razor him. You know I wouldn't be here in person or alone if I was." Johnny tried to inject as much exasperation and impatience as he could into his tone. As Giuseppe had pointed out, he was still the head of the Black mob. Surely to hell that must still count for something?

Giuseppe grinned again. "Now I come to think of it," he said. "Leo does sometimes take a wander in here about four o'clock some days. Who knows, maybe today might be one of those days. Why don't you order yourself a beer and try your luck?"

"You still calling that fizzy pop you serve in here beer, are you?" said Johnny. Over the last months, he'd developed a taste for the more continental brews, but he wasn't about to let Giuseppe know that. "Go on then." He slapped down a couple of coins and waited while Giuseppe busied himself at the bar.

It was gone half past four before Leo Danelli showed up. Johnny had watched Giuseppe pick up the telephone almost as soon as Johnny had sat down and conduct a hushed, urgent phone call, punctuated by glances in Johnny's direction. But Johnny had figured that although he would be burning to know what the Blacks could possibly want with him, Leo wouldn't want to pass up the opportunity of keeping the head of the clan waiting around for as long as possible. And that was something Johnny was just going to have to put up with this time.

But eventually Leo did swagger in. The intervening years had not been kind to him, thought Johnny. His youthful, Latin good looks had roughened and he looked gaunt and haggard. This was not helped by the numerous small scars and pocks on his face, from countless knife fights and skirmishes over the years, most prominent of which, Johnny noticed, was the one he'd given Leo himself on Regent Street all those years ago. He was surprised at how pronounced it was and again remonstrated with himself for his heavy-handedness when it came to personally doling out violence. It was clearly not his forte.

Leo glanced at Giuseppe who nodded, almost imperceptibly, in the direction of Johnny's booth. He saw Leo's hand drift towards his jacket pocket where he was no doubt packing a cat-stabber and Johnny suddenly wished he'd brought something himself. It hadn't occurred to him till now that Leo might possibly still be holding a grudge after all this time.

"Alright, Johnny?" said Leo warily, as he slid into the booth. He was dressed in a black suit that would have once been well-cut and expensive but which Johnny was pleased to note was now frayed, patched and baggy. Leo had clearly fallen on harder times and this suited Johnny's purposes perfectly. "Been a while. Heard you'd disappeared off the face of the earth. Got collared down on the coast somewhere or something like that."

"Sounds like your information is out of date, Leo," said Johnny smoothly. "Because here I am."

"So you are," sneered Leo. "And all on your ownsome too. So, any reason why I don't just carve you up right here and now? I believe I still owe you a cut. More than one."

"Because you ain't all that, for a start, Leo. I reckon I could put you down pretty easy, solo or not. And that was all a long time ago. What's the point of keeping score like that?" Johnny talked quickly and insistently. The longer he had Leo listening, the less the chances were he'd do something stupid. "Besides, I hear you've got the Law on your case these days, so the last thing you'd want to do is draw attention to yourself like that. And anyway, I'm here to offer you a job so you'd be kind of dumb to pull anything, at least before hearing me out."

Leo smirked. "Since when do the Blacks come to the Danellis with work?"

"Times change, Leo. It's a different world out there these days. Everything's turned upside down."

"Yeah," said Leo. "You got that right at least."

"Heard they interned your old man. Your brothers too."

"Bastards," spat Leo. "What the hell they want to do that for? Lock up an innocent old man."

"With respect, Leo," said Johnny, with a thin smile. "The last thing anyone could really accuse Aldo of was being innocent."

"Or the Blacks," countered Leo evenly.

Johnny could make a guess at what had happened. It made sense that the Law would make use of the war and the Enemy Aliens Acts to smash what was left of the Danellis. It was lucky that the Blacks were as British as roast beef otherwise he could see those kind of tactics being used to tear up their firm also. All's fair in love and war and all that.

"Look, do you want to hear about this job or not?" he asked.

"Sure," said Leo, with a wholly unconvincing attempt at cool. "Why not? But you still haven't explained why you've come to me when you've got a whole outfit at home ready to come running the minute you click your fingers."

Johnny smiled at Leo's bitterness, allowing himself to enjoy a little moment of professional schadenfreude at seeing his old rivals' empire in tatters while (as far as he knew) his was still intact.

"What can I say, Leo?" he said. "I just thought you could do with the money. I'm sure times must be tough out there for you at the moment. But if you're not interested..." He made a theatrical show of sliding out the booth and, as expected, Leo placed a restraining hand on his arm.

"No, wait," he said. "I'm listening."

Johnny smiled. This was going to work. Leo was clearly desperate and that made him easy to control. But he was still a Danelli and therefore not to be trusted. He had to proceed very carefully.

"Right up your street," he began. "Demolition job. I can handle the fireworks, that's no problem, but I need someone to watch my back and do the rest of the lifting. Two hundred quid in it for you if it comes off."

The mention of the money lit up Leo's face. Johnny knew that his offer was a good-but-not-great take and it showed him just how hard-up Leo actually was. He hoped that that desperation would be enough to offset the distrust and lack of loyalty that there would undoubtedly be between them. He didn't like the idea of pulling a job where half your concentration would be on making sure your back-up man wasn't waiting to stick a knife in but what choice did he have?

But despite his obvious need for the pay-day, there was still deep suspicion on Leo's face. "All sounds a bit too easy to me. What's the bloody catch?"

"No catch, Leo. And I've got my reasons for not using my own people on this one. You're just going to have to trust me."

Leo sneered at him, not without reason, thought Johnny. The one thing there wouldn't be on this job was any kind of trust. "What's the target?" asked Leo.

"You don't need to know that just yet. Let's just say, it's worth doing."

Now it was Leo's turn to start sliding out the booth. "Sorry, but I ain't going into a job like this blind, especially with Johnny bloody Black, without knowing the target. You either tell me the whole bloody thing or I walk. Two hundred quid or not."

"Right, so you can walk into the nearest station and spill to the Law?"

"I'm an enemy bloody alien, Johnny. I could walk in with Adolf himself under my arm and they'd still be locking me up. Come on, tell me. Because I ain't doing nothing for you until you do."

Johnny took a sharp breath. This was the danger point. Leo Danelli was unpredictable at the best of times and while he might be on the enemy list, Johnny still had no way of really knowing just how far his patriotism – or lack of it – would stretch. He had hoped that he'd have been able to keep him in the dark about the actual nature of the job until he'd reeled him in a bit further. But it was clear that wasn't going to be an option.

"Alright," said Johnny. "It's an aeroplane factory. Down Hertfordshire way."

Leo was silent for a moment, processing this potentially tasty piece of information and the triumphant smirk returned to his face. "Are we talking sabotage here, Johnny?" he said finally. "What is this? You throwing your lot in with the Jerries?"

"Why?" said Johnny. "Would that be a problem if I was?"

Leo thought for a moment. "Nah," he said finally. "Fuck 'em, eh? If it's good enough for Benito, it's good enough for me."

Johnny almost sighed with relief. God knows how the hell he would have pulled this off if Leo had walked. And the Italian wasn't stupid. He'd probably been able to read at least that much. He'd known he was Johnny's last hope. While Weiler and Behrensdorff had said there was a network of other Nazi agents working in England, they had been careful not to give Johnny any details. For fear of compromising them, they had said, although Johnny suspected that it could be just as likely that they simply didn't trust him enough to reveal that kind of information yet. It was Leo or nothing and this just wasn't the kind of job he could pull on his own.

"Alright then," he said. "But keep your bloody voice down, will you? This is the sort of caper that could get us both shot."

Leo held up his hands placatingly. "Sure, sure. You're the boss. Alright, what happens next?"

"Next," said Johnny. "We have to find some stuff that goes 'boom.'"

THREE

"HERE you go, Harry."

Illingworth dropped the simple, brown envelope onto Harry's desk. Harry stared at it for a moment before looking up at Illingworth, who once again had a look of disapproval on his face.

"What?" he asked irritably. Illingworth's constant air of moral superiority was really beginning to grate.

"This," said Illingworth, eyeing the envelope with obvious distaste. "You really going to go through with this?"

"Any reason why I shouldn't?" said Harry. "The kid's broken the law. And last I heard enforcing it was what we did round about here."

"Yeah, I don't know if you noticed but we are up to our necks in dead gangsters round here at the moment. Don't you think we should be trying to collar the Blacks for something a bit heavier than this? Quite apart from the fact it's not exactly our jurisdiction, is it? Isn't it just a bit... petty?"

Harry shrugged as he picked up the envelope and slipped it into the inside pocket of his jacket. He got painfully to his feet. "Petty sometimes gets the job done. Look at Al Capone," he muttered, before adding, "You coming?"

Illingworth raised an eyebrow. "What, you're going to deliver it yourself? We still have an excellent postal service, you know."

"No," said Harry. "I don't want there to be any doubt. I want them to know that it was me that did this."

"I don't think there'll be any doubt about that, do you, Harry?"

"All the same, you coming?"

Illingworth shook his head. "No thanks, Harry. I think I'll pass."

Keith swung open the front door and groaned when he saw Harry standing there. "Oh Christ, not you again. I've got orders not to let you in, so unless you've got some kind of a warrant, you can bloody forget it."

Harry gave an almost cheerful chuckle that unnerved Keith more than any blustering threat could possibly have. "Don't worry, son. It's you that I'm here to see."

Suspicion and also some fear flickered behind Keith's eyes. "Oh yeah?" he said. "How's that then?"

Harry produced the envelope and stuffed it into Keith's unresisting hand. "Remember I said I thought there must be something up with your call-up papers last time I was here?" he said. "Well I did a bit of asking around and it turned out that I was right. Must have got lost somewhere along the line so I chivvied them along a bit for you."

Keith stared in horror at Harry, not daring yet to even look down at the envelope in his hand.

"Congratulations, son," said Harry, a savage smile on his face. "You're going to go and do your bit for your country at last."

"You really are a bastard, aren't you?" was all Keith managed to muster.

"Hey, I'm not the one trying to backslide out of doing my duty. If it was me, I'd be right in there. But I suppose you're too much of a coward for that, eh? Anyway, consider yourself lucky that we're not taking this further. You could have all been looking at charges over this." He neglected to add the reason they weren't was that no amount of ferreting around had been able to come up with a firm link between the Blacks and the mislaid papers.

He gave one last smirk at the shocked boy and then turned on his heel and walked up the street. It was petty, as Illingworth had said, but he did not care. It was a victory of sorts. Not much of one, to be sure. But still enough to show the Blacks that he was out there and he had the power to upset their plans. And until something better showed up, he was happy to take any little piece of victory he could get.

When Jack returned from his early-morning walk, he found the boy sitting alone at the kitchen table. Jack liked to stretch his legs before breakfast and was usually the first up in the house. He would get out and buy the papers and any supplies that might be needed, assuming they were available (and to the Blacks they were always available) enjoying the milky, early morning light, the sharp air on his skin and the sound of his footsteps on the still largely empty streets.

"Alright, Keithie?" said Jack, with a joviality that was not his usual style but which he felt was somehow required. "Everything alright?"

"Not really, Jack, no," said Keith. And for a moment Jack thought the boy was going to burst into tears.

"Why, what's up?"

Keith slid an envelope across the table top. Jack could see that it was something official. Buff envelope. Typewritten address. Official stamps over one corner. He didn't need to read it to know what it said. He put down the bottle of milk he'd brought in and sat down opposite Keith and went through the motions of reading it anyway.

"When did this come?" he asked finally.

"Just now," said Keith. "Special delivery. Courtesy of your pal Harry Blum."

Jack grimaced and looked down at the letter again, staring hard at the ragged, typewritten lines, more to avoid looking at Keith than anything else. Here was someone else he'd let down. It was getting to be a habit.

"What'd he have to go and do something like that for, Jack?" demanded Keith. "I mean what's it got to do with him anyway? What did I ever do to him?"

Jack shook his head and said, "I don't know, son. Because he can, I suppose." He scanned the letter again. "Week after next down in Bexhill for your basic training," he read. "They're not hanging about, are they?"

"I don't suppose…?" Keith left the question hanging in the air, perhaps wishing that its air of futile hopefulness would take wing in the early morning sunlight.

"Sorry, son," said Jack. "They've got your number now. There's nothing we can do."

"That's what I figured." Keith was silent for a moment, before saying, "I'm not a coward, you know, Jack. It's not that I'm afraid to fight or anything."

"Oh Christ, son," said Jack. "I know that. We all do. You wouldn't be working for us if you were."

"It's just that I've got things I want to do. There's no crime in that, is there? And what the hell good am I going to be with them anyway? I saw what the last one did to my old man. I don't want to end up like that, Jack. I don't want to come back all mashed up. Pissing myself with fear every time a car backfires or hobbling about like a bloody cripple."

Jack said nothing. All he could do now was let the boy talk. Let him vent his rage, give his frustration free rein before life reeled him back in and crushed him to its will. There was nothing else he could offer him.

"My old man," Keith went on, "he came back from the last one. And he was fucked. One lung gone altogether, the other one all burnt up by mustard gas. He could barely cross from one end of the room to the other without coughing his guts up. And he said it was all bullshit. All of it. Load of old toffs in their clubs gassing away over the brandy and cigars and it was us that had to die for it. And now they want to do the same thing to me." The boy slammed the table with his chunky fists, so hard that it rattled the unused tea-things upon it. "It's not bloody fair."

Jack had to agree. And he felt just as angry at himself for not having the words to comfort the boy. "You don't know how it'll turn out, son," he said. "The way thing are going, it could all be over before you've even finished your basic."

It occurred to Jack to suggest to Keith that he go out and turn over a house or something and just make sure that he got collared for it. After all, he could only assume that it was Jack's record that had prevented him from being called up himself. But Keith was the kind of kid who would be ruined by prison. Not that he wouldn't survive it – he was more than tough enough – just that it would change him too much. It would set his path for life, thought Jack. And right at this moment, the kid still had choices open to him. There were other paths his life could take. And Jack would be damned if he'd take that away from him, war or no war.

That was part of the reason he'd put him on house duty so early, to take him out of the corrupting influence of the streets, for at least long enough to let the kid decide what it was he really wanted to do with his life. And the war wasn't going to last forever, was it? There would come a time when the kid would be able to walk away from it, assuming he survived it. But once the Law had got their claws into him, that would be it for him for the rest of his days.

"Maybe it won't be so bad," added Jack. "If you keep your head down and out of trouble till it's all over. Half the Army's bloody desk jobs these days anyway. You might never even set foot out of England."

But Keith was shaking his head fatalistically. All the fight went out of him and he seemed to visibly diminish as he let his fate wash over him. "No," he said. "They're going to kill me. I can feel it."

Jack said nothing. There was nothing else he could say.

Billie entered the kitchen, dressed for the day. "Alright, you two?" she said breezily.

Her arrival seemed to break the spell of intimacy between the two men and Keith stood up, almost guiltily, suddenly aware that he should be at his regular post. He scooped up his letter and stuffed it into his pocket. "Thanks, Jack," he said, before hurrying to the door and back along the passageway, with little more than an embarrassed and mumbled "g'morning" in Billie's direction.

"What's up with him?" asked Billie, joining Jack at the table.

"His call-up papers came. They're sending him down to Bexhill week after next."

"How come?" said Billie. "I thought we'd fixed that."

"Yes, well, Harry Blum unfixed it."

Billie shook her head. "That bastard again. Just what is it with him anyway? I mean, what the hell is his problem?"

"You know what."

"But that was years ago now. If you're going to play the game then you've got to learn to take your lumps. He should know that. Even if your name is Harry bloody Blum."

"I told Johnny," said Jack. "I told him there would be consequences. Harry Blum is not one of those coppers you tangle with lightly."

"You think…" Her voice trailed off, surprisingly unsure of itself, tangled in thought.

"Think what?"

"That we should deal with him? You know, finish what Johnny started?"

Jack shook his head, smiling at the audacity of the suggestion. "No, that would be a really bad idea. You take out someone like Harry Blum, you'd have the entire Yard gunning for you. We ain't ready for that."

Billie smiled and nodded. "You're probably right. But he's never going to leave us alone, is he? I mean, what's it going to take, Jack?"

"Don't worry," he said. "I'll think of something."

She smiled and reached across the table for his hand, but he was already standing up and moving away. As he did so, he was aware of the look of almost sly, taunting cruelty that flashed across her features. Nothing had ever been said by either of them about that night they had spent together, but Billie had more than once wordlessly alluded to it – and it seemed to him in a way designed to mock him, to flaunt the power she now assumed she had over him.

He wondered what would happen when Johnny did come back. Would Billie tell him what had happened between them? Would they make him go this time? It was not the first time these thoughts had crossed his mind but now that he knew for sure that Johnny was back, they had a sickening solidity to them. He had become used to things as they were. He liked it being just him and Billie and he wanted to hold onto that for as long as he could. But that wasn't going to be for much longer, it seemed. And there was nothing he could really do about that.

Was there?

FOUR

JOHNNY threw himself into the explosives job with enthusiasm. He'd had enough of waiting around, both in Jersey and in France and to be actually doing something seemed to him to be far preferable to sitting around and brooding over the increasingly complicated mess he seemed to be making of his life. And while it could hardly be said to be the most ambitious caper he'd ever planned, it was still rather like coming home.

It wasn't strictly necessary, of course. He could have built some homemade explosives that could have done the job just as well. A major part of his training in Nantes had been in volatile chemicals and he'd picked up a lot. But despite his knowledge and relative aptitude for the subject, he'd had more than a few near-disasters at the villa. Timings and measurements using home-made fertiliser bombs and the like were inexact and the explosives created were often unpredictable, and he didn't want to attract unwanted attention before the operation itself by blowing up a garden shed somewhere. Nor did he want to have to worry about lugging unstable mixtures around that might explode in his face while he was planting them.

Instead, he preferred to steal what he needed so that he could be assured of a more professional quality. He was used to working with gelignite and knew how to handle it, besides generally preferring it over other forms of explosive. Anyway, word of the jelly getting stolen would hopefully get back to Nantes and provide some corroboration to his radio messages to Weiler and the others that he was embroiled in the mission.

However, his main motivation was that he wanted to pull a low-level job just to keep his hand in. He decided that the best idea would be to head to somewhere quieter and less urban. The city just had too many coppers and soldiers and other officious types milling around these days for his liking. It was getting harder and harder to go about your business without some herbert sticking his nose in where it didn't belong, especially after the hours of darkness. And so he had chosen a stone quarry in Essex which he knew would have to have some decent blasting equipment and which also hopefully wouldn't be sealed up like the Bank of England.

Not that he still didn't have serious misgivings about embarking on a relatively simple job like this. He felt exposed, naked almost without his old team and especially, Jack to back him up. He would even have liked to have had the likes of Krause or Fleischer with him right at that moment. Instead, all he had was Leo Danelli and he had been regretting recruiting him almost from the moment he had done so.

Johnny peered through the metal grille across the gate, scanning first for the location of the supply hut and secondly for any sign of the watchman that he knew must be on duty somewhere. He could feel Leo fidgeting impatiently at his shoulder and that alone was making him irritated. It was like trying to pull a job with a child in tow, constantly pulling on your coat and demanding to go to the toilet.

"Well?" hissed Leo, his feet shuffling on the frosty ground in a vain attempt to keep warm. It was a bastardly cold night, but all the same, Johnny couldn't remember ever embarking on a job where his sole back-up was someone who, it was becoming increasingly obvious, simply didn't have the basic wherewithal for this kind of work.

Ignoring the temptation to tell Leo to shut the hell up, Johnny squinted back through gate. Security was lax, which was why he had chosen this particular target; it consisted mainly of one night-watchman who looked as if he were a hundred and two. Johnny had already spent several hours out here watching the doddering old fool shuffle his way around the site and was confident that he was not going to provide any kind of a problem.

"Can't see anyone," he whispered. He assumed this meant the old man was currently ambling his way around the main quarry site, leaving the supply huts next to the entrance unguarded. His plan was to make this a quick in-out job and this was probably his best window of opportunity before the old coot got settled for the night. He slid the crowbar from his belt and used it to prise off the padlock and chain that was securing a smaller access door built into the wide, wooden gate. As previously instructed, Leo deftly caught the lock and chain as they fell, to prevent them clattering on the stony ground.

They waited silently for a moment to make sure that what little noise they had made hadn't alerted anyone before Johnny cautiously pushed the wooden door open.

What lay beyond was a yard with a collection of rudimentary brick and wood huts, a few fuel tanks and a couple of lorries and diggers parked between them. A wide track, churned by countless tyre tracks but now frozen solid, led to the quarry beyond. Johnny scanned the huts critically. One had a couple of large windows and also had what appeared to be a light burning within it. That was probably the guards' hut and was the one to be avoided. But there was one at the far end of the yard, windowless, and all but hidden in the shadow of the looming rock. It looked to Johnny rather like it could be a storage hut and was certainly a good place to start looking.

Once they were through the gate, Johnny gently pushed Leo into the shadows. "Right, you know the score," he whispered. "This won't take but a minute. Watch my back."

"What?" hissed Leo. "You want me to just hang about out here?"

"If that wouldn't be too much trouble," replied Johnny, through gritted teeth, before moving off.

Balancing his movement between speed and stealth, Johnny set about tearing the locks off with a combination of crowbar and screwdriver and he was inside in a matter of minutes. He was pleased to find that his instincts still served him well, after what was now coming up to a couple of years of essentially living (more or less) on the right side of the law; he hit pay dirt first time. Inside the hut was an arrangement of shelves and lockers that held everything from torches to pickaxes to overalls and helmets. And, most importantly, one shelf where detonators and sticks of gelignite were carefully arranged, framed by stark safety warnings. He padded his way to these shelves and began methodically stowing the detonators and jelly in his knapsack, carefully ensuring that each was amply wrapped in the rags he'd brought with him for this very purpose.

He was so intent on the job that for a moment he didn't realise he was no longer alone in the hut. He turned to see the stocky, dumbfounded watchman framed in the hut's doorway. He was old, well into his 60s at least, and slow too, as attested to by his astounded silence. As well as surprise, Johnny could see consternation etched on the old man's face. He knew he'd gauged it right that the watchman wouldn't be a threat. There was no challenge, no aggression on the man's face. Just confusion at this disruption in his normal routine, and an apprehension as to what was going to happen next.

The watchman still hadn't said anything, but now the expression on the sagging, craggy features turned from astonishment to pain. With a hoarse, rasping whimper of agony, the old man suddenly pitched forward, landing on the wooden planks of the hut with a crash that made Johnny wince for fear of further discovery.

The old man's place in the doorway was now taken by Leo, who stood there with a grin on his face, the cat-stabber in his hand slick with the watchman's blood.

"Jesus Christ," hissed Johnny in the darkness, disgust dripping from his voice. "What the fuck do you think you're doing?"

"Watching your back," said Leo. "Or rather this old bugger's." He knelt down beside the old man's head. The old man gave an agonised gurgle as Leo forced his head back, clearly preparing to cut the his throat.

Johnny leapt forward and pulled Leo roughly to his feet, anger giving him the strength to wrestle the bigger man off his intended victim. "Leave him, leave him," he said furiously. "We've got what we need. Let's just get the hell out of here."

Leo shrugged and all but danced out of the hut, still high on the action. Johnny checked the old man's pulse before following. It was weak and already there was a dark pool of blood forming on the floor where Leo had stabbed him. He looked into the old man's eyes, which were still full of fear but also bewilderment, as if struck by the sheer absurdity that his life might end in a cold, wooden hut in the middle of a quarry, and for no good reason at all.

"Just hang on in there, Grandad," Johnny whispered to him. "You'll be alright. They'll find you and you'll be alright."

The old man didn't look as if he had heard Johnny or was even aware of his presence. He was now fully enveloped in the spreading numbness in his lower back and the prospect of his own death. There was no room for anything else.

Johnny cursed under his breath and hurried out of the hut, anxious to make his escape, before anything else went wrong, as well as to comfort himself with the knowledge that the old man was at least still alive when he had left him.

FIVE

HARRY had always hated hospitals.

This had been true long before his prolonged stay in one in '36. Even as a child he had found them slightly scary places, the nurses otherworldly, the doctors aloof, patrician and forbidding. He'd lost count of the amount of time he had spent in them as a boy, either sitting beside his mother as she recovered from the latest gin-fuelled kicking from his father or waiting for his father himself as he was stitched up after picking a fight with someone he shouldn't have or yet another drunken tumble into a gutter. And there were the countless professional visits he'd had to make over the years. The endless domestics that had ended in violence or even murder, the traffic accidents, the street brawls, the tavern knifings, glassings and bottlings. The fragile and already damaged lives that were just one bad night away from unshakeable tragedy and horror.

They were not places in which he ever felt he belonged. Not that he thought there were many who didn't feel the same way. These were the places where the membrane between life and death was at its thinnest and most fragile. He'd lived much of his adult life – and a significant chunk of his childhood – in the shadow of violence and blood, but, it wasn't that that bothered him so much as the fact that hospitals represented nothing so much to him as bad news. They were places where people's lives were changed, and seldom for the better.

Walking through starched, clinical wards with Illingworth, it was all being brought back home to him. He was walking past men in a similar state – and worse – to the one he had been in. You would have expected to hear more complaint, he thought. More cries of pain, more tears, more rage. But, no, the hospital had the aura of a church. Just hushed voices, prim, precise footsteps and purposeful, healing activity. Yet even so, above that, barely detectable was something Harry recognised all too well. The bitter note of human despair, of lives being stripped away until all that was left was the stark, elemental choice of life or death.

They'd come to see a man called Davy Royce. Royce was a retired copper, now well into his 60s, but who, like everyone else it seemed, had been pressed back into service due to manpower shortages and had ended up as a night-watchman at a quarry down in Essex. This, by rights, should be an easy job and certainly not one in which you'd expect to get knifed in the back. But this is exactly what had happened to Royce the night before last.

"There were two of them," said Royce. "At least. Might have been more, but I didn't see 'em." He was obviously in some pain, his torso trussed up tightly in bandages, and it showed in the clenched jaw, the eyes narrowed with constant discomfort. But there was also a spark of inextinguishable pride there too. He was a copper again, albeit briefly. Back in the midst of action, not pensioned off to the sidelines any more. Harry understood completely. The war had given Harry a second chance, a fluke opportunity to reclaim what Johnny Black had stolen from him. And he imagined, whether rightly or wrongly, that Royce must be experiencing something similar.

"And they took all your jelly?" asked Harry. "How much did they get?"

"A lot," said Royce grimly. "Enough to blow the Bank of England sky high if they took the fancy."

"And you think that's what they're likely to use it for?" asked Illingworth, who had accompanied Harry down on this trip. "Did you get that impression?"

Royce gave Illingworth a scowl that was not wholly out of physical pain. "I didn't get no impression whatsoever, son," he said. "But they were a professional mob, that's for sure. Made short work of the locks. Knew exactly what they were looking for. And I don't think they took all that jelly just for an interesting conversation piece, do you?"

Harry smiled. He liked Royce. He seemed exactly the same sort of truculent pain in the arse that no doubt most considered him to be. And a quick glance at Illingworth's sour expression seemed to bear this out.

Illingworth picked up the chart at the bottom of Royce's bed and scanned the hasty scrawls scribbled upon it. "Three separate stab wounds," he read. "All of which seemed to have missed any vital organs more by accident rather than design. By all accounts, you're lucky to still be here, Mr Royce. Doesn't sound like the work of a professional to me."

"No," admitted Royce grudgingly. "They made a right bloody mess of me and no mistake."

"Panic slashing probably," said Harry. "Maybe didn't expect you to come bursting in on them. Did you get a look at any of them?"

"Only the one in the supply hut. Youngish feller. Maybe 28 or 29. Thin as a lat. Pencil moustache. Spiv type, you know."

Harry and Illingworth exchanged a glance. Harry took out his wallet and produced a tattered newspaper cutting. It was from the Jersey newspaper's reporting of Johnny's trial and was accompanied by a photograph of a dishevelled-looking Johnny at the time of his arrest. Ignoring the knowing smirk on Illingworth's face, he passed the cutting to Royce.

"Is this him?" he asked.

Royce squinted at the creased, tattered clipping. "It's not the best picture, but, yes, I'd say that's him. Why, an old acquaintance, is he?"

"You have no idea, mate," said Illingworth. "You've just made Harry's bloody day."

Symons rubbed his eyes and exhaled wearily. He was suffering from a migraine. The same one he got every time Harry Blum walked into his office these days.

"And you're sure, absolutely sure that it's Johnny Black?" he asked, wearily.

"Positive ID from the night-watchman," said Harry.

"Who is still recovering from an almost-fatal attack, you said," mused Symons. "I wouldn't blame the bugger if he thought Adolf himself had shivved him. Are you sure he's entirely reliable?"

"I believe him," said Harry.

"Forgive me, Harry, but if someone waltzed in here and told you they'd just seen Johnny Black, Hitler and Genghis Khan sharing milk stout in the Midnight Bell you'd believe them. But that's by the by, what do you want me to do about it?"

"Take it to the Blacks. Kick down some doors. Drag Johnny to jail where he belongs."

"And what about that Pickering bloke? He made it quite clear that they're taking an interest in Black. Best thing we can do is hand over this information to them and let them get on with it."

"And Johnny Black disappears for good. You can't do that."

"Why? Because it means an end to your little vendetta? Because I tend to think that might be the best thing all round. Plus I'd finally have Johnny Black out of my hair for good."

"But it's not just about Black, is it? You've got Billie and her mob carving up rivals all over town. That's not going to go away. Kicking in a few doors. Making a few arrests. It's the best way to send them a message. Now's a good chance to do it. Plus it'll earn you some brownie points with the brass. And isn't it better if it's us who hands over Black to the spooks? Put that snotty herbert Pickering in his place?"

"And the honour of Harry Blum will be satisfied." Symons grimaced. Harry was playing him, he knew that, but at the same time, the bugger was making at least some sense. He hated when that happened.

"Alright, Harry," he sighed. "I'm going to look the other way. For the next 12 hours, anyway. What you get up to in that time is your business. But if Pickering comes sniffing around in that time, then you're on your own."

"Thanks, Guv. You won't regret it."

"I think I already am. Just make sure I'm smiling this time tomorrow, that's all."

SIX

IT WAS a moment Harry had dreamed of for years.

At just after 6am on a cold, crisp Thursday morning, a posse consisting of Harry Blum and another four or five members of the Heavy Mob, assisted by various enthusiastic uniformed volunteers emerged from a series of cars and thundered up the cold pavement towards the Black house.

The combined strength of half a dozen of the uniforms meant that the door gave way relatively quickly. The three 'minders', who for the first time were actually called upon to defend their employers, burst out into the street and began trading blows with the intruders. While Stott and a couple of the other Heavies pitched into the battle that took place halfway on the street and halfway on the threshold of the house, Harry and Illingworth led another team past the melee and into the hallway.

"Right," Harry barked. "You know what you're looking for. Tear this bloody place apart."

Billie came tearing down the stairs, still in her dressing-gown and her face white with fury. "What the hell is going on?" she demanded, storming in Harry's direction, her red-painted nails as tense and ready as talons. "What the bloody hell do you think you're doing?"

"Where is he, Billie?" Harry demanded.

"Where's who?"

"You know who," said Harry. "Your fucking no-mark husband. Where's little Johnny hiding then?"

"You've lost your bloody mind. Get out of my house."

"Sit down and shut up!" bellowed Harry. He thrust his face into hers, his features contorted with fury.

Billie looked angry enough to sink her nails into Harry's eyes and a couple of the uniforms squared up next to her, ready to drag her away if she got violent. Harry himself was unconcerned, although he noted that Jack had also appeared at the top of the stairs, ready to join the battle if required.

"I mean it," growled Harry. "Sit down and stay out the way or I'll fucking drag you out of here myself."

By now, Jack had sidled down the stairs and had taken Billie gently by the arm. "Come on, Billie," he said gently. "Let them have their fun." He gave Harry a look. "We'll have ours later."

"It's a disaster, Harry," said Illingworth gloomily. "A bloody disaster."

Harry lit a cigarette and stared at the curious neighbours on the other side of the street who had started gathering to see the commotion of the splintered front door and the now gradually dispersing policemen.

"We got nothing?" he asked. "Nothing at all?"

"Not so much as a dodgy bacon voucher. Let alone anything like Johnny Black sitting on top of a big pile of jelly and wrapped in a swastika. Symons is going to do his nut."

Harry was inclined to agree. If the Blacks made an official complaint, as Harry was sure they now would, then they would bring a lot of pain into Symons's world, and he would not be shy in passing that on. Not that Harry could really blame him.

"I suppose," said Harry, "that I better get in there and try to smooth things over."

The idea of Harry Blum managing to smooth anything over, even with people who didn't hate his guts, seemed highly unlikely to Illingworth, but he thought it wise not to say as much. Instead, he nodded, and ambled away to a group of uniforms who had less of the aura of the marked man about them.

Harry found Billie in the kitchen, busily restocking the cupboards and dressers that had been left ransacked and dishevelled by the raid, watched, as ever, by Jack from the opposite end of the room. Her face was white and her entire body taut with rage as she slowly reassembled her violated domain. Harry now wished they had conducted the raid with a little more tact and care. It might have possibly made things a bit easier now.

"Sorry about that," he said, in a tone that seemed to convey precisely the opposite, although he righted a kitchen chair in an act of pseudo-contrition. "Seems like our information wasn't quite as good as it might have been."

"I should say not," said Billie. "You haven't heard the last of this. If you think you can just waltz in here whenever you like—"

"It was an honest mistake, alright?" said Harry, unsurprised to find that he'd already reached the end of his patience. "What more do you want me to say?" He imagined that by tomorrow the Blacks would have reeled in one of their tame lawyers to kick up hell and there was bugger all he could do to change that.

Billie gave a contemptuous snort before turning back to her work.

"I notice you haven't asked what we were looking for," said Harry after a moment.

"I really couldn't care less, Harry," said Billie. "I just want you gone. You and the rest of your bloody flatfoots."

"We're leaving now," he said. "But I'm going to ask you one more time. Where's Johnny?"

Billie stopped what she was doing and turned around to look at them. "You really have lost your bloody marbles, haven't you? Johnny's still stuck in Jersey – as well you bloody know."

"Do I?" It now occurred to him that if he intrigued her enough then he might get more out of her than he would by bullying her. And it might just make her forget her anger at them almost ripping her house apart. "Because I think he's back."

Billie looked at him with conflict, intrigued and maybe even hopeful despite herself. "What on earth makes you think that?" She exchanged a glance with Jack who was looking blankly at Harry, impassively poker-faced.

"When was the last time you saw him?"

"You haven't answered my question."

"So answer mine. When was the last time you saw Johnny?"

She shrugged. "I don't know. The day he went to Jersey, I suppose."

Harry watched her closely, scanning for any sign of falsehood. "You sure about that?" But the question was superfluous. He was pretty certain that she had no idea what he was talking about.

"What about you, Jack?" he said, turning to Spinks. "When was the last time *you* saw your old mucker?"

Jack's face was impassive, a lot harder to read. "Jersey, I s'pose," he said. "Went down to see him just before he got sent down."

"And neither of you have seen him since?"

"Of course we bloody haven't," said Billie. "It might have escaped your notice, but the island that he's on is currently crawling with Jerries. Makes it a bit bloody difficult for him to get the boat home, doesn't it?"

"What's all this about, Harry?" asked Jack quietly.

"A quarry in Essex had its supplies hut raided night before last. Seems like somebody made off with a serious load of gelignite and detonators."

"And you think that it just had to be Johnny?" said Billie, her voice dripping with contempt. "He wasn't the only one who used jelly. And you know it."

"We got a positive description of Johnny at the scene."

"Yeah, I'm sure you did," she sneered. "You never did have too much trouble sorting that kind of thing out, did you, Harry?"

"They also carved up a night-watchman pretty badly," said Harry, his gaze falling on Jack.

Jack shrugged. "I know nothing whatsoever about it," he said.

"And for once, Jack, I'm inclined to believe you. But who would Johnny use as a knife-man if he didn't want to use you, that's what I'm wondering."

"You're talking rubbish, Harry," said Billie. "If Johnny was back,

Jack or I would bloody know about it. I'm his wife, for God's sake. And Jack's his best mate. I mean, why wouldn't he come to us?"

"I have some ideas about that," said Harry. "You see, I think the reason he didn't come to you is that he's got some new allegiances these days. If you know what I mean. I mean, if he's been stuck down in Jersey he will have been keeping some pretty questionable company."

"You're full of crap, Harry," said Billie. Her voice was full of distrust and venom, but he could see the doubt flickering behind her eyes.

"Sure about that are you?" he said. "Because the war is changing a lot of people. They're doing things they never thought they'd ever have to do. And I'm guessing that probably goes for scum like your Johnny too."

"Look, just get out, Harry, will you?" said Billie. "I'm really getting fed up of this bloody sad little obsession of yours. It's making me sick just to look at you."

"Gladly," said Harry, turning on his heel to walk out.

Jack watched him go. His expression was, as usual, completely unreadable, but behind his dark eyes several new – and surprising – ideas were starting to compete for his attention.

SEVEN

JACK stepped out of Sharkey's office, folding the sheet of paper containing the list of London properties into the inside pocket of his Crombie. The craggy Irishman had squinted at him through wreaths of Woodbine smoke, but Jack had determinedly not told the wily old brief anything. He didn't want to run the risk of anything getting back to Billie.

There was no guarantee that he would find Johnny at any of the places on the list, but it struck Jack as being his best option. He knew Johnny and if he was indeed planning some kind of job then he'd want some kind of bolthole, and there was no reason why it wouldn't be one of the places on this list. There was no reason why it would be either, of course, but Jack had a hunch that if he was denied the chance to use his old team on this job (whatever it was), he would at least want some safe or familiar ground from which to operate.

Now all he had to do was find him. A great many of the properties on the list could be struck off immediately as being too high profile or just by being unsuitable, such as the various clubs and businesses the Blacks had an interest in. But there was a significant number private properties, mostly used as safehouses or for storage of one kind or another, that Jack thought might fit the bill.

He struck lucky about halfway through his search. A former safehouse in a terraced row deep in the East End. It hadn't actually been used by the Blacks for several years now and had been all but forgotten, which was partially why Jack thought it might be somewhere Johnny might choose.

The place was actually in a pretty poor state. The street had been hit by some bombing and although all of the houses were still standing, most had been damaged in some way or another. Quite a few had lost their roofs and most were boarded up and obviously unoccupied. This again struck Jack as being something that might appeal to Johnny, meaning there would be less in the way of nosy neighbours to poke their nose in.

The house in question was in slightly better shape than many of those surrounding it but still had a few gaping holes in its roof, and the windows of its upper floor had been blown out completely.

Grateful for the uninhabited state of the street, Jack scurried across the road and picked his way through the small front plot, which was littered with rubble and old junk to peer through the grimy window. Looking through a gap in the filthy, sun-faded curtains, he found what he had been looking for. Johnny was curled up on an old sofa, reading a book and Leo was planted in an armchair, a dissatisfied scowl on his face, a bottle of beer in his hand.

It felt odd to see them. To be on the outside looking in at his oldest friend shacked up with someone who had once been one of their bitterest enemies. More than once, Jack had to fight back the urge to tap on the window, to go inside. But, no. He had lain awake all the previous night arguing with himself whether or not to go through with this and he couldn't turn back now.

He stepped away from the window, for fear of being spotted by the house's occupants and went to do what needed to be done.

Jack approached Harry in the Midnight Bell. He trailed the detective from the police station until he saw him popping into the Midnight Bell for an early evening pint and followed him inside. It was as good an opportunity as any.

"I might have known you'd be the type who had to drink alone," said Jack, taking the stool next to Harry's.

"I like the peace and quiet," replied Harry, not condescending to turn around to face Jack.

"Going to buy me a drink, Harry?"

"Not a chance, Spinks."

"Then let me buy you one." Jack raised a finger to attract the attention of the barman.

"I don't want to drink with you, Spinks," said Harry. "I just want to put you behind bars."

"Not much chance of that. Or at least not tonight at any rate." Jack ordered half a mild and told the barman to get Harry another of whatever he was drinking. Harry did not object.

"So," said Harry, as he supped his fresh pint. "To what do I owe this singular pleasure?"

"Did you get your bollocks handed to you over that thing at the house?" asked Jack, unable to suppress a slight smile. "Is that why you're being so sore?"

"Is that why you're here, Jack?" asked Harry. "Spot of gloating? Well, hate to disappoint you, but all we did was turn over a house full of known criminals. No one is going to much care if you feel hard done by. There's a war on and people have got other things to worry about."

"Yeah, but I bet you still got your knuckles rapped for it."

"Go away, Spinks. I'm asking nicely."

"Anyway," continued Jack. "That's not why I'm here. I actually think I might be able to help you out."

"Why do I find that so very hard to believe?"

"All that stuff you said, about Johnny being a Nazi."

"Did I really say that?" asked Harry. "Can't remember." He was aware of the dim view that spook Pickering would take if he thought that he'd been flapping his gums to the likes of the Blacks which is why he'd been very cagy about what he actually did say. Not that it would have mattered, given the level of popularity he was enjoying with the brass at the moment.

"Do you really believe that?" asked Jack.

"You're meant to be his best mate. Do you believe it?"

Jack was silent for a moment. He couldn't say for sure that Johnny couldn't be a Nazi because he honestly didn't know. That has always been the trouble with Johnny. You could never tell with him. He'd say one thing one day, and the complete opposite the next. The question was, thought Jack, what was he going to do now? How was he going to play this?

"Johnny is back," he said. "I've seen him."

Harry stared at him. "Is that right?" he said eventually. "And when was this?"

"Few weeks ago. A month maybe."

"And you didn't mention this before because?"

"Billie doesn't know. Nobody does. And I'd like to keep it that way."

Harry continued to look at Jack with amusement. "Just what are you up to here, Spinks?"

"Tell me, Harry. Just what is Johnny worth to you?"

"And just what's that supposed to mean?"

"Just what I say. What's Johnny worth to you? For you to get your hands on him, I mean?"

Harry raised an eyebrow. "Are you making me some kind of an offer here, Jacky-Boy?"

"Might be," said Jack.

"Now, tell me, why would you want to do something like that?"

Jack wanted to get up and walk out, to forget the whole thing. But it was too late for that. He'd come this far. "What's it worth to you?" he repeated.

Harry shrugged. "Depends. What did you have in mind?"

Jack didn't think he'd ever hated Harry more than he did at that moment. His scars caught the low light of the pub, giving him the appearance of a sneering death's head. For the briefest moment, he thought about the cat-stabber in his coat pocket. Maybe that would be simpler, he thought. Just stick Harry right here and now and then walk out and forget about all this craziness.

"I want you to back off," he said. "I want you to leave me and Billie be. That's the deal."

Harry almost laughed in his face. "You and Billie," he repeated. "So, *that's* what all this is about. Well, I can't say I blame you, I suppose. She's quite the looker." He gave another wry chuckle. "Jack, I'd never have thought it of you. To be honest, I was beginning to think you were inclined in another direction entirely. And what about Billie? Does she know that you're here now trying to stitch up her old man?"

"She doesn't know a damn thing about it," said Jack. "And she never will. That's also part of the deal."

Harry laughed again and took another sip of his pint. "Alright, Jack," he said. "I'll tell you what. If I get Johnny – and only if I do – then alright, I'll wipe the slate clean as far as the Blacks go. But that's all, mind. If you get up to your old tricks in the future, which I've no doubt you will, I'll still come down on you like a ton of bloody bricks. And you stop all this bloody running around carving up the opposition. And I mean immediately."

"A truce," said Jack. "Is that it? Is that all you're going to offer me here?"

"Best you're going to get. Take it or leave it. You get to walk away, sod off with your one true love into the bleeding sunset. But only if you deliver Johnny."

Jack nodded. "Alright."

He took a piece of paper from the pocket of his Crombie and slid it along the bar discreetly, allowing it to rest just next to Harry's pint.

"What's this?"

"It's what you've been looking for. It's where you'll find Johnny, if you're quick."

Harry stared at the paper but did not pick it up. "Why should I believe a bloody word of this?"

"Because you've got nothing to lose. Not really."

Harry reached for the paper but Jack, quick as ever, placed has hand over it.

"Do we have a deal?"

Harry sneered at him again. "Look at you, Jacky-Boy. Never seen you so rattled. I suppose that's what love does to a man. Yes, we've got a deal. If Johnny's there and if I get the cuffs on him."

Jack lifted his hand and Harry took the paper, slipping it into his own pocket without looking at it. He knew the drill enough not to call attention to when an informant has coughed up the goods, not when there still might be prying eyes around.

"You know, Jack, if this pans out, I'm sure I could find you a little something from my snout fund."

Jack bristled, as Harry had hoped he would. "I don't want your bloody money. I just want you to leave us alone. Both of us."

Harry drained his pint and got off his barstool. "I'll see what we can do." He took a note from his wallet and placed it on the bar. "Thanks for the drink. Have another one on me. Oh, and give my best to Billie, won't you?"

He walked out the pub, leaving Jack nursing his drink and letting the cold tendrils of guilt and dread spreading through his gut take hold.

EIGHT

"THIS is driving me bloody crazy," spat Leo.

You're not the only one, mate, thought Johnny as he watched the Italian pace the length of what had once been the lounge before the Luftwaffe had knocked seven shades of hell out of the place. Leo's footfalls raised tiny puffs of plaster dust and the whole house constantly creaked and groaned around them like an ancient ship on unforgiving seas. Only the front end of the ground floor of the house was remotely inhabitable and they seemed to live with the constant risk of the whole thing coming down on top of them at any moment.

Since the quarry job, Johnny had decided that they should lay low for a bit before carrying on. He wanted to make sure that the knifing of the night-watchman hadn't stirred things up too much, but he needed a safe house in order to do that. Racking his memory, he had come up with this place, hoping that its sorry state would mean that no one would come sticking their nose in where it wasn't wanted. And then he'd contacted Nantes, telling them that everything was in place and that he was just waiting for the best opportunity to go ahead.

"And when is that going to be?" Leo had asked him.

Johnny sighed and put aside the book he'd been trying and failing to read. How could anyone manage to concentrate with a stir-crazy Eye-tie pacing all around them?

"I told you," he said, "when things have died down again."

He got off the ancient, mouldering sofa from which he'd hardly moved for the last few days and reached for his jacket.

"Now where are you going?" demanded Leo.

Johnny stifled the urge to punch the Italian in the face and said, "Going to get us another bottle. I'm going to need it if I'm up to put up with your constant bloody whinging."

Leo didn't even bother to look offended. The feeling was quite obviously mutual. Not for the first time, Johnny considered the merits of just paying Leo off right now but, as usual, rejected it. As much as he hated to admit it, he needed him. For the time being at least, he was stuck with him.

Johnny grabbed his hat and began padding along the darkened, mouldy hallway and pulled away the heavy plank that was the only thing holding the front door in place. The fresh night air was shockingly cold on his skin for a moment and made his breath feel cold and fresh. How long had it been since he'd last stepped out from the fetid air of the decaying, half-destroyed house? Too long.

The feeling that something was wrong hit him almost immediately. It was nothing obvious. The street before him was empty and dark, with the misty wall of rainy fog adding to the gloom. Was that a figure just lurking in the darkness at the corner? And was there maybe something familiar about them? He couldn't be sure but something was definitely wrong. There was an unmistakable feeling of dread rising within him with every passing moment.

He retreated back inside the house and replaced the plank against the door before hurrying back along the hallway to the lounge.

"That was quick," said Leo, who had taken up residence in Johnny's usual spot on the sofa. "What? What's going on," he added, alarm beginning to edge into his voice as he saw Johnny scamper to the window and peer out through the moth-eaten curtains.

"Something's up," muttered Johnny. "I think we're being watched."

"You're imagining things," said Leo, but there was worry in his voice.

"Maybe," said Johnny, continuing to peer out into the street. He had been right about the figure at the corner. It had now stepped forward further into the light and he could now recognise it as one of the minor Heavies. What was his name again? Illington? Illingworth? Something like that. And emerging from the darkness behind him, like some lumbering ogre from his nightmares, was Harry Blum. There were more of them behind Harry, now scuttling across the road towards the house. It was a raid.

"Move!" cried Johnny, turning from the window. "Fucking move."

Leo leaped from the sofa while Johnny grabbed the knapsack that contained their purloined jelly and various other documents connected to the op. Already he could hear the angry shouts and the determined thuds as the Heavies tried to kick in at the front door so that way wasn't an option. He turned in the hallway towards the back of the house. This was less than safe and halfway blocked by rubble and fallen beams, but there was no choice. The commotion at the front door had already unsettled fine clouds of dust from the ceiling and the growling voices of the Heavies seemed louder now. They were almost in.

Johnny turned abruptly, almost bumping into Leo who was hard on his heels. He headbutted the Italian violently, sending him staggering back down the hall, clutching his now-broken nose. Leo swore with muffled outrage, but before he'd managed to get a chance to recover, Johnny piled into him with three or four savage kicks which left Leo curled up defensively on the grimy floor. Johnny turned and fled up the hall, aware that the Heavies had by now managed to dislodge the plank and were pouring into the house. He had hoped that Leo's prostrate figure would provide another momentary obstacle and sure enough they piled on top of him, prompting further cries of fear and alarm from the Italian.

Johnny hurried through what was previously the kitchen, squeezing through a gap in the fallen slab of wood and masonry that had once been the floor of the upstairs bedroom. He kicked away the plank that had been securing the back door and burst through, hauling himself immediately over the wall of the rubble-strewn back yard and into the safety of the night.

NINE

"FOR GOD'S sake, how the hell could he have got away?"

Illingworth shrugged. "Must have just missed him. He's a slippery little sod, ain't he?"

Harry scowled, his face still black with anger and stepped further into the wrecked lounge where, until very recently, Johnny Black and Leo Danelli had been bunked up. It was a miserable hole of a place, thought Harry, trying to take a glimmer of comfort at the straitened conditions Johnny had now found himself.

"There's a radio set and a book of Jerry codes in the backroom," offered Illingworth. "Look on the bright side, Harry. It proves you were right, don't it?"

Cold comfort, thought Harry. He could already feel that creep Pickering on his heels, just waiting to jump in and take over. And he had no doubt that Symons was going to be more than happy to let him. He'd blown his chance.

Something caught his eye, hiding just under the sideboard at one end of the room. He bent over, ignoring the discomfort it caused to his leg and picked it up between his thumb and forefinger.

"What's that you've got?" asked Illingworth.

Harry held it up. It was a narrow strip of off-white paper that had once been attached as a loop but which had now been torn apart. Printed upon it in bold, Gothic lettering was the world *REICHSBANK*. It was clearly a money band, once holding together a wad of banknotes.

"Well, that kind of settles it, don't it?" said Illingworth. "So, what do you want to do now?"

"Evening, Jack."

Genuine alarm flitted behind Jack's normally cool, inexpressive features when he opened the front door to see Harry Blum standing there, a grim smile upon his face.

"Jesus, what the hell is this?" he hissed, aware of the three minders looking curiously up at his back.

"Don't worry. I'm here in peace. Thought you might be able to help us with our enquiries like."

Jack cast a nervous look over his shoulder. "Do you seriously think that I'm going to let you across the door of this house after what happened last time?" he asked.

"Yes, Jack," said Harry, levelly. "Yes, I do."

Jack cursed and grabbed the detective by the arm, ushering him into the house and slamming the door behind him. He ignored the curious looks from the minders and all but shoved Harry into the first room by the front door, one of the bedrooms for the live-in muscle.

"What the hell do you think you're doing?" said Jack, as soon as the door was shut.

"We lost him," said Harry. "Bastard must have seen us coming and did a runner. Slippery little shit your pal Johnny."

"Well, that's not my bloody problem, is it?"

"Yes, Jack, actually, I'd say it is, wouldn't you?"

For the first time in what felt like years, Jack could feel panic rising within him. He should have known better than to get involved with Harry Blum like this. The bastard was trouble, always had been. "Look, I kept up my side of the deal. If you can't get your bloody act together—"

"So, where would he go?" Harry cut in. "You want me to help you, so help me. Where would he hide out?"

Jack shook his head. "I don't know. I gave you everything I had. If you've messed that up, then I can't help you. And for you to come here like this—"

"Look, Jack," said Harry. "You started this and now it's up to you to finish it. You know it's not safe for you otherwise. If Black shows up here..." He paused, letting the threat hang in the air. "You want me out of your hair for good?" he went on. "Then you know what you've got to do."

"Except I don't know anything, do I? He could be bloody anywhere now, thanks to you."

"What about his missus?" asked Harry, nodding in the direction of the door. "Think she might know something?"

"Now wait a minute," said Jack, his panic levels rising again. "This is bullshit, Harry—"

"Don't worry," said Harry, clapping Jack on the back with exaggerated matey-ness. "I'm not going to drop you in it, am I? Not now we're all friends together."

Billie had been waiting for them ever since Jack had led Harry through the front door. In a surprisingly short time, she had come to be able to recognise Harry Blum's rumbling baritone and she could hear their low voices during their conference in the other room. And it filled her with dread. She was irked enough that Harry had been let back into the house, but what the hell was this scuttling off in private?

Her suspicion was plain to see the minute they walked through the parlour door and Jack did his best to give her a reassuring smile as he stepped round the table. Billie ignored him, keeping her face set and grim, not even looking in his direction.

"It's Harry," he said.

"Yeah, I can see that. The question is what the hell is he doing here? And what are the two of you playing at skulking off on your own back there?"

"Now, you mustn't blame Jack," said Harry, a sadistic smile on his face. "He's got your interests at heart here. Trying to protect you, he is."

"Is that right?" Billie looked from Harry face to Jack's, not particularly liking the look of shifty guilt she saw in the latter. "Jack, just what the hell is going on here?"

"It's about your Johnny," Harry went on.

"Oh, Christ, not this again."

"He's back," Harry went on. "We know that for a fact now. Just like we know for sure he's working for the Nazis."

"You're off your rocker."

"We got a tip off," said Harry, deliberately not looking in Jack's direction. "We found this." He put the torn paper strip down on the table in front of her. "Do you know what it is?"

"Why don't you tell me, Harry?" she said, icily.

"It's a money band, the kind that holds wads of banknotes together. I'm sure you've seen them before. Only this one is in German, meaning it probably came from a bank in Berlin. Probably used to hold Johnny's pay together."

"If you say so, Harry. But isn't that, what do they call it, circumstantial evidence?"

"We also found radio equipment, German codebooks, the works, everything your Nazi spy-about-town could possibly need."

"But you didn't find Johnny?"

"No, he managed to slip by us. But we did find Leo Danelli. And he positively puts your Johnny right in the middle of all this."

"Leo Danelli," repeated Billie with contempt. "And why should I believe anything that no-mark has to say? We've been carving up the Danellis since Leo was in short trousers. And there's no way in hell Johnny would have anything to do with him."

"It's true, Billie," interrupted Jack softly. "He is back."

She turned to look at Jack. "You've seen him?"

"Yeah."

"When?"

"Not that long ago. He collared me across the road there."

"And why didn't you say anything?"

"He told me not to. Said he had some work to sort out before he came back. Wouldn't say what it was."

"And you think what he," she nodded at Harry, "is saying is the truth? That he's working for the Nazis?"

Jack shook his head. "I don't know, Billie, pet. But I'm starting to think it could be."

"No way," she said. "No bloody way in hell is my Johnny a Nazi."

"Listen to me," urged Harry, leaning forward on the table towards Billie. "I don't like you. Either of you. Or any part of your crooked outfit. Any more than any of you have got any love for me. But I will say this for you, you usually kept it among yourselves. You only carved each other up – or us on occasion – as a rule. You left the ordinary folk on the street out of it if you could. Well, Johnny's crossed that line now. He's thrown in his lot with the ones who've declared war on the whole bloody lot of us. The ones who don't care who they kill or who gets hurt. And if you let him do that then you're just as much of a traitor as he is."

"I'm telling you," said Billie, "he would never do that."

"Then help me find him. Give him the chance to tell his side of it."

"Yeah, you'd like that, wouldn't you? Getting him in a cell finally so you can pay him back for what he served up to you. And for me to be the one that helped you do it. Well, you can bloody forget it, Harry Blum. There's no way in hell that's going to happen. Not now. Not ever."

"This isn't about me and Johnny," said Harry. "Not anymore."

"Oh, yes it is, Harry. It's never been about anything else. Now, I'm getting bloody tired of saying this but get out of my house. And don't come back."

Harry stared at her for a moment, but this time there was no anger there, just frustration and a sense of resigned defeat. He didn't say anything more but simply turned and walked out.

Jack walked from his place behind Billie and closed the parlour door. Billie said nothing, deep in thought. Eventually she said softly, "What the hell are you playing at, Jack?"

Jack thought of the dozen little speeches that he'd replayed constantly in his head and that now would be the time to make but instead he just shook his head sadly. "I don't know. What I've always done, I suppose. Just trying to make sure things work out the way they should."

She nodded but didn't say anything more. She wasn't even looking at him now.

"You need anything?"
"No, Jack. I don't need anything at all."
He turned and left the parlour.

TEN

IT WAS not often these days that Billie left the house. Her life ran on regular tracks from her bedroom to her parlour and there was seldom any deviation from this settled routine. She had the house to run, mouths to feed and business to transact, and she found that this all was done most efficiently from her little nest at the back of the house. Anything in the outside world that required taking care of she could leave to Jack or one of the others. And she really didn't mind. She'd had her days of gallivanting about, of the clubs and pubs and being out to all hours. Her world might have become a lot smaller, but she was perfectly happy for it to have transformed as such.

Now, however, she had to get out. It was the last place she wanted to be, at least for a while. The house now held memories of both Johnny and Jack and neither man, it seemed, was entirely what she had thought them to be. She wanted to be away from the influence of both of them, needed neutral ground where she could be free to figure out this whole bloody mess for herself.

And so she walked. She walked for hours, without any real

destination or any real goal. As night fell, it got colder but she didn't care. She already felt much colder on the inside than anything this freezing evening could muster. She couldn't remember feeling this alone in her life.

She couldn't get Harry's words out of her head. Was Johnny a Nazi? She couldn't believe that. She really couldn't. But at the same time, she knew that Johnny was liable to leap off the deep end and end up needing someone to fish him out. In the old days that had usually been Jack. But not this time, it seemed. He'd gone out on his own, turned his back on them and it didn't take an idiot to figure out the reason why.

She realised that she had begun moving in a certain direction almost without conscious intention and the knowledge of it made her smile to herself. There was one place that he might yet go, she thought to herself. One place that she doubted even Jack would have thought to look. And so she let herself be led there, feeling almost as if part of her was homing in on Johnny's 'signal' somehow.

Her destination was a small garage tucked away in an old warehouse district close to the docks. Like everywhere, the streets around it had seen some bombing, but the buildings still looked more or less intact. She slipped around to the grimy alleys behind the street, ignoring the slightly threatening figures shuffling in the darkness and felt her way to the back door of the garage.

It was locked, of course, but she was already fumbling in the bottom of her bag for her purse. She'd carried this key around for years, more for sentimentality than anything, a talisman of the bond between Johnny and herself, rather than any real expectation that she would ever have to use it. It glinted in the darkness, still as shiny as the day Johnny had had it cut for her. She slipped it into the lock and opened the door carefully.

The door opened into a narrow, pitch-black corridor that was cluttered with broken ladders, discarded paint tins, rusting toolboxes and other rubbish. She picked her way along it, cursing to herself more than once as she kicked something over. As she got closer to the inner door that led to the garage, she saw a glint of light and the low sound of a gramophone playing told her that her instincts had been right.

The garage was dominated by the bulky but imposing shape of the Bentley. The canvas that had normally covered it had been pulled back and its back door was open. An old gramophone had been set up on upturned crate in one corner of the garage, a small pile of records next to it, and was now playing softly.

Her arrival had triggered a flurry of panicked shuffling from the back seat and a pair of boots emerged from the car, followed by the rest of a lithe, male form, as Johnny slid in alarm from his repose in the back of the Bentley.

The mere sight of him took her breath away for a moment and for what seemed like the longest time, they just stood and stared at each other. Johnny dug his hands into the pockets of the oily boiler-suit he was wearing and gave her his best roguish grin. Billie herself wanted to laugh, but she was as yet unable to muster up any kind of control over herself. Seeing Johnny again after all this time seemed to have left her unusually numb.

"Alright, Bil?" he said eventually.

"Johnny," she said, a smile spreading across her lips. The whole thing felt surreal. How long was it since they'd last seen each other? And how much had changed in the interim? Lifetimes. Several lifetimes.

Billie was struck by just how aloof and awkward they were being with each other. She wanted to walk over to him and kiss him right there and then, but it somehow didn't seem quite right. It was still too soon. And it was unutterably strange. They were all so different to who they had been before. They all seemed to be living in different worlds to each other, and none of them resembled the one she had known before the war.

"How did you find me?" asked Johnny, finally.

"Stands to reason, doesn't it?" she said, stepping further into the garage now and closer towards him. "Where else would you go to lick your wounds?"

Johnny smiled. He ran his hand along the back of the car. "I love this old bird," he said. "I always have. Remember that first time I came to pick you up in her?"

Billie smiled. "Yeah, I do. You showed up outside my place with this thing and said 'coming out for a spin'? 'Don't mind if I do,' I said. 'Where are you taking me'? 'Anywhere you like,' you said. 'I'll take you to the Moon if you like.'"

"That's right," said Johnny, with a grin. "I seem to remember we only ended up as far as Brighton though."

Billie laughed. "Brighton. The Moon. What's the difference?"

"It's not too late," he said, taking a step forward and tentatively taking his wife in his arms. "I could still take you to the Moon. If you like."

"No, Johnny," said Billie, a note of melancholy in her voice. "I don't think the Moon's an option. At least, not right now."

Johnny held Billie close. It was not a time for kisses. There was still too much sadness, too much confusion, between them for that, but they held each other, clinging to each other tightly. The years of separation, and the doubt and fear they had brought with them, began to melt away and for the moment that was enough. Eventually, they released their hold, relaxing in each other's arms rather than gripping each other with palpable, rigid, anxiety.

Finally Billie disentangled herself from him and took a step backward. Her face hardened into seriousness. "What's going on, Johnny?" she said. "Is it true what they're saying about you?"

Johnny grinned. "I don't know. What is it they're saying about me?"

"That you've turned Nazi. That's what Harry Blum is saying anyway."

"Oh well, if Harry Blum's saying it then it must be true, mustn't it?"

"I'm serious, Johnny. Tell me what's going on."

"It's not as easy as that, Bil," he said, pacing the garage himself now. "It's complicated. It's all got terribly complicated."

"Not really, Johnny. It's actually quite simple. Are you working for the Nazis or not?"

"Bil," he began evasively. "Listen—"

"No, Johnny, *you* listen. You've got to stop this. You've got to get out of this right now."

"I can't, pet. I've got..." He laughed bitterly. "I've got responsibilities."

"To who? The bloody Führer? Don't make me laugh."

She stepped further away, turning her back on him for a moment.

He could see how angry she was. He would have expected this sense of moral outrage in Jack maybe, but in Billie it seemed to be something entirely new. Maybe she and Jack had more in common than he thought. Perhaps more than even Billie herself realised.

She turned back to him. Her face was scowling, serious. "You always used to say that it doesn't matter what we do just so long as the civilians don't get hurt. Do you remember? We know what we're in for but they don't, that's what you used to say. Harry Blum reminded me of that today. And he was right. How many civilians are going to get hurt now, Johnny? Hundreds? Thousands?"

"No one's going to get hurt, Bil," he said, genuine hurt in his voice.

"Aren't they?" She glanced down at the factory plans that were now lying on the backseat of the Bentley. She caught sight of the scrawl of a wing, a propeller. "What is it? Aeroplanes? The way I see it, the fewer planes we've got, the more chance the Luftwaffe has of getting its bombs through. And I've seen what those bombs do, Johnny. And it ain't pretty."

"You don't understand, Bil."

She put her hand on his face, touched by the clear torment she saw there. This kind of conflict, of doubt, was almost entirely alien to Johnny and it pained her to see it.

"Then *tell* me," she said. "Make me understand."

He looked at her. There was still something there, thought Billie. Something inside, eating away at him. But it was coming to the surface now. He was in the process of letting her draw it out of him. He was going to let her give him some peace. She just had to wait for it, that's all.

And then the screeching of tyres. Several cars from the sound of it. Followed by the barking of male, officious voices. And at least one of them was aggravatingly familiar to both of them. It was a voice that Billie had let harangue her only a few hours previously.

Johnny looked at his wife with alarm and hurt. "Jesus, Billie," he said. "Tell me you didn't."

"Of course not," she said, vehemently. "They must have followed me." She cursed inwardly, furious at herself for not being more careful. Of course they would have been tailing her. Harry fucking Blum, she seethed to herself. God, how she despised him.

Johnny was already moving, scooping up the plans from the garage floor and slinging the knapsack that still contained the jelly and the detonators over his shoulder. The sounds of the coppers outside were getting closer and this garage was severely limited in its escape routes.

"Johnny, wait!" Billie cried after his retreating back as he made for the back door of the garage. The last thing she wanted was for him to be caught, but she was also afraid that if she lost sight of him now then he might disappear forever.

But Harry was already framed in the doorway, blocking Johnny's path, a look of the most intense grim satisfaction on his face. Johnny tried to skid to a halt in the face of the clearly immovable form in front of him.

The punch, when it came, was dramatic, with years of pent-up hate, resentment and anger behind it. There was the sound of breaking bones, splintering teeth and hard bone upon bone as Johnny was sent flying back into the garage, bouncing off the back of the Bentley and skidding along the floor to land almost at Billie's feet.

"Guess what, Johnny?" said Harry, his voice thick with satisfaction. "You're bloody nicked."

ELEVEN

THE ride back to the station was conducted in absolute silence. Harry sat in the front seat, enveloped in quiet satisfaction, while Illingworth drove them through the blacked-out streets. In the back seat, Billie administered to the handcuffed Johnny's busted nose and bleeding lips.

"Alright, Mr Pickering?" Johnny managed to say through his bloodied handkerchief and mangled mouth. "Fancy meeting you here!"

Harry's spirits sank in what seemed to be an almost exact inverse to Johnny's rising ones as they approached the station to be faced with Symons and Pickering waiting sombrely outside for them. Harry glared at Symons.

"You had to go call them in, didn't you?" he said bitterly.

"Yes, Harry, I did," said Symons. "This is way beyond our ken now. And you know it."

"I'm afraid I have to agree," said Pickering. "Do you realise just how much work you've endangered here?"

"Blimey, Harry," lisped Johnny, his voice was muffled through his busted mouth but the tone of glee was unmistakeable. "Sounds like you're in the shit here."

"Take him inside and get him cleaned up," said Pickering to Illingworth. With a final worried glance at Harry, Illingworth led Johnny and Billie into the station.

"Now, Mr Blum," said Pickering, the irritation quite palpable in his voice. "Perhaps you'd also step inside and we can sort this whole bloody mess out."

"You don't need to bother, I know where this is going," said Harry, as soon as the door to Symons's office was firmly closed. "You want to debrief Black, find out what he knows about the Jerries. I understand that, but can't it wait until we've charged him at least?"

"Charged him?" said Pickering, raising his eyebrows, his tone halfway between exasperation and contempt. "I'm afraid there's no question of charging him. And our ambitions for him are bit loftier than a few debriefings."

"I might have guessed as much," said Harry. "You want to use him yourself. Well, I'm telling you—"

"Harry!" broke in Symons sharply. "Will you just shut the dickens up and let the man talk?"

"Thank you. I'm afraid, Mr Blum, that we're way ahead of you on this one. The debriefings and interrogations have already taken place. We've been working with Black for quite some time now. Shortly after he arrived back in England, in fact. And it was Black who first came to us actually."

"But I don't understand," said Harry. "The aeroplane factory—"

"Is a legitimate German target and thanks to Black we know all about it. And the sabotage attempt upon it will go ahead. With certain modifications. We've had Black under discreet surveillance for weeks now and he's been operating more or less with our knowledge and our blessing."

"And what about Royce, the night-watchman? Black damn near nearly killed him. Was that done with your blessing too?"

Pickering was unruffled by the accusation. "I'll admit that we might have given Black more latitude than was strictly sensible. Believe me, I was all for keeping a much tighter rein on the whole operation. But it was generally considered that Black was a special case and that we would have to make certain allowances for his, ah, independent spirit. That might have been a mistake, I concur. But it's done now and everything has more or less worked out satisfactorily."

"Tell that to Royce. And what about Leo Danelli?"

"Why, he'll stand trial, of course. He is, after all, a petty thug and a suspect alien to boot. But I'm sure with the correct inducement he'll agree to amend his testimony to our ends. Yes, I think it's all going to work out very well."

"Especially for Johnny bloody Black," said Harry, unable to keep the bitterness out of his voice. "Sounds like you've got it all figured out just to your liking. Too bad little things like justice don't seem to figure in it."

"My dear Mr Blum," said Pickering. "I really don't know what you're complaining about. You wanted to charge someone and here we are offering you a very likely candidate on a plate. It was always the intention to hand Danelli over to you fellows anyway. We need the trial and the newspaper reports to lend the whole thing some credence. For the Abwehr's benefit, you see."

"But I already have Leo," said Harry. "And Johnny too for that matter. Do you really expect me to just let you walk out of here with him?"

"Actually, I do. Look, I realise that you have something of a vendetta going on where Black is concerned, but frankly I couldn't care less about it. Black is leaving here with me today and that's the end of it. If it wasn't for the fact that your blundering around nearly destroyed the entire operation I wouldn't be condescending to having this conversation with you now. I urge you, for your own good, not to cause any further difficulties."

"Harry," said Symons firmly, but not without understanding. "Let it go. Although, I have to say, Mr Pickering, things would have gone a whole lot easier if you'd actually let us in on what you were up to."

"Need-to-know basis and all that," said Pickering smoothly. "The police force, if you'll forgive me, is one big bureaucracy. The more of a paper trail we leave, the easier it is for the whole operation to be compromised. Sure you understand."

"All the same," insisted Symons, "it's an awful lot of bother to go to, isn't it? Why go through all this palaver?"

"Because Black is not the only Nazi agent operating in this country and they will no doubt have been keeping a watch on him. He's put us onto at least one other agent so far. The Germans aren't stupid and for us to get them to sufficiently trust Black they have to be absolutely satisfied that he's their man. They'll be scrutinising every inch of this operation and there's no part of it that we can afford not to have the utter ring of truth about it."

"You can't trust Black," said Harry. "How can you be sure that he's not playing you the same way he's playing the Nazis?"

"I'm in Intelligence, Mr Blum," said Pickering, with a wry smile. "I don't trust anyone. But I do know that there's more to be gained from having Black operating in the heart of the Abwehr and the off-chance of some further use from him later on, rather than having him languishing uselessly in some prison here. Even if he does end up betraying us later."

Harry shook his head, his anger already dissipating into disbelief. "You're making a mistake."

"Possibly," agreed Pickering. "But it's one we have no choice but to go ahead and make. And consider this, at the moment you're more guilty of aiding the enemy with all this floundering about than Black is. From a certain point of view, it is *you* who is the traitor here, not him. So, I suggest you do as your superior says, sit back and stop being such a bloody idiot about the whole thing. Because I can promise you that there are others, in my department and elsewhere, who would not be quite as forgiving as I about this entire situation."

Harry said nothing but stared out of the window of Symons's office, where Johnny was being uncuffed and handed a coat.

"You're making a mistake," Harry said again, almost to himself.

Despite its bruised and bloodied condition, Johnny's face was again wearing the insufferable grin that Harry could remember from way back. It was the same look Johnny had had on his face when he had approached him in that alley back in 1936.

He turned from the window in disgust as Johnny put his arm around Billie and gave her a kiss and Harry heard the familiar, triumphant guffaw.

He's won, he thought. Johnny Black had beaten him once again.

TWELVE

JOHNNY lay in his bed listening to the sounds of the morning gently unfolding outside the blacked-out window. Billie was still asleep in his arms but he himself had been awake for hours, lying in the dark listening to the night fade away. It had been a surprisingly quiet one, with no bombs, no sirens. Just the quiet fear of a city in an uneasy, suspicious sleep.

He had finally got to spend a few weeks back at home with Billie before being sent back to his hopefully unsuspecting German paymasters. It had certainly been blissful and part of him couldn't imagine that he'd managed to get home after what had become well over a year of trial and effort. He would lie on his bed, or wander the house and everything seemed familiar, comforting, and he was delighted to be back home. But it wasn't the same somehow. And while he and Billie seemed to fall back into their old routines relatively quickly, there was still something wrong, something indefinable but at the same time definitely discernible, like hearing a previously loved song being played on a slightly out-of-tune instrument.

That things had changed at home became evident to him almost immediately. For one thing, Jack wouldn't seem to give him the time of day anymore. In fact, he would barely even look him in the eye and seldom joined them for meals anymore, preferring to skulk away in his attic for most of the time. At first, Johnny had tried to engage with him, offered to take him out for a drink, revisit their old haunts, but to no avail. Johnny didn't press the matter further than that. His time was limited, after all, and he wanted to spend as much of it with Billie as he could. But it unsettled him all the same, although he could guess what probably lay at the back of it.

He felt Billie stir in his arms.

"Morning," she said, her voice still full of sleep.

"Good morning. Sleep alright?"

"Yeah. Probably for the last time in god knows how long though."

Johnny didn't answer. This was a moment that had been waiting to haunt them ever since Pickering had given him these few weeks grace before sending him back out into the field. Both he and Billie had been doing their best to avoid it but now they could no longer do so. Reality had come crashing back into their lives.

"Do you really have to go?" she said, her thoughts once again echoing his own. With those words, he felt that they'd invited the real world back into their lives to smash them both to hell again. The holiday was over.

"You know I do."

"I don't want you to go."

"I know you don't," he said. "Neither do I." This was true. He would have given anything to remain in that room with her, even for just one day longer. And not so long ago he would have done just that, done what the hell he wanted to and damn the consequences, but that time was long past. He was going to go. Indeed, part of him was already gone, already on that lonely and dangerous road back to Berlin or wherever they were going to send him. He knew it and so did Billie.

She sat up and looked at him. "Then why don't you stay?"

"Because Pickering would probably have me arrested as a German spy for starters. Believe me, he might look like butter wouldn't melt, but you'll never meet a worse son of a bitch." This was also true. He thought back to the six days he'd spent in the MI6 internment camp when he'd first given himself up on his arrival back in England. Where the Germans had attempted to win him round with jovial camaraderie and the promise of great financial rewards, the British had used nothing more than hostility and threats and the prospect of the firing squad. So much so that he was still unsure if he wasn't doing entirely the wrong thing by throwing his lot in with them.

"Besides," he went on. "I have to go back. I just do."

"But why?"

"There's a feller I met in Jersey. Name of Albie. Nice bloke, you'd like him. Anyway, he's still stuck over there in a prison in Paris. They'll kill him if I don't go back. I owe it to him to go over there and get him out. And if this thing has gone according to plan then I should have earned enough Brownie points with them that I'll be able to do just that."

"And if you haven't? What if they figure out exactly what you're up to? What if they just turn around and shoot you?"

Johnny shook his head. "I don't think they will. Besides, I've got to try. I can't leave the poor bugger to swing in the wind. Not when it's my fault that he is where he is."

"Christ," she murmured. "They're bastards."

"Yeah, they are." But when he thought about it, it wasn't as simple as that. Weiler and Krause and a lot of the other guys, yeah, they were wearing the swastika, but they weren't what he would have called bastards. And then you had people like Pickering and Harry Blum and the like, and that's *exactly* how he would describe them. This wasn't a war of countries, or territories, or nationalities, or even of ideas anymore, he thought. It was a war of the bastards against the rest of us. And when the dust settled, nothing would ever be the same again. Not if he had anything to do with it.

"Come on," he said, kissing her once more and spanking her backside, as he reluctantly got out of the bed. "Let's bloody do this thing. Before I change my mind and chicken out of it altogether."

His little 'holiday' back home had been his reward from Pickering. Unlike the Germans, the British had been extremely reticent on the subject of paying Johnny for his services and instead, he had been offered protection from prosecution (and persecution) from the police while arrangements were made for his return to France. But it had always been clear to all of them that it would ultimately come to an end and that the war would once again intrude upon their lives.

And come to an end it had. Pickering had called him up a few days beforehand and driven him to Hertfordshire to the plane factory to see "the results of his handiwork". The courtyard of the factory had been transformed with huge canvases painted to resemble bomb damage spread over the walls and roofs of the factory. Fake masonry and the twisted remnants of generators and boilers had been built and strewn liberally around the main courtyard of the factory.

"What do you think?" Pickering had asked him proudly.

Johnny had thought that it didn't look more convincing than the stage sets of your average school play and said so. He thought of Weiler and Behrensdorff and found it hard to imagine that they'd be taken in by something so amateurish. "Do you really think they're going to fall for this?" he asked, hefting a chunk of balsa wood "generator" in his hands.

"Oh, yes," said Pickering. "I know it doesn't look like much up close but at a distance, at night, under cloud cover, I think this will look highly convincing. You'd be amazed at some of the stuff we've managed to get the Jerries to swallow. Trust me."

And so, despite his reservations, Johnny radioed Nantes to tell them the deed was done. Pickering had arranged for a few tame newspapers to carry some column inches and this must have helped convince Weiler and the others because his next message was one of ecstatic congratulation and started laying the groundwork for his "escape" from Britain.

"How do I look?"

Johnny stepped into the parlour. He was dressed in the denims, donkey jacket and black woollen cap of a dockworker.

"Do you like it?" he asked.

Billie had been preparing some sandwiches for the trip, as much to give her something to do and to take her mind off Johnny's imminent departure as anything else. But now she turned around to take in her husband's new look.

"Well, you look the part, that's for sure," she said, laughing. "Though I have to say that I've always preferred you in a nice suit."

He sniffed. "Look a bit bloody conspicuous down the docks with my tin flute on, wouldn't I?" The plan was for him to get to Liverpool where passage on a steamer bound for Portugal had been laid on for him. Once he got to Lisbon he was on his own, although he'd been given access to his radio set once more in order to radio Weiler and tell them to prepare for his return.

"Here, sit down," Billie said. "You've got time for a cuppa before you go, ain't ya?"

"Yeah, a quick one." He turned and bellowed upwards towards the attic. "Oi, Spinksie! Get your arse down here! Ain't you going to see me off?"

Johnny took a leap towards Billie and scooped her up in his arms, spinning her around and finishing with a deep kiss.

"I don't even know when I'm going to see you again," she said bleakly, when they disengaged once more. "Or if I even will."

"Don't say that," he said. "Of course you'll see me again."

"You can't know that," she said. "You don't know what's going to happen."

"True," he said, grinning. "But that's the whole fun of it, ain't it?"

Billie shook her head and smiled in spite of herself. "Just what are you playing at, Johnny Black? I mean, really," She laughed as she saw his guileless expression and punched his shoulder. "You don't even know yourself, do you? I really did marry a mad bugger, didn't I?"

He grinned. "The maddest." He kissed her again. "It'll be alright, Bil," he said. "I promise you. And when it's all over, we'll be out on top again. Just you wait and see."

"Well, look at you. All done up like a Jolly Jack Tar."

They turned and disengaged to see Jack standing by the doorway, a rare, but genuine smile on his face. There had been something decidedly strained in the atmosphere in the house since Johnny had returned, with Jack seldom emerging from his room, no longer eating with them despite Johnny's best efforts to coax him out. And whenever he tried to quiz Billie about it, she was always noncommittal, even dismissive.

"That's Jack," she would say. "He always was a funny bugger. You know that."

Johnny wasn't so naïve as to not realise that something was amiss and the obvious answer was that something had been going on between Billie and Jack. Yet, he just didn't get that impression from Billie, that this was the case and she showed an absolute disinterest in Jack. Johnny had half-intended to try and get Jack on his own to see if he could get any further with him but the opportunity never presented itself. And in truth, Johnny was relieved. Partially for fear of what he might find out – besides he felt in no place to take the moral high ground after his antics in Jersey, no matter how much had taken place in the meantime. But he also only had a few weeks left before he had to leave again and he didn't want to leave everything in a state of discord. It was better to keep his mouth shut and look the other way, at least for now.

For now it seemed, for the briefest moment, that everything was as it should be and that all the complications of their lives as they were now had briefly melted away. As the three of them stood in the parlour, it felt almost as it had when they were younger. Together. United in conspiracy. It was a feeling that Johnny had been yearning for ever since he'd found himself banged up in Jersey and it bothered him that it wasn't going to last, that he might never feel that way again.

Johnny stepped out of the front door, Jack and Billie at his elbows. He stared up at the ashen clouds worriedly. "Don't look too pretty, does it?"

"Pack a brolly, did you?" asked Billie.

He gave her a smile. "Nah. Not my style. Think I'll risk it." He hefted his kitbag more securely on his shoulder. "Come here," he said.

Billie stepped towards him and they kissed long and hard, gripping each other tightly, reluctant now at the moment of parting to let go of each other.

"You take care of yourself now, pet," he said. "And don't you be taking no nonsense from anyone. Not the Heavies, no one."

"Don't you worry, pet. We've got that all under control."

Johnny turned to Jack, who was watching the both of them from the threshold of the front door. "Take care of her, Jack. Keep her safe. And yourself too."

Jack reached out and clasped his hand. "Count on it." Johnny was heartened to see that the clouds of doubt and suspicion that had lurked in Jack's dark eyes for the past weeks seemed to be gone. This seemed a lot more like the Jack he used to know.

"Don't worry," said Billie. "We'll keep everything ticking over here. You just be bloody careful out there. Don't do anything stupid."

"I thought you always said I never do anything else but," said Johnny with a grin.

"And so you do. But I'm serious this time. I need you, Johnny."

"Just as well you've got me then. Never doubt that. Right, better get going then."

He turned back to Billie and kissed her again before adjusting his cap and taking a step back. "Right, best be off. You all have a nice war now, do you hear. Don't wait up."

He turned on his heel and began marching up the street, whistling a nautical tune. Neither Billie nor Jack were remotely fooled by this jaunty facade as they watched him go until his receding form gradually disappeared into the drizzly mist.

Jack put his arm on Billie's shoulder, instantly feeling dismayed at the cold, unrelenting tension he could feel in the strong bone and muscle. She neither flinched nor relaxed under his touch.

"He'll be alright," he said awkwardly. "You know Johnny."

"I know," she said. She shrugged out of his grip and turned to face him, pushing him against the doorway. He staggered back against the wall and the two minders on duty in the hallway looked at them curiously.

"Beat it," said Billie. They knew her tone well enough by now to not need telling twice and both disappeared down the passageway towards the parlour.

Billie took another step forward towards Jack. He could feel her body up close against his as she looked up into his eyes, while one hand slipped into his jacket pocket and took out his cat-stabber. She flicked the knife open with a smooth, practised jerk of her wrist and held the blade between them, hard up against his abdomen.

"You've been practising," he said.

"You've no idea, Jack, love." She pushed the blade, held lengthways, against his gut, exerting just enough pressure until he flinched. "I know what you did, Jack Spinks," she said. "What you did to Johnny.

At least, what you tried to do. And I want you to know that you're going to answer for it. Some day you're going to answer for it."

Jack held his breath as he felt the unyielding hardness of the knife through his shirt. He looked into Billie's eyes to see nothing but a similar implacable mercilessness there too. "But not today," he said.

She held the blade against him for a moment longer and then released it, flicking it back into its resting place in the knife's handle. She then slipped it back into his pocket.

"No, Jack. Not today."

She stepped back, closed the front door to and walked back towards the parlour.

"Come on," she said. "We've got work to do."

NOTES & ACKNOWLEDGEMENTS

Historians of the period will notice that many of the characters in this book are based on genuine events and people. However, I have also taken significant fictional liberties and have felt in no way bound by historical fidelity. I've also conflated several historical characters and events for dramatic purposes. For a more factual look at the period and the people within it, the reader could not do better than seek out the excellent non-fictional works of the likes of Juliet Gardener, Ben Macintyre and Norman Longmate, which I hope you will find just as interesting and invaluable as I have.

But aside from the authors above, I'd also like to thank the friends and family who painstakingly assisted in the creation of the book, with particular heartfelt thanks going to Garry Scott and Leonie Gregson — but most of all to my long-suffering editor and general creative foil Claire Spinks.

CM

Printed in Great Britain
by Amazon.co.uk, Ltd.,
Marston Gate.